THE WATCHERS
THE WATCHERS SERIES: BOOK 1

EILIDH MILLER

Cover Photography by TJ Drysdale

Cover Design by Matthew Weatherston

Griffith Cameron Publishing

ISBN - 978-1-7345367-5-1

FOREWORD

I felt incredibly honoured when Eilidh asked me to write the foreword for her fabulous book as the emotional connections I felt whilst reading it went deeper than me just being a supportive friend.

I was drawn into this book not only because I am also a Guardian of history or because I know its author but like every good book should do, it made me want to know more about what was next for Watcher Grace. Surprisingly, it also made me want to know more about my own heritage.

As a Yeoman Warder of HM Tower of London, I too am a Guardian. The Palace is steeped in history and I see the visitors touching walls as I too have done, hoping to catch a glimpse of its past to try and feel connected in some way.

Reading 'The Watchers' gives you that glimpse, that connection but it also takes you deeper on a more personal level and allows you to see it through modern eyes that makes history come alive.

I really connected with this book and Eilidh's writing, so many parts of the book were familiar and elicited many memories: Chapter 6: 'She enjoyed the silence and the stillness of the woods as, inside, Aileen and Euan slept. To Grace, these moments always felt as though she was sitting much as a Guardian would, making sure no harm came to anyone.'

I have never visited the area of Achnacarry but like most of the West Coast of Scotland the similarities were there to behold. With the clever wording of this talented author I could see it, feel it, sense it. I could see the trees in the forests, the water in the river and loch, I felt the pull of the heather clad hills and the peace and the sense of stillness you can only find when you feel truly at home.

This book is like coming home and historians and lovers of Scotland will feel at home with this series of books and Eilidh's writing. Maybe in these troubled days we all need some Watchers to watch over us.

The thought of people looking after us and keeping us on the right track is comforting and to learn from history to ensure we don't make the same mistakes is especially important. However, we must remember to have balance as in the words of Sen. George Graham Vest, "In all revolutions the vanquished are the ones who are guilty of treason, even by the historians, for history is written by the victors and framed according to the prejudices and bias existing on their side."

Moira Cameron – July 2020
The first female Yeoman Warder of HM Tower of London

CHAPTER 1

All is ready for the attack, and we await the final orders and regimental positions from Lord Murray.

The sound of the quill scratching upon the parchment as she wrote was the only sound that filled the tiny room the Watcher had called home for the last week. Inverness was currently occupied by Jacobite rebels under the command of Prince Charles Edward Stuart, the Young Pretender, but that would all end in two days, and it would end because she was about to ensure it.

Pausing in her writing to think, Grace looked out of the window onto the street below. People bustled to and fro, moving through the daily hum of life. She could hear the hawkers calling out to passersby, offering anything from eggs, to wildflowers, to used shoes as they carried their baskets through the muddy streets. The town was busier than it might normally be with the influx of the Highland regiments and those supporting them all preparing for the battle to come. She watched with curiosity as two men in Highland dress, easily identifiable by the colors they wore as being members of rebel clans, stopped to speak to each other. Would they be alive after to-morrow? Judging by the badges they wore that distinguished them as officers, probably not. Officers didn't fare well after Culloden.

With a small shake of her head to clear it, she turned her eyes back to the task at hand. This letter needed to be believable so that when she handed it over to Cumberland's men, they would take it seriously and act on it. If the English failed to do so and the Jacobite ambush succeeded, then the prince and his army would win the Battle of Culloden and change everything in history which came after it. The ripples such a change could cause, if allowed to happen, were impossible to fathom. She resumed her writing.

The meeting point has been set, and you will find us massed in the woods near Culloden House for the march to the Nairn encampment. We will march out as soon as it is dark and, if all goes to plan, should arrive a few hours before dawn. Such time will allow us to surround the camp, so as to raid it from all sides, and catch all in the middle. No quarter will be given, as our aim is to disrupt them entirely and prevent them marching toward Inverness. If God is with us, he will deliver Cumberland into our hands, and his fate will depend upon his cooperation. Victory in this endeavor, and this war, is within our reach. If we defeat Cumberland's army, England's forces shall be severely weakened and less likely to attack us as long as he is our prisoner.

God save the true king!

Grace signed a name to it, thankful for the information in her dossier that allowed for such minute details. Sitting back, she examined her work with an air of practiced detachment. There was a part of her that almost wished she didn't have to do this because she knew full well what was coming. The defeat of the Jacobite Army in the coming battle was also the death knell for the entire clan system and the Highland way of life. So much would be lost to history, and the human cost was great. It was tragic, as war so often was, and unnecessary. It was why she was here, why she did what she did. Those who had sent her, The Council, had managed to eliminate war, and any change in history that threatened that peace could not and would not be allowed.

Despite her best efforts, Grace hadn't yet been able to discover what was spurring the timeline change. This meant it was time to use cleverness, deception, and manipulation to achieve her goal, and the result was this forged letter. It would do the job if she played it right with its delivery. Standing up, she folded the letter, then crumpled it and proceeded to make it look a bit worn. Looking at herself in the mirror, it took a moment to register the reflection she saw there. On missions like this one she was meant to fit in, and that meant changing her appearance to reflect what someone in this period would look like. The real Grace would look far too healthy here and stand out immediately. The vibrant golden hair was, instead, a dull yellow. Her eyes, normally one of her most striking features, were changed to a lighter blue, and her complexion was far paler. Her clothes, too, were rather ordinary, nothing fine. She was here as an employee of a tavern known to be popular with the rebels in order to listen and see what secrets slipped out with too much ale. Grace grabbed her cloak and pulled it around her shoulders, raising the hood over her head before opening the door. Shutting it behind her, she made her way down the stairs to the street.

The blast of cold air that met her should've made her shiver, even beneath the cloak, but she didn't feel it. The body she was in while she worked was impervious to the elements, as well as to injury, death, or anything else. However, The Council ensured she would always blend in with the local people by giving her all the languages, manners, clothing, rank, and other details she'd need, no matter where or when in history they sent her.

Grace made her way to a stable near her lodgings, where a horse was waiting for her, just as she'd requested when she'd made her progress report to The Council last night. The stable hand, a very young man who found himself tongue-tied in her presence, saddled it quickly and brought it to Grace, who mounted the side saddle with trained ease. She passed him a coin with a word of thanks and a smile, pretending not to notice his inability to look away from her. Adjusting the reins in her hands, she started north toward the edge of town. Once she'd reached open road, she moved the horse from a walk to a fast trot. She had a 12-mile ride before she reached the encampment at Nairn, where Cumberland had been since the previous day, and it would take her at least a few hours to reach it.

These ordinary journeys always gave her time to think through the next parts of her plan, about possible scenarios she might encounter when she arrived, and any myriad number of things that came to mind. She had the opportunity to be moved forward to precisely where she wished to be at any given moment, but at times like these it was a better cover to use the traditional way. Her horse would be tired, she would be seen upon the road, small details that could prove important if she needed to prove herself later.

"Halt!"

Grace pulled up on the reins as the sentry challenged her upon her arrival at the English encampment.

"Who are you and what is your business here?"

Grace pushed the hood back from her head to show her face and smiled. "My name is Miss Evans, and I have an urgent message for His Grace. I mean no harm."

The sound of an English accent seemed to ease his tension, and the young man shouldered his rifle and took hold of the horse with one hand, while offering her the other to help her step down. "You are English? What are you doing here? It is dangerous! We are at war, miss."

"I know full well, sir, and that is why I am here. I really must see His Grace, it is urgent." She kept her tone even and measured, her speech pattern showing her to be decidedly middle class.

"For what reason?"

"I have intelligence that may prove vital, private, so if you wish to remain alive, I suggest you get me to His Grace with all due haste."

He looked at her curiously, but Grace didn't miss the fear that flashed through his eyes. "Yes, of course. Johnson!"

The other young soldier standing at sentry approached.

"Go and inform His Grace's aides that there is a visitor with intelligence to share."

Johnson nodded and turned, threading his way quickly through the camp to attend to his duty.

"Thank you so much for your assistance," Grace said. "I wish no harm to come to any of you, and I have come such a long way, it would be a shame if I was not able to pass on what I know."

"It is good of you to do so."

"What is your name?"

"John Holmes, miss."

"A pleasure to make your acquaintance. Where in England do you hail from, Mr. Holmes?"

"Kent. Maidstone, to be exact."

"Oh! Kent is lovely. I know where Maidstone is."

"Do you? To know such a small village, you must be from nearby." Holmes relaxed a bit more now, eased by the idea that someone from home was in this godforsaken place.

"I wish I could say so, but no. I passed it on the road once, a lovely little place. You must have been sad to leave it."

"Not at first, but yes, sometimes I am now."

"As in this moment?"

"As in this entire campaign," he said, his smile rueful.

His admission amused her, and she couldn't say she blamed him. "Yes, I suppose I can understand that."

"Where are you from, Miss Evans?"

"I am from London originally."

"Indeed! You are a long way from London now."

"Yes, quite," Grace replied as Johnson returned.

"His Grace will see you, miss," Johnson said. "You are to come with me."

Grace nodded in acknowledgment. "A pleasure, Mr. Holmes. I will pray for your continued safety."

"Thank you," he replied. "I will see to your horse."

Grace turned and followed Johnson, the sight of a young woman alone in a military encampment earning her curious stares. There were a great many men here, 8,000 by historical count, and the sprawl of tents and small fires was massive. She kept her eyes forward, not looking at any of them as she passed. The fewer people she met, the better, as it left fewer witnesses to the presence of a young woman who should never have been there.

When they reached the command tent, Johnson stopped and bowed to her. "Good day to you, miss."

"And you," Grace said as he left, and another man emerged. He surveyed her with a critical eye and Grace didn't flinch, her expression fearless.

"What may we do for you, miss?"

"As I told the sentries, I have an urgent message for His Grace."

"You may give it to me, and I will see that he gets it."

"No," Grace replied, her firm tone a warning that she had no intention of backing down on this. "I must deliver it into his hands myself and tell him what I know."

"Send her in for heaven's sake!" A voice called from inside.

With an irritated expression, the aide pushed aside the tent flap to allow Grace access, and she stepped inside without hesitation. When her eyes adjusted to the dim interior, she saw the Duke of Cumberland seated in a chair, a glass of wine in his hand. At twenty-five, he was the same age as Grace and in full control of the royal army, sent by his father, King George II, to tamp down this rebellion against their authority and their right to rule both countries.

Grace made a low curtsy. "Your Grace."

He motioned for her to rise, waiting to speak to her until she had. "What is your name?"

"Grace Evans."

"And what are you doing here, Miss Evans? This is quite a dangerous place to be just now."

"It is, and that is precisely why I am here. I have something you need."

"Is that so?"

Grace pulled the letter from the pocket of her dress. "It is. I have this," she said, holding up the letter to get his attention before offering it to him.

Leaning forward, he took it from her, clearly expecting it to be nothing, for what would a woman know about what was important? Setting his glass aside, he unfolded the letter, his eyes going wide in an instant. "Where did you get this?"

"It was left in the tavern my father owns. Someone dropped it, I think, I cannot be sure, but I found it while I was cleaning. I knew I needed to get it to you immediately, for I believe they intend to attack tonight. The only way was to come myself, for no one would suspect a young lady, and I had to be certain you actually saw it."

The Duke stood from his chair. "Is this all you have? Have you overheard anything?"

"I have not, but I was not often allowed around where the soldiers were congregating. It was not safe. They are savages, all of them."

Grace hated the word and hated to use it, particularly in this instance, for the Scots were anything but. She needed to play to his prejudices, however.

"Of course they are, and it was wise of your father to keep you safe from them. Burke!"

"Yes, Your Grace?" The summoned aide stepped inside almost immediately.

"I want men stationed on perimeter watch tonight. There is to be an ambush and we need to be prepared for it."

"An ambush? We have not heard —"

Cumberland held up the letter to silence him. "*We* have not, but *she* has, and she has put herself in considerable danger to make sure we knew. I am sorry to have to relieve men of liberty, but it is absolutely vital."

"Of course, Your Grace, I will see to it immediately," Burke said with a bow before he departed.

Cumberland returned his attention to Grace. "I am afraid you cannot leave, Miss Evans. It is far too dangerous, and you will never make it back to Inverness before dark. I must insist you remain here."

"If you command it, then I must."

"You will be safe here. It is my birthday," he said, looking like an elated child for a moment. "The men have a day at liberty and have all been given brandy to celebrate."

"Then I have chosen a good day to be confined here," Grace replied, smiling.

"Indeed, you have. Please do remain inside and help yourself to anything you wish. If you need a rest, you are welcome to the cot over there," he said, pointing to one corner. "Otherwise, there are books and maps, or simply conversation with me."

"You have far more serious demands on your time than conversation with a woman so beneath you, Your Grace."

"Beneath me?"

"I am not of noble blood. I am the daughter of a tavern keeper and nothing more."

"Your bravery in coming here says otherwise, and I find it intriguing. May I offer you wine?"

"That is very kind, but no thank you, Your Grace. I wish to keep my senses sharp in case we need to escape."

Cumberland laughed. "I assure you that will not be the

case, but I understand you perfectly. If you will excuse me, there are some things I must attend to."

"Of course," Grace replied, curtsying again as he departed and left her alone.

Grace rolled her eyes, allowing herself a few moments of freedom from her persona while he was gone. Being a simpering, helpless girl was so antithetical to her true self as to be laughable, and she found having to fake it an annoyance. Making her way over to the map spread out upon the table and studying it, it was easy to discern that this was the battle plan for the following day. She was half tempted to shift a few things and make it a bit more evenly matched, but that would be against the rules. She wasn't allowed to change history in the course of any mission.

"Why would you choose such a place," she whispered to herself. "There are so many places which are much more suitable. I understand about the road to Inverness, but how could you possibly choose to defend it here?"

Reaching out, she drew a finger along the lines which marked the enclosures of Culloden Park. The moor itself was, at this time, called Drumossie and not Culloden; only later would it take its name from the manor house nearby. There were tokens representing soldiers stationed behind the Culwhinnie wall, hiding to ambush fleeing Jacobites, something they would end up accomplishing quite effectively.

In a box on the table were other, unused, resource tokens and Grace picked them up. Walking around the table, she put herself on the Jacobite side of the field and proceeded to arrange the tokens as she would lay out the army in response to the Hanoverian formations. Once she was done, she surveyed it and moved the tokens in the way she intended, the result being an overwhelming Jacobite victory after the Hanoverians were hemmed in on all sides.

"You should be glad I am not in charge of them, Your Grace," Grace whispered, her lips turning in a wry smile.

Not that the Jacobites would've allowed such a thing anyway, or even listened to her. The limitations of her gender were usually quite clearly defined in whatever period she visited, and she always had to play within those confines and still achieve her objective, no matter how irritating she might find them. She'd never failed and didn't intend to start now.

The sound of approaching voices caused her to clear the pieces with a swift movement of her hand and put them back where she'd found them, so that when the Duke re-entered the tent, he found Grace studying the map with a confused look on her face.

"Would you like me to tell you what this means, Miss Evans?" he asked, his smile dripping with condescension as he came up beside her.

"Oh, no, I think it is far beyond me, but thank you for the offer, Your Grace."

"Yes, well, that is why we men handle these things."

At his comment, Grace found herself wanting to drop the act and ask him if he'd like a detailed rundown of all the flaws in his battle plan, but somehow managed to refrain.

"Come, make yourself comfortable, and let us talk and game to pass the time, hm?"

"If Your Grace wishes it."

He turned his back on her and made his way to another table after picking up his glass of wine. He was so trusting, so solid in his belief that a woman wouldn't be capable of any sort of treachery. How wrong he was, she thought to herself as her hand slowly closed around the handle of a knife left sitting on the table. Staring at his back, she had a fleeting thought of driving the knife into it, at once changing history and preventing the horrors to come from his rampage through the Highlands after the battle. Women, children, and innocents were murdered under his orders, and Grace loathed him for it, no matter how polite she had to be in this moment. He was a sociopath who would not only take pleasure in the retribution he unleashed but would consistently fail to understand the public sentiment against it. However, that was not her job, and she shoved the thought away as she released her hold on the knife.

Later that evening, when the Duke had fallen asleep, Grace made her way out of the tent. She had one final piece to complete in this mission. Making her way toward the nearby woods, she intended to use the excuse of needing to relieve herself as a reason for her progress if she was questioned, but no one seemed to notice, and that was just as well.

Keeping off the road, she made quick work of reaching the spot nearly four miles from Nairn, where her next target would soon be passing. The ambush had already been called off due to the exhaustion of the Jacobite soldiers and an inability to get to the English encampment in enough time to secure the element of surprise, and O'Sullivan had been sent by Murray to inform the prince of the changed plans. In the darkness, Grace heard the sound of hooves approaching on the road and, when they drew near enough, she stepped out of the darkness. The horse saw her even if its rider didn't and startled, rearing up.

"Jesus Christ!" O'Sullivan cried out, trying to regain control of his horse.

Grace receded into the darkness before he had any idea someone had been there, and the horse bolted while he tried to control it. This would take him far enough off course to miss the prince and his wing of the army.

Grace smiled in satisfaction and closed her eyes. *"Watcher Evans reporting mission completion,"* Grace said as she felt the connection with The Council open.

"Copy, Watcher Evans. Are you requesting extraction?"

"Yes," Grace replied. *"Bring me home."*

CHAPTER 2

In the next moment, the woods around her faded, replaced by the smooth walls of one of the debriefing rooms at The Council's headquarters. Gone were the simple clothes she'd been wearing, the standard white dress of the Watcher uniform in their place. Grace took a deep breath and released it, knowing she had only a moment to ground herself once more. Behind her, a door opened, and a young woman entered. Though she was dressed in a uniform like the one Grace currently wore, it was a bit more ornate and there was something in the way she carried herself that gave her an air of authority. Long, sandy-blonde hair curled over her shoulders and down her back, and she wore a kind expression on her delicate features.

"Watcher Evans, welcome back."

Grace turned around and bowed to her. "Thank you, Councilwoman Rochford."

"Another stellar mission on your part. The timeline has returned to normal, and all is well."

"Good," Grace said, her relieved smile betraying her outward calm. "It got a bit tricky."

"Is that ever *not* the case with your missions? That is why we send you and not the others, after all."

"Fair enough," Grace replied, chuckling.

"I am sure you are ready to debrief so you can get home."

"Very much so. It should be short work, as there is really not much to say about it."

"Then let us get started. Caia has already been alerted and will be waiting for you."

When debrief was over and she was released from the mission body, Grace's eyes fluttered open to the darkness created by the blackout curtains surrounding the bed, and she yawned and stretched before sitting up. Her head was pounding, and it made her feel dizzy, forcing her eyes closed again. Groaning, she placed her hands to her head. She never failed to wake up with a headache post-mission, and it was the part she hated most.

"Grace?"

Her name called out in a familiar, soothing voice made her smile despite the pain. "Yeah, I'm here."

The curtains parted and Grace looked up to see the smiling face of her Guardian, Caia, and this truly meant she was back in her own home and her own time once more. As a Guardian, it was Caia's job to watch over Grace while she was on a mission, and Grace was her sole assignment. It was Caia who made sure she remained hydrated, nourished, and moved her body to keep it from getting stiff if she was down for more than a day. More than that, Caia had become a very dear friend, a stable presence who was always there to greet Grace when she returned. The two women had bonded quickly when Caia was assigned to Grace at the start of Grace's tenure as the Evans Watcher. The death of her grandparents had been traumatic for Grace, but Caia's care had helped her to get through it.

"Headache again?"

"Of course."

"Here," Caia said, holding out a cup of tea.

"*Angel*," Grace said, the word slipping from her lips in a sigh as she took the offered cup and sipped it. "Have I ever told you that you make the perfect cup of tea?"

"Probably," Caia said, "but you are always welcome to tell me again."

Grace laughed. "This should get me back to normal soon enough."

"Here are the tablets for the pain," Caia said, placing them in Grace's hand when she reached for them.

There was a routine after two years of working together, and Caia had it down to an art form. A cup of tea, aspirin, a plate of biscuits. Placing the tablets in her mouth, Grace washed them down with another sip of tea before grabbing a biscuit.

"Thanks," she murmured between bites.

"You're welcome, of course," Caia replied. "Where to this time?"

"Scotland, 1746."

"Oh, well, that is a dangerous place to be at that point, right?"

"Definitely," Grace said, happy to hear the return of her own speaking cadence instead of the one she'd been using in the mission.

"What was the change?"

"The night attack at Nairn by the Jacobites was going to succeed for some reason, which would give them the upper hand and the win at Culloden."

"Oh dear. What happened that they were going to end up succeeding?"

"A good question. I never was able to find out."

"How did you stop it, then?"

"Forged a letter between two regimental aides for Perth and Murray with details of the planned attack, then handed it to the Duke of Cumberland so he could put men on watch."

"And did he?"

"Of course he did."

Caia grinned. "You really are clever, you know that?"

"Clever is a point of view, I think."

"Well, it is *my* point of view."

"Then thank you very much."

"So, what was he like?"

"Who? The duke?"

"Yes!"

"Pretty much entirely as you would expect him to be. Pompous, arrogant, condescending. You know, a prince."

"Yes, well, I am sure you were perfectly charming."

"On the outside, perhaps. Inside, I considered grabbing a knife and stabbing him in the back."

"Whatever for?" Caia asked, shocked.

"If only to prevent the things he did after the victory at Culloden. Innocent people were murdered by his orders. They didn't call him Butcher Cumberland for no reason."

"Yes, I would think one would not earn such a nickname lightly," Caia said, grimacing.

"And trust me, he didn't."

"It is a good thing you are able to control such impulses. I cannot imagine what that would do to history."

"If I couldn't, I wouldn't be a Watcher."

"True, but all the same."

"I know, I know. Everything good here?"

"Yes, no problems at all. It is always so quiet here. I appreciate the music you left, that was kind. The little candies were delicious, too."

"I'm glad you like them."

Grace always made sure to leave a treat in the mission room for Caia. It felt like such a small thing to do for someone who protected her so diligently, and there wasn't enough candy in the world to thank her for that.

"They were my favorite so far," she replied.

"I'll have to remember to get more then," Grace said, smiling before taking another sip of tea.

"Tell me what else you saw."

"They had me working in a tavern, so mainly I saw a lot of drunk Scots in Highland dress, blustering about war and the true king."

The description made Caia laugh. "Any worth looking at?"

"No," Grace said, joining her in laughter. "Nothing extraordinary, really."

"Shame, that. Oh, I do wish I could go with you just one time!"

"Whatever for?"

"It must be so exciting to do what you do, Grace. You go back in time, meet famous figures, protect history. You have to use your wits to succeed while making people think you are not doing a thing."

"You make me sound like some sort of superhero! It isn't as simple as that, and not always particularly exciting, especially when those famous figures are nothing like you thought they were. A bit disappointing, actually."

"All the same. You do all these important things, and you are so very good at it. Your grandmother was not this good, I know that much."

Grace's heart ached at the mention of her grandmother, Jean, who had been the Evans Watcher before her. "I think, perhaps, she didn't have to be. Besides, don't you also go to the past? I mean, you're here right now. To you, this is 400 years in the past, and what you do is extremely important."

"I had not really considered that, but I suppose you are right."

Grace winced and put a hand to her head. "Really bad this time," she murmured.

Caia frowned and took the teacup from her. "Poor Grace. Would you like something to eat? Maybe you can wash up while I make you something, and then we will get you into bed for a proper rest."

"That sounds like a good idea," Grace said, pushing herself from the bed. "Maybe some soup?"

"I can do that," Caia replied before she caught Grace as she stumbled. "Easy. You always try to go too quickly."

Recovering herself, Grace made her way out of the mission room and into her own bedroom with Caia's assistance. The mission room was used for that purpose only, and once she returned from the mission Caia would return it to its previous state by replacing the sheets, removing any trace of her having been there, and locking the door until the next time.

Turning on the water in the shower, Grace stripped out of the loose linen clothing all Watchers wore while they were down for a mission. It was comfortable and regulated their body temperatures to optimum levels, all part of the extreme care taken with the real bodies of the Watchers while they were in the field. Stepping inside, she closed her eyes in relief as the hot water washed over her, bringing with it a wave of relaxation. Grace just stood there for a few long moments, letting the heat ease the tension from her muscles. While her body might have seemed to be asleep in bed, it had been far from it. Her mind was still going at a fast pace while she worked, and a return always left a Watcher with aching, tense muscles and an energy level that lingered dangerously near exhaustion. Grace was no exception.

After her shower, she caught sight of herself in the bathroom mirror and it was, as always, a relief to once more see the face she recognized. Changing into pajamas, Grace shuffled out to the kitchen where Caia had a bowl of soup and some bread waiting for her at the table. Grace slumped into the chair, not sure if she'd even make it through a meal, but she had to try.

Caia sat down across from Grace and watched her stir the soup absently, then shook her head. "Did you want me to stay a while? That way you can sleep and not have to worry about anything. I do not mind," she said, her voice gentle.

"That'd be lovely, if you really don't mind."

"Of course I do not. It is my job but, more than that, you are my friend. I know many Guardians cannot say such a thing about their Watcher, but I can. Staying here with you is a privilege, not a chore, and I know you rest better after a return when someone else is here."

"You're right," Grace replied, her exhaustion plain and only getting more pronounced the longer she sat there. "I really do. I appreciate it."

"I know you do. Now eat." Caia gave Grace's hand a gentle squeeze.

Of anyone, Caia knew how truly alone Grace was, though she'd never admit to being lonely or ask Caia to stay even when she desperately needed it. It wasn't her way, though Grace sometimes wished it was. The times she'd considered doing it had only led to frustration for her when she couldn't make the words come, instead defaulting to telling Caia she was fine, as she always did.

Grace ate what she could before the fatigue got the better of her and caused her to push the bowl away. When she stood up, Caia was there to help her and walk with her to her room. Grace was barely awake as she crawled into her regular bed and was asleep by the time Caia covered her with the blankets.

With a concerned expression, Caia reached out and ran a hand over Grace's hair. "Sleep well, my friend, you have more than earned it.

CHAPTER 3

"Someday, Grace, you are going to take over for me, doing a very important job."

"Doing what, grandma?"

"Protecting history and the whole of the world."

"Protecting it from what?"

"Itself."

Councilwoman Rochford let go of a heavy sigh as she watched the moment play out on the screen before her. Jean had always made sure that Grace realized her place in the world, in what was to come. She'd never shied away from it, wanting Grace to be ready, to know what was expected when her turn came. It had paid off, this education, and Grace had reported for duty far more prepared than any of them could have realized. There was still, however, so much Grace didn't know, and they couldn't possibly tell her. Not yet.

"Councilwoman."

She turned around to find one of her fellow members and gave a nod of acknowledgement. "Yes?"

"It is time."

With a frown, she turned back to the screen, looking at the innocent face of the small child sitting upon her grandmother's lap. "I know, but I am not sure she is ready."

"Whether she is or is not is irrelevant. You know that better than anyone."

"Do not remind me," she muttered.

"It cannot be delayed any longer."

"You make it sound as if we have delayed it at all."

"I simply mean we cannot delay it even if we wanted to. It must be done, and you must give the order."

Rochford stared at the screen silently for a long moment.

"Then let us begin."

CHAPTER 4

Grace put her fork down when the familiar feeling of a mission notification swept through her. For her, it always felt like that momentary heaviness and dizziness you might get in a moment of déjà vu. Knowing Caia would be arriving within moments of the notification, she stood and quickly cleaned her plate, putting it in the dishwasher, and then starting the machine so the dishes wouldn't be sitting for however long she was gone. When she worked, it would be a day here but a week in the mission location.

The familiar knock at the door made her smile, and she heard it unlock as Caia placed her security key fob against the reader. "Good afternoon, Gracie!" Caia said, her tone bright as she entered and shut the door behind her.

Past Watchers had often lived remotely to avoid detection, but present Watchers could and did pay handsomely to live in well-appointed buildings with excellent security, covered by The Council's payment for state-of-the-art technology, as Grace did.

"Hey Caia! Good to see you as always."

"Ready to go again?"

"Nah, not really. I was just in the middle of watching the 'Steve Wilkos' show and having lunch. Can we wait another half hour?"

Caia gave her a confused look. "The what show? Oh, wait, is that what was on the television in the daytime in this time?"

"Yeah. It's a talk show. People come on, tell their host

about their problems and then the host tries to help them or something. There's all sorts of drama, especially when they have lie detector results."

"That sounds … interesting. A lie detector; is it the sort of thing Dr. Fraser does in Medical?"

Grace laughed at her reticence. The television wasn't on. "Not even close. It's kind of my guilty pleasure when I'm home, but I was just kidding, Caia. Of course I'm ready to go."

"Now I rather want to watch it once and see what you are talking about."

"We can when I come back," Grace offered.

"Something to look forward to! Other than your return and the stories that come with it, of course. But we had better get started."

"We can skip the shower, I just did that this morning," Grace said as they turned and walked back to the mission room.

"Great, that just means you can get on the ground faster," Caia replied as Grace unlocked the door and handed her the key.

"The sooner I go, the sooner I'm back. Any idea what I'm in for?"

"None, but you know they never tell me."

"I always ask just in case you overheard something," Grace chuckled.

"As if they would have such a conversation anywhere that I could overhear it?"

"That's true," Grace said as she grabbed a set of linens from a small dresser, ducking behind a screen to change into them. "How is everyone?"

"Oh, well, Councilwoman Rochford is always herself. Stoic but kind. Dr. Fraser has been working hard on something I cannot, unfortunately, tell you about, but he is well. The rest of The Council are all fine. Things have been quiet."

"Have they? No one else has worked?"

"They have, absolutely! Just small things."

"Ah," Grace said as she re-appeared from behind the screen. "That's a good thing, though. Large changes are always a bit of a disaster."

"And you know full well you are the only one who works those when they come up."

"No reason the others couldn't, but that isn't my choice to make," Grace said, giving a small shrug as she sat down on the edge of the bed.

Caia picked up a brush and started to run it through Grace's long hair. "What have you been up to on your break?"

"Not much, really. Did some hiking, hung out with Vanessa a couple of times, read, things like that. Nothing exciting."

Grace, like the others, always had a break of at least a couple of weeks in between missions. This last one had been three, and she'd appreciated that.

"That sounds fun! I do wish I could meet Vanessa; she sounds like quite the character."

"She is," Grace said. "You'd love each other, I'm sure."

Vanessa was, other than Caia, the only other close female friend Grace had. She kept her distance from everyone for her own personal reasons and was reluctant to let anyone get close enough to her to be emotionally invested. Vanessa was an exception due to her early persistence in rebuffing Grace's unconscious attempts to shy away from her.

"Maybe someday," Caia mused before she smiled and set the brush aside, then started to braid Grace's hair so it wouldn't turn into a tangled mess while she was down.

"I'll try to make it happen at some point; I promise. It's just a bit tricky."

"I understand entirely. I would have to be very mindful not to slip up, and I would not want to take the chance until I knew I could completely trust myself not to do so," she replied as she tied off the bottom of the braid with an elastic band. "Right, all set."

Grace nodded and moved forward to lie down on the bed.

Once she settled herself into position, she smiled at Caia. "See you in a while."

"See you in a while. I'm looking forward to hearing all about your assignment when you come back. Good luck, Grace," Caia said.

"Thanks," Grace replied as Caia pulled the curtains shut around the bed. Taking a deep breath, she released it before she closed her eyes.

In the next moment there came that strange tug which let her know she was now out of her present body and on her way to wherever she was meant to be. Another tug brought her eyes open, and she sat up to look around her. She felt dizzy, as though she'd sat up too quickly, and closed her eyes to let it pass. Arrival was always slightly disconcerting as her brain fought to register what had happened. That catch up ran parallel to the immense amount of information flooding in from the mission dossier, the one containing the details on her target and all she'd need for the period she was in.

Grace took several deep breaths as she tried to steady herself. Where was she? Scotland. April 1746. Again? Damn, she hated this timeline point. She'd just been here, but that was a different timeline altogether, one of several that ran all at once. Who was she looking for? Euan Cameron, an officer in Lochiel's Cameron regiment. His face flashed behind her closed lids as though it was projected on a screen for her to study. Dark hair, blue eyes, tall. At least he was easy on the eyes but that didn't mean anything. She'd met more than her fair share of handsome jerks. On to the next piece. Was he a Jacobite or a loyalist? Neither. Interesting. Her job was to make sure he didn't join the Jacobites at Culloden. She had no idea why, only that he wasn't to join the coming battle so that he survived the war.

"Well, that will be easy enough," Grace thought to herself, even her internal voice registering the sarcasm at the very idea.

She stood up and looked around her, finding herself in a

beautiful clearing, and a bag containing extra clothing was beside her. There was a gentle river in front of her, coming from a loch nearby, and she made her way to it to look at her reflection in the still water of a pool. This time she saw her true reflection, and that told her that this mission wasn't going to be about blending in. Her hair was done up in a simple style, her dress made of warm blue wool with a matching length of wool to pull around herself for warmth. Not that it mattered, as she wasn't really here, but it was all part of the game.

As she looked around her, she took a moment to admire the beauty here. The silence and solitude seemed almost a blessing to her, so far removed was it from the world she knew. Grace closed her eyes with a smile and listened to the breeze rustle the leaves of the trees in the woods around her. The air smelled fresh and clean, tinged with the earthy scent of leaves and wet earth. Picking up the bag, she turned, making her way toward the road and the loch, and when she reached the edge of the shore, she looked out across the expanse. On the other side, hills rose, covered in ancient trees. To her left, the water reflected the mountains, still covered with snow, and the loch turned into the river on her right.

Her body suddenly jerked forward at the same time the crack of a gunshot reached her. She cried out in pain as her body collapsed to the ground, her mind forgetting momentarily that this was a mission body, one that diminished or eliminated dangerous sensations. Pain, heat, cold, hunger, exhaustion, and the like had to be reduced to a mere nuisance for a Watcher to be effective. Wounds healed nearly instantly, and she couldn't die here. There were many reasons Watchers were referred to as supernatural beings and this was one of them. Grace pushed herself up onto her knees and placed her hand against her shoulder, where a dull ache let her know there had been an injury. When she felt moisture there, she pulled her hand back to find it covered in blood.

"Really?!" Grace exclaimed in irritation.

At that moment she saw several young men hurry out of the woods toward her and all of them looked concerned. "Christ, lass, are ye all right?"

Grace looked over at them as her target approached and quickly knelt at her side. "Yes, no thanks to you," she sniped.

"I was nae the one who shot ye," Euan Cameron said, casting an angry look at one of the other men, who looked dismayed.

"Well, it does not matter who shot me — just that one of you did," she huffed. "Help me up, would you?"

The men looked at each other in confusion. The woman in front of them should be dying or screaming in pain, and at this moment she was doing neither of those things. Euan held out a hand and helped her up, and then Grace quickly fashioned a sling out of the length of wool around her waist. She didn't really need it, as the wound would already almost be gone, but these men needed to believe otherwise.

"We should take her to Lochiel," one of the others said.

"Aye," said the rest in unison.

"No, thank you," Grace replied. "I have had quite enough of your help."

Euan surveyed her with curiosity. "No, I will take her to my mam. She would be sent for by Lochiel to help the lass, so I might as well just take her straight there."

"Ye are nae going to tell anyone I shot her are ye?"

"I will nae lie if questioned further than this, but I will say ye thought she was a poacher, Duncan."

"Thank ye, I can at least get out of that if asked," Duncan replied.

Grace rolled her eyes. This was not an auspicious start to things. "If we are to go to a healer could we please make our way there?"

"Aye, of course. Lads get ye gone from here and say naught," Euan said before he picked up the bag she'd been carrying and draped Grace's good arm about his shoulders. The young men quickly dispersed, and the two of them started to walk back into the woods. "What is yer name?"

"Grace," she replied, trying to tame her irritation since she was now with her target and he was assisting her. She wasn't really irritated with him anyway.

"Grace, hm? An English name but ye dinnae sound English. Well, nae exactly anyway," Euan said.

Grace's speech had the lilt of the English accent to it after spending over seven years living there, but there was something slightly different about the cadence that she was unable to do much about because she was born an American.

"Because I am not."

"Where are ye from, Grace?"

"Someplace you have never heard of. What is your name?" Grace asked, trying to change the subject.

"Euan. Euan Cameron."

"I would say it was nice to meet you, but …" Grace said, trailing off as she gestured toward her injured shoulder with a small movement of her head.

A small laugh came from Euan at her sarcasm. "Aye, I can see how ye may nae feel so welcomed at the moment. I cannae believe ye are both alive and nae in pain."

"I am tougher than I seem."

"I dinnae know a man alive so tough as this."

"A good thing I am not a man then," Grace said, offering him a smile as sarcastic as her words had been.

Euan's lips parted into a smile of his own and then laughter. "Ye have a quick wit."

"I have been told that before."

"It was probably no less true when last ye heard it."

"I would not know, but I am not judging my own wit."

"Nae asking ye to," Euan said as he helped her up a small hill. At the crest of it sat a simple stone cottage. "Mam!"

At his call, a woman stepped outside. Her red hair stood out immediately, but her features were gentle and kind, and Grace felt she couldn't be more than 40.

"Aye, s —" but she froze when she saw Euan holding Grace. "Heaven help us!"

"She has been shot and needs help," Euan explained as he helped Grace inside.

"Shot! Shot by whom?"

"Duncan got a bit eager."

"Christ, it is a wonder that boy is still alive," Euan's mother muttered. "Sit ye down, lass."

Grace sat down upon a stool beside a warm-looking fire as her arm was unwrapped, and Euan set her bag aside. The wool at her shoulder was covered in blood and Euan's mother gasped when she saw it.

"How are ye still conscious!"

Grace bit her lip. She hated this part and, though she didn't always have to do it and could stay working in the background, this clearly wasn't one of those times. Having to explain what she was and why she was there, she could never be sure how anyone would react to it. Euan's mother had begun unpinning the side of the gown from the stomacher to get a better look at her arm, but Grace gently pushed the woman's hands away from her. Grace slipped her arm from the sleeve and lowered the neckline of the shift. There was no wound to be seen.

Euan's mother inhaled sharply and jumped back from her, crossing herself. "Jesus!"

Euan stared at her shoulder in shock and then looked at Grace. "How? Ye were shot! I saw ye! There is blood!"

Euan's mother grabbed Grace by the arm and dragged her from the chair. "Out of my house, demon!"

"No, wait," Grace said as she resisted. "Please …"

"Get out! Ye are nae wel —" she shouted at Grace before she stopped, her face going pale as she lifted Grace's left wrist to eye level and then dropped it, backing up. "Oh Lord … God …"

"Mam?"

"A Watcher. Ye have shot a Watcher!"

"A Watcher? Mam, those are only old tales."

A Watcher. At least this woman knew her for what she was. Grace looked at Euan in momentary silence, and then held up her wrist. "They are not."

Euan's eyes went wide, and the color drained from his face. The mark was clear, two female figures, one holding a watch and the other a book and quill; and only one creature bore that mark: a Watcher. "No. It cannae be true …"

"Who are ye here for, Watcher?" Euan's mother asked. "We will send ye to them so ye need nae delay yer purpose."

"My name is Grace, and I am here for *him*," she said as she looked back at Euan.

Euan backed up until the wall stopped him, shaking his head, as his mother burst into tears.

"No, please, I beg ye! Dinnae kill him!"

"What?" Grace looked at her in confusion. "Kill him? Why would I do that? I am here to save him."

"The tales say the Watchers come to kill those who may prevent what should happen from happening," Euan explained, everything about him showing how wary he was.

"No," Grace replied. "We never do that. We make sure that everything goes as it should, and that involves making sure that the people who are supposed to live and go on to do other things do so. It does not involve killing them. I am here because you must be considering doing something that will change your future and ours."

Euan's mother looked at him with shock. "Euan … what have ye done …"

"Naught! I …" he replied as he trailed off, though the look on his face showed he was trying desperately to think over his recent actions.

"Where did ye go last night? Where did ye truly go!"

"I went to Achnacarry. Lochiel let us know we have been called back to go north to join the prince and the rest of the army."

"Euan! Ye said ye would nae join them again!"

Grace backed away to let them argue, slipping her arm back into the shift and the gown before re-pinning it. This was not her fight. She was only here to make sure Euan didn't continue upon the path he'd started down.

"I said naught of the sort! I am an officer! I have a company under my command. Do ye really think I can stay here while they go? It is my duty, Mam."

"No! It is nae! Nae when what he is calling ye for is treason! I dinnae care what he believes about the bloody Bonnie Prince! I will nae have ye lose yer life over a man who will nae care if ye live or die because ye are just another young body to put before English guns!"

"I am nae going to die! I am here now, am I nae? I would nae be if I was nae good at what I have been trained to do! Lochiel would care if I died, trust me. I am too valuable to him for it to be otherwise."

"Nae going to die? If ye were nae *she* would nae be here!" Euan's mother said, pointing at Grace. "Do ye nae see what this means? Ye are meant for greater things than this and she is here to make sure ye do them!"

Euan ran his hands over his face and Grace knew he wasn't convinced. She had only a short window of time to show him otherwise. "She is right. I do not know what you are meant to do, only that you must not join the Jacobites again."

"Ye are welcome in our home, Watcher, and I apologize for my earlier treatment of ye. I am Aileen Cameron."

"Please, call me Grace, and believe me I understand. That was rather tame compared to other reactions I have gotten," Grace replied, offering a reassuring smile. "It is refreshing to actually be called what I am instead of having to pretend otherwise. Not many people know those stories."

"I grew up with them and told them to Euan," Aileen said. "May I get ye anything?"

"No, thank you," Grace replied. "I will not need anything."

"No food or drink?"

"No. I am not like you in that way. Just like that gunshot wound healed, this body does not go by the normal rules. I do not need to eat, or drink, or even sleep."

Euan, still wary, eyed her. "It is unnatural."

"It is, but that is how it works. We are not natural, and neither are our tasks."

"Where are ye from," Euan said. This time it was not a question but a demand.

"A place that, to you, does not yet exist. I could not explain it to you because it would make no sense. It is easiest to say I am from the colonies, but a place even they have not yet discovered."

Euan frowned. "Explains yer strange way of speaking, then."

"I suppose it does."

"So, ye know what is going to happen in the future then?"

"Yes, if you do what you are supposed to."

Euan made a derisive sound. "And who are ye to tell me what that is? How do we know ye are nae some spy or, worse, a demon as my mother called ye?"

"She has the mark, Euan!" Aileen chided.

"A mark that could be faked!" Euan shot back.

"If you think it is fake, try to rub it off," Grace said, nonchalantly.

Euan closed the space between them with an almost surprising rapidity and grabbed Grace's wrist roughly. Before he got a chance to try to touch the actual mark on her wrist, however, a strange look crossed his face, as though he might be sick. He yanked his hand away from her wrist and stumbled back, leaning against the wall as he tried to catch his breath.

Grace looked at him in curiosity and concern. That was a reaction she'd never seen before. "Are you all right?"

"What did ye do to me?"

"Nothing." Grace replied.

"I heard … I heard things. I cannae think …"

"I have no idea what you mean. That is not something that happens."

"Perhaps it is yer own guilt," Aileen said.

"No," Euan replied, still leaning against the wall and seemingly trying to get his bearings. "I dinnae want her here. Please Mam, she has to leave. There is something nae right about any of this."

"I will nae throw a Watcher out of my home, Euan. Ye brought her here with yer actions and now ye must let her do what she was sent here to do."

There was something about Euan's sort of reaction that never ceased to wound Grace no matter how detached she kept herself. She wasn't wanted despite what she was there to do, and it was part of the reason she kept her distance from others in her own time.

"I do not have to stay with you," Grace interjected. "I can go elsewhere."

"Where would ye go, lass? Into the woods to sleep upon the ground? No, nae while I live and breathe. Dinnae listen to him. Ye are welcome here," Aileen said with a nod, letting Euan know it was the final word.

Euan frowned but said nothing else, and Grace looked at the fire for a moment as it danced in front of her, wishing she could feel it.

"At least let me help you," Grace said, looking up at Aileen. "Did you need anything? Perhaps I can help you prepare supper or fetch water?"

"Aye, if ye wish," she said before Euan stormed out, and she shook her head. "The boy is a fool. Dinnae mind him. He has nae been the same since he first left for the war."

"I am not sure he is any more of a fool than any young man, and no one is ever the same after a war."

Aileen chuckled. "Sure ye are right, lass. Thank ye and to those who sent ye for trying to save my boy. He is all I have."

"What happened to your husband?"

Aileen sat down at the table. "Dead, long ago. Euan was just a wee lad. His father, Alexander, took fever and died."

"I am sorry," Grace replied. "I am sure that made things very difficult." Those things were something with which Grace was now intimately familiar for a host of reasons.

"Aye, and I fear that is the reason Euan is doing what he is doing now. He thinks Lochiel cares about him and his well-being, but the only thing he cares about is the young men willing to work for him, follow him, and fight his cause. Euan seeks a father."

Grace nodded. It made sense and it was a cycle that repeated throughout history. "I will do all I can to dissuade him. I could not kill him even if I wanted to, so you need not fear that."

"That is good to hear, though, I warn ye, ye may be tempted to because he can be a stubborn one. Just like his father."

Grace was unable to stifle her laugh, though she knew she probably should. "His death would mean I failed at my mission, and my mission is to make sure he lives and does not join the Jacobites. Or, at least, not this time."

"Ye dinnae have much time, I think," Aileen said. "Perhaps ye should go after him."

Grace sighed. "Yes, probably."

"First, ye should let me get that blood out of yer dress," Aileen said. "For now, ye can wear a spare arasaid to cover up."

Standing, Aileen went to a basket and pulled out a length of tartan along with a belt and a fresh shift, before returning to Grace. She helped Grace to undress and change into the fresh shift before putting the petticoats she'd arrived in back on her. Draping the tartan over the young woman's head, she let it fall before gently taking the two ends and pulling them around the shoulders. Once it sat like a shawl, Aileen put the belt around her waist to secure the two loose ends to her sides, the vibrant red of the tartan striking against the blue of her petticoats.

"There," Aileen said, smiling and pushing the hood she'd created away from Grace's head. "Ye look a proper Cameron lass now.

CHAPTER 5

Grace stepped out of the door of the cottage not long afterward in search of Euan, her shift, stays, and gown left with Aileen for cleaning. Making her way down the hill, she let her sense of his direction guide her. One of the helpful things about any mission was the tracking sense that led the Watchers to their targets, allowing them to always know where they could find them. For a Watcher, it was a feeling that guided them, a sense of knowing where something had been placed even if it could no longer be seen.

Grace reached the tree line and saw Euan bathing in the water of the loch. Placing one hand against a tree, she watched him, taking stock of the man she was assigned to. His hair was long and, while it had been tied back before, it no longer was. The gentle waves hung around his neck and shoulders, dripping with water from having just been washed. He was muscular and fit, precisely what she'd expect from a young man who trained for battle and was currently embroiled in a war. His shoulders were broad, and, on his torso, Grace could see scars. Most of them were small, but there was a large, more prominent one still healing, and she wondered where they'd come from.

Before she could think more on it, Euan turned and started to walk out of the water. Grace caught herself and turned away before she saw anything she shouldn't, closing her eyes and giving a gentle shake of her head. There was something beautiful about him, something in his eyes and bearing that told her he was full of fire, darkness, and rebellion. But there was something else too, something he kept hidden, and she wanted to know what it was. It wasn't something she'd really thought of before.

"I thank ye for leaving me a bit of privacy," he called out in irritation as he started to dry himself off.

"I did not mean to intrude," Grace said.

"And yet, here ye are."

"I am not your enemy, Euan."

"How do I know? It is my job to see everyone as a potential enemy and ye are no different."

"Because if I were, you would be dead already."

Euan paused in his movements with an irritated look that would transfer into his tone with his next words. Grace would hear it even if she couldn't see it. "Perhaps. Why is it so important to whoever sent ye that I nae do my duty?"

"I cannot say," Grace replied. "Not because I know, but because I do not. That is not information they give us."

"So ye dinnae know my future."

"No, I do not. I do not know what becomes of you after this. I do not even know what my own future is," she said, keeping her back to him as she ran her fingertips over the rough bark of the tree.

"Ye can turn around now."

When she did so, she found him with his kilt back around his waist, but that was all. She made her way out of the trees to where he stood. "If I did know, would you want me to tell you?"

Euan's expression was immediately curious. "I cannae rightly say. I can see the bad in each choice," he replied as he gestured to a large rock near him, a silent offer to sit. "It is strange to see ye in our colors," he said, with a nod to the arasaid.

Grace accepted the invitation and sat down. "Your mother was kind enough to let me borrow it while she washes the blood from my dress. It seems as though someone shot me,"

Grace said, her tone at once teasing and sarcastic.

"Is that so? We should find the villain and string him up immediately."

Grace laughed. "See? I am not so bad, am I?"

"When ye are being normal, it seems nae."

"And I suppose trying to do my job is not being normal?"

"Aye."

Grace smiled and shook her head at him.

"How is it that ye healed so quickly?"

"A benefit of the job," she replied. "I am here but not here. My real body is somewhere safe while I am here with you." Grace toyed with the edge of the arasaid for a moment. "I cannot die when I am working a mission. If I could, I would be useless."

"Have people actually tried to kill ye?"

"Oh yes. Usually the ones whose plans are being foiled by my pulling my target away from them. I will admit it is rather amusing to see their faces when they realize I am not going to die, though."

"Is this what ye really look like, then?"

Grace gave him a curious look at such a change of topic. "Yes, why?"

"I thought perhaps ye could take a different shape if ye wished it."

"No, that is something I cannot do. It would be helpful if I could, though. Sometimes they will alter my appearance in small ways, but what you see here now is what you would see if you were with me in my own time."

"Which is?" Euan asked.

"271 years in your future."

Euan's eyes widened. "Christ, that is quite a long way."

Grace laughed. "Yes, it is."

"Yet ye fit so well here."

"Another feature of the job. They instill us with all we will need to fit in wherever we go, each time we go."

"Do ye have a husband waiting there for ye? What does he do while ye are at this?"

Grace raised an eyebrow. "No, I do not. I honestly do not have time for that kind of a relationship, so I do not know what a man would do if I had one."

"Tha e duilich nach eil a leithid de bhòidhchead air a chall," *A shame such beauty is going to waste,* Euan muttered to himself as he looked down at the ground.

"Tapadh leibh airson smaoineachadh gu bheil mi àlainn," *Thank you for thinking I am beautiful,* Grace replied with a wicked smile. "What about you? Do you have a sweetheart here?"

Euan whipped his head up and looked at her in utter shock. "Ye speak Scots Gaelic?"

"Of course. I will not when I return home, but I do now."

"I cannae hide anything can I? What about French, do ye speak that? And no, I dinnae have one at present. I have been a *wee* bit busy with fighting a war."

Euan's dip into sarcasm made Grace laugh. "Yes, that too. You speak French?"

"Oui. J'ai appris il y a longtemps," *Yes. I learned long ago,* he replied, handing back the same wicked smile she had given him.

"Interesting. I would not expect that."

"Why nae?"

"Well, it is not as though you are a noble, so I am not sure what use you would have for it."

It was Euan's turn to laugh now. "That is a fair observation and ye would likely be right. However, after my father died, Lochiel took me under his care and educated me so that I might serve as an officer when I was old enough."

"Really? Fascinating. So, you can read and write?"

"Aye, I can."

"Did you like learning?"

"I loved it. I remember being so distraught that I could nae continue on, but Lochiel would nae pay for it because he did nae feel I needed it for what he wanted me to do."

Grace frowned. "I am very sorry to hear that."

Euan shrugged. "It is the way things are. As ye said, I am nae the son of a noble, nor will I ever have to marry some noble lass or take over as chief. Lochiel has sons for that. So, what use would I have for it?"

"Does 'use' matter? What about just to further the love of it?"

"Here, it matters. What about ye? Did ye get lessons?"

"Oh, yes of course. We all did."

"All?"

"Every child goes to lessons from the time they are five until they are 18."

"Ach, that must be a struggle for some. Lessons are nae cheap."

Grace smiled. "It is free for all of us."

"What!" Euan exclaimed in surprise.

"If you want to go to university, though, you must pay."

Euan turned toward her quickly. "University. Did ye go?"

"I did."

"They truly let lasses go to university?"

"Yes, of course they do. We can do anything men can. Well, almost anyway."

"Amazing," he said. "What did ye study there? What was it like?"

Grace could tell from his reaction how much Euan had desired to go to such a place. "It was incredible. So many books and so much knowledge." She chuckled to herself before answering his next question. "And I studied history."

Euan's expression turned to one of amusement. "History. And now ye spend all yer time in it. Have ye always been a Watcher?"

"No, not always. I only began a couple of years ago when my grandmother died. That is how it works. When one Watcher passes, the next in her family takes her place."

"Did ye wish to?"

"More than anything."

Euan was quiet for a long moment. "Ye say ye cannae die. Clearly ye cannae be wounded. Ye did nae seem in pain earlier."

"No, I was not. Well, not really. It was a dull ache but nothing more."

"A dull … ye were shot and that is how ye describe it!"

Grace laughed. "It is the best description I can give you. Here, let me see your dirk."

Euan eyed her with suspicion but unsheathed it from where it hung on the baldric he had set aside with his shirt and coat and handed it to her. Grace held out her arm and raised the dirk, bringing it down, but just before it touched her skin, Euan grabbed her wrist and stopped her.

"No," he said. "Dinnae do that."

"Why? It will not hurt me."

"Does nae matter. Please, dinnae. I have seen enough blood to last me for centuries. Enough men cut open by my own hand with the same weapon ye now hold. I have no desire to have yer blood on it too, and I admit that the thought of seeing that steel red with yer blood sickens me."

"All right," Grace said as he released her. "You did not have the same reaction to touching me that time."

"I am glad I did nae."

"You said you heard something. What was it?"

"Battle. The sounds of musket fire and cannons, clashing steel and colliding bodies. A woman screaming my name."

Grace looked at him with the same curiosity and concern as she had when it happened. "That has never happened before. You have already been in battle have you not?"

"Aye, how did ye know that?"

"Your mother said something about not joining them again, so I just assumed," Grace replied, though it was a lie. She didn't want him to pull back because he realized she knew so much about him already. "Which ones?"

"All of them. I have been there from the start, but more recently Falkirk, Stirling, and Fort William."

"Did some of those scars come from those?" Grace asked as she gestured to his torso.

"Aye, most of them. Some came from training."

"What was it like?"

"What do ye mean?"

"War. Battle. I have never seen it." She'd made sure it would happen as it was supposed to, but she'd never had to remain behind to see it.

"Do they nae have war where ye live?"

"They do, but it is far away, and people volunteer to fight. I am not one of those people."

"Ah," Euan said. "It is … well, it is a horrible thing. Death everywhere, so much blood ye can smell it. The screams of dying men and the overwhelming stench of fear."

"Were you afraid?"

"Of course I was. If ye are nae then something is wrong with ye."

"But you have survived."

"Aye, and I will again."

"No, you will not. Not this time."

"Ye said ye did nae know my future."

"I do not know what your future is if I am successful. I know what it is if I am not. If I am not, you do not have one."

Euan frowned. "How is it so?"

"The Jacobites will be massacred at Drumossie. That battle will end it all, and there will be great retribution visited upon those who rebelled. Most of those who go will never return."

"Most."

"You are among them if you go. You will never come home again."

"Then help me make it so we dinnae lose."

Grace shook her head. "I could not do that even if I wanted to."

"Why nae?"

"Because that is too great a change. I do not know what

40

that would do to the future, and that is not my job. My job is you. That is all."

"If ye want to save me, Watcher, then that is how ye will have to do it. Otherwise, I go where I am called," Euan said as he pulled his boots on and stood up.

"You do not have to. You could make another choice."

"Spoken as someone who has never known what it is like to be called upon to defend her homeland," Euan said.

Grace shot up from her place on the rock, her eyes flashing with anger. "Just because I do not do it by charging into battle does not mean I do not defend my homeland. I do. I defend mine and yours and everyone else's too. My battle is for the soul of history and what comes from it. Yours is for an invisible line on the ground and a king who does not even know you."

"Ye are nae as placid as ye seem," Euan said, his voice low and quiet, and he watched as Grace checked herself, realizing she'd gotten close to him as she'd spoken and backed away.

"I am sorry ... I ..."

"Dinnae apologize for answering a slight as ye should. I did nae expect it from ye."

"But I insulted your cause and I know you believe in it."

"No, I dinnae."

"What?" Grace looked at him in confusion. She knew he didn't take a side, but to not believe in it at all surprised her.

"A king is a king no matter his name as far as I am concerned, all of them the same, but Lochiel believes in it and I am one of his officers. Where he directs me, I go. It is as simple as that."

"But why stay committed to something you do not believe in if you know it means your death?"

"Because that *is* my life. It was what I was born to and what I will die for if I must. I know ye dinnae understand that, but it is the truth of it. Ye can do yer best but ye will nae sway me."

As Euan walked past her to leave, she reached out and grabbed his hand. "Wait —"

It was the only word she got out. Something so strong swept through her that it felt like a shockwave and sent her to her knees. She couldn't breathe. There was pain, screaming, the acrid smell of smoke, the sight of Euan dead on the ground. It was followed by the sound of his laughter, the sight of him kissing someone's hand, the sound of a child's laughter. His two futures. It was gone just as soon as it had come and left her gasping for air.

"Grace?" Euan looked shocked as she fell to her knees and he knelt in front of her. "Look at me, come on lass, come on …" he said as he cupped her face in his hands and patted it. "Grace."

"No!" she cried out as she slapped his hands away from her, stumbling backward and trying to make sense of what had just happened to her. It was something she'd never experienced before, and the intense emotional impact was overwhelming. As she struggled to breathe, she could feel the tears on her cheeks, hot and fast.

"Grace, what happened?"

"I saw you. I saw you dead and then I saw what you have if you stay. I do not understand!"

"Ye saw me dead? What do ye mean what I would have?"

"You have a life. Someone you love and a child. You are happy. I want that for you. Please, you have to stay." Grace was, in an instant, confused by her own pleading. It was never something she'd needed to resort to or even felt inclined to.

"I may still have it, but that is up to ye," he said as he turned and walked away.

***

As Euan handled the few chores he had at Achnacarry later that day, his thoughts drifted to their mysterious visitor. She'd come bearing the news that he'd die in an upcoming battle, and while that bothered him, knowing she'd seen him dead in a vision unnerved him far more.

He wasn't proud of his initial behavior toward her, either. Calling her a spy or worse? Before the war he would never have thought to call anyone here such a thing, but now no one could be trusted. Ever. Then again, she'd been right when she'd said she could've killed him while he was bathing and he would never have known, but did the fact that she hadn't not count for at least something in her favor? It still irritated him that he'd he dropped his guard so low, but perhaps it was an after effect of what he'd experienced when he'd touched her.

Euan then thought back to the moment when she'd finally shown him that there was something beneath that tranquil exterior; her passion and her anger still surprising him. He'd challenged her and she'd stood up to him and called him on it. It impressed him, not an easy feat, and it was interesting to see a flash of greater emotion from a woman who had been so maddeningly calm up to that point. She had no fear of him, that had been clear, but if he couldn't harm her why would she need to?

Then there was her appearance. No matter what her reason for being here was, there was something comforting in the knowledge that what he'd seen was a true representation. She was beautiful, and he certainly could not and would not deny that. Not overly tall for a woman, she had hair that was almost golden in color and eyes that were a strangely intense shade of deep blue. It was a color he'd never seen before and nothing like his own. Her features were delicate, and she didn't look like someone you would expect to do such a dangerous task. Euan had to admit to himself that he found her quite compelling to look at. There were plenty of women here and he knew he could have his pick of any of them, though he'd avoided such attachments since the war began. Not that he'd wanted them even when he wasn't at war. In fact, he'd entirely avoided it for a myriad of reasons. However, none of the women here looked like *her*, and that could prove problematic.

Euan shook his head to clear it, needing to banish thoughts like this from his mind. She was here to stop him from doing what his position and his duty to Lochiel commanded of him, and he wasn't about to let her win.

CHAPTER 6

Later that night, Grace sat outside in front of the cottage. She enjoyed the silence and stillness of the woods as, inside, Aileen and Euan slept. To Grace, these moments always felt as though she was sitting watch as a Guardian would, making sure no harm came to anyone. At least for now, she had time to try and process what had happened to her earlier. She'd tried to reach out to The Council but had received no response. That wasn't normal, and the fact that she'd heard nothing at all bothered her a great deal. She wondered if it had anything to do with the visions she and Euan had experienced, but she'd keep trying.

Drawing her knees up to her chest, Grace pulled the arasaid over her hair. She wasn't cold, but that wasn't the point anyway. It made her feel more alone, and that was what she wanted right now. A crackle from the trees brought her attention back to the present just as a massive buck emerged from the woods. Grace sat up in a slow movement and watched him. He was a magnificent creature and she was glad he hadn't fallen to a hunt. The two of them stared at each other before the buck made his way forward toward her. Smiling, she held out her hand and he placed his nose into her palm, sniffing around.

"Sorry, I do not have food for you," she whispered to him. "I would give it to you if I did." Reaching up, she smoothed her fingertips over the bridge of the buck's nose. "You are lovely. I bet you do not have many worries do you?" The buck stared at her in silence. "No, of course not."

The buck turned, walking back into the woods, and Grace watched him go. If she were normal here such a thing would never have happened, but her life was filled with moments like these now, moments no one else would or could understand.

***

From inside, Euan watched her in the darkness as the buck came right to her. It intrigued him, and he wondered what sort of magic she possessed that such a thing might happen. She looked unreal in the faint moonlight, ethereally beautiful, and he couldn't help but think about how sad it was that such a creature was so rootless as to not even feel she should have someone waiting for her whenever she returned from wherever she'd gone. He turned over to look at the wall as he once again caught himself with thoughts that didn't belong in his mind right now. She had her job and he had his.

When Euan woke in the morning, he was surprised to find Grace wasn't there. His mother's arasaid hung on a chair, neatly folded, and Grace's cleaned clothing was gone. Had whoever sent her decided it was a lost cause and moved her on? He sat up and stretched before sliding out of bed and dressing himself. Grabbing the buckets for water, he took them out so he might fill them for his mother and leave one less task for her to do.

As he neared the loch, he could hear the faint sound of someone singing. Raising an eyebrow, he followed the sound, hearing it grow louder the closer he got. As he came to the edge of the trees, he saw it was Grace; she hadn't left after all. She was barefoot and sitting on a boulder with her feet in the water as though it were a fine summer day, a strange sight with how cold and unpredictable the weather still was. As she swirled the water around, she sang to herself, a song that was in Scots Gaelic, but he didn't recognize it. As he listened, he realized she was singing about the Highlands.

"I see right away the place of my birth
I will be welcomed in a language
which I understand
I will receive hospitality and love
when I reach there
That I would not trade for tons of gold."

The small smile that spread across his lips as he leaned against a tree and listened to her was involuntary. She had a beautiful singing voice

.

"I see woods there, I see thickets
I see fair, fertile lands there
I see the deer on the ground of the corries
Shrouded in a garment of mist

High mountains with lovely slopes
Folk abiding there who are customarily kind
Light is my step when I go bounding to see them
And I will remain there a while willingly."

There was something sad in her voice as she sang the last words, and he heard her repeat the last line not in song, but in a whisper to the gentle wind that rustled the water of the loch. Was she ever in one place for long? The sound of it made his heart ache in a way he didn't understand. That she was troubled bothered him, but he knew she was troubled because of him. If he let these feelings in, she would change his mind, and he couldn't allow that.

"Ye there! Dinnae move!"

The shouted words caused both to turn their heads toward the sound as if they were the same person. Grace didn't move or seem distressed in the least as several men approached her, and Euan recognized all of them. They were Cameron men, but not officers, and he made no immediate move to alert them to his presence.

"Who are ye and what are ye doin' on Cameron land?"

"My name is Grace, and I —"

"She is English, look at her," one said angrily, cutting her off.

"No, I am not." Grace replied.

"What are ye doin' here? Are ye spyin' for the illegitimate king?"

"If I were, would I be out in the open?"

Euan smiled and bit his lip to check a laugh. There was that wit again.

"Shut yer mouth, woman!"

Euan saw Grace sigh, her expression one of annoyance. Given what she'd told him about where she came from, it didn't surprise him that being spoken to in such a way chafed her.

"Tell me what ye are doin' here."

"You told me to shut my mouth."

Before Euan could see it coming, the man slapped Grace across the face so hard that her entire upper body turned with the blow and it made Euan wince. She turned her head back toward him slowly, fixing him with a gaze so cold Euan was sure the man could feel it.

"Answer my question and dinnae back talk me again."

Grace wiped the blood from her mouth. "I am here to visit a friend."

"Who?"

"Me," Euan said as he stepped out of the trees before Grace could answer. All the men quickly touched their hats in salute.

"Euan? Ye did nae mention ye were having visitors when last we saw ye."

"I did nae know I reported to ye or needed to make ye aware if my mam and I had kin visiting." Indeed, they reported to men who reported to him.

Grace's eyes shifted to him at the mention of family, and the men's looks turned questioning. "Kin? What kin is she to ye? She does nae even sound as though she is from here."

"Because she is nae. Her father and mother were from another branch and moved to the colonies. She has come back to find herself a husband, and I would kindly ask ye nae to lay hands on her in violence again."

The men looked from Euan, to Grace, then back again before they seemed to relax a bit. That one of their superior officers was able to explain her presence was all they needed. That it was Euan made it more so.

"Apologies, Euan. Ye would do well to teach her she cannae speak to a man the way she just did while she is here in the Highlands."

Euan shrugged. "There are many who would have no problem with a wife who had a quick wit. I think, perhaps, those are the ones she should concern herself with. And ye should apologize to her, nae me." Euan looked at Grace. "Ye left yer arasaid back at the cottage, lass. Ye should nae go out without it in times like these. I know ye dinnae need such where ye are from, but it is different here."

"Of course. I was not thinking of it," Grace replied, though there was something different in her voice when she did so.

"My apologies for strikin' ye lass. Come on men, let us get on. We have more land to check," the man said before he mounted his horse again and they departed.

Grace lowered her head, and it was only then that Euan noticed her hands were clenched in fists so tight they were white and shaking. He set the buckets down and made his way to her. Reaching out, he kept the movement slow and deliberate, not wanting to startle her. Taking one of her hands, he closed it in both of his own.

"Come now. It is over and ye are safe. I know ye are angry."

"I hate being spoken to that way. Hate being talked about as if I am not here," she said, seething.

"I can believe it. Such would leave me aggrieved as well."

"Thank you for intervening. You did not have to."

49

"I did or it would have gotten worse. I knew they would nae challenge me, and how would ye explain how quickly ye healed from that strike he gave ye? Grace, lass," he said, his voice softening before he began to sing back to her the song she'd sung just moments ago. Euan felt her hand relax and release, but it felt warm and wet, and he realized she'd dug her fingernails so hard into her palms that they'd bled. He slid onto the rock beside her. "How does the rest of it go? I have never heard it."

"Of course not. It has not been written yet and will not be for another hundred years." But she continued the song before he joined her at the part he remembered.

When they came to the last line, he saw a tear make its way down her cheek. Reaching out, he brushed it away. "Why do ye cry?"

"I am thinking of all that is to come. All that will happen here and all over the Highlands, and it makes my heart ache. So much death and destruction." Her voice sounded as far away as her gaze. "All of it for nothing."

"Nae for naught," Euan replied. "Perhaps it may seem so to you —"

"It is for nothing, Euan," Grace asserted as she cut off his thought. "Nothing comes of it except the destruction of the Highlanders and the entire clan system. The Stuarts do not come back, and there is so much lost."

"Then help me stop it. Help us change the outcome. Ye know how."

"I cannot! I cannot change history that way because the future depends on it staying as it is."

"Then why should I worry about dying when everything I know will be destroyed anyway?"

"Because you are meant for more than this. I do not know what, but clearly it is important, or I would not be here."

Euan looked down and stroked her palm as he watched the wounds heal right before his eyes. He heard her breath catch just a little, though she remained unmoving. The skin of her hands was soft and delicate, nothing like his own, but there was something oddly familiar about the way it felt to hold them. "I will have to get ye an arasaid to wear while ye are here, or ye can continue to wear the one my mother lent ye. It will help ye avoid further suspicion," he said, changing the subject.

"You sing beautifully."

"Thank ye," he replied. "So do ye. Singing is one of my favorite things to do."

"Mine too," Grace said in a quiet voice. "Why did you help me? You could have let it happen and I would have been out of your way."

Euan looked back up at her. "I dinnae know," he answered with complete honesty. "It angered me to see ye treated such when ye have been naught but kind. Ye did nae deserve it."

"Does anyone?"

"No. I have never struck a woman and never would. There is no cause for it." He reached up and touched her face where she'd been hit. "Already gone. That is incredible," Euan whispered, leaning closer to her to study her face.

When he cupped her chin in his fingers, she didn't stop him from turning her face one way, then the other, while examining it. As he brought her chin back to center, he found himself looking directly into her eyes, and he couldn't look away. The vivid intensity he saw there made him almost forget to breathe. She was so different, different than anyone he'd ever met. Smooth, unmarred skin, perfect teeth, a vision of health in a way no woman here could ever hope to match. He wanted to touch her, craved it in some strange way. Euan brushed a thumb across her lips, watching her expression change to one he couldn't read. Everything in him ached with that wanting, screamed at him to do what he wished to and to hell with consequences. It was overwhelming, terrifying in its strength and the way it threatened to swallow every excuse he had for keeping his distance from her. He'd never felt this, never thought he could, and yet again there was that sense of the familiar. Euan pulled her forward just a bit before his reason caught up with him, causing him to pull himself back with haste and slide off the rock to get away from her and everything he'd just felt.

Euan said nothing as he fetched the buckets he'd come with, filled them, and began to walk back. There was something about her that pulled at him, something just out of reach urging him to remember what was hidden just beneath the surface, and he couldn't even begin to explain what it might be. Whatever it was, it was distracting, and it allowed him to open up to her in ways he knew he shouldn't if he meant to keep his word.

CHAPTER 7

$\mathbf{A}$s night settled once again, Grace took up her post outside. This was her time to think, to strategize, to process. She was still troubled by all that had happened that morning, and the moment they'd shared where they'd each seemed to forget who and what the other was. He'd done his best to avoid her when she returned, and then had taken himself off to his work at the castle. When he came back later in the day, he'd acted as though she wasn't even there. This bothered her, but she wasn't sure why. It had never bothered her before but, for some reason, he was different. There was something about him that drew her in, whispers in her mind of safety and the trust she'd never given anyone, and it was something she'd never experienced with any of her other targets. He was, however, almost infuriatingly changeable. One minute he was as kind to her as he had been at the loch, and the next he was ignoring her. Another moment he was open with her, and the next he pulled back and shut the door again. His signals were so mixed that it left her confused and off balance, but why should she care? He was just another target and her job was to make him go the right way.

"But he isn't just another target. He isn't. He feels like something more, but you can't even say what that is."

The thought repeated in her head and she brought a hand up to her forehead to rub it as if the action would somehow silence the words. Again, it was the beauty she'd glimpsed in him before it was shuttered and hidden once more. It was not his looks, though he was beautiful in that way too, but it was his heart, his empathy, his tendency to kindness. That he was either of those things surprised her, but even that surprise was confusing. Why *wouldn't* he be any of those things?

She jumped as she felt him sit down beside her. She'd been so lost in her thoughts that she hadn't heard him come out. "Why are you not sleeping?" Grace asked in a whisper.

Euan gave a gentle shrug. "I could nae, so I thought perhaps I would come sit with ye a while. I have had a difficult time finding sleep some nights ever since Falkirk, and I find I like speaking with ye."

Grace turned her head to look at him and could see him smiling in the light from the moon filtering through the trees. "I like speaking with you, too."

"Do ye usually like it? Speaking with those ye are here for."

"Sometimes, but then it is usually not anything like this."

"I apologize for ignoring ye today. It was nae kind and ye did nae deserve it from me."

"Why did you?"

"I dinnae know. It is the strangest feeling when I am with ye. I both want to talk to ye and dinnae. I barely know ye, but at the same time I feel like I have known ye always. I dinnae usually say this much to anyone, dinnae speak this much, and I am nae even sure why I am telling ye any of this now. Ye confuse me."

"You are not the only one. I am confused, too. Not only by your treatment of me, but by why I even care. I usually do not care if my target likes me or not. Whether they do or do not is irrelevant."

"But this time ye do. For some reason ye do. I feel the same way," Euan said. "What is it ye do out here all night?"

"Think," she replied. "Mostly think. Try to process all that happened and think on what to do next. I also stand guard, in a way, so no one might harm you."

"Have ye thought of what to do next with me?"

"No," Grace admitted, though a small smile passed over her lips. "I am having a difficult time thinking of anything when it comes to you."

Euan chuckled. "I dinnae know what ye would do either, if I am honest. If I were ye, I think I would just leave me to my fate."

"I cannot," Grace replied, a hint of sadness underlying her voice.

"What would ye do if someone came to do us harm in the night?"

"Stop them."

"Aye, but how?"

"I can stab someone just as well as you can, Euan."

Euan raised an eyebrow. "I thought ye said ye did nae kill people?"

"I said we did not kill our targets. I said nothing of anyone else."

Though it was frowned upon, a Watcher could do it in defense of their target, but that was the only time it was allowed. The shocked look on Euan's face as he realized she was right, that she hadn't said that and he'd just assumed it, was amusing to her. It was clearly not the answer he'd expected.

"Have ye?"

"Not yet."

"Tell me; what is it like to know ye cannae die?" Euan asked, the question coming out of the blue.

Grace looked over at him, her gaze questioning. "I can."

"But nae here. Ye cannae die when ye are here with me."

"No."

"How does that feel? Here ye are invincible and, as a soldier, the thought intrigues me. Are ye ever afraid? Does it make ye feel powerful?"

Grace understood what he was getting at. She had a power he did not. Death always lurked in the shadows for him. Each battle, each journey, each day a chance to never come home again. "Of course I am, just as you are. Even though I know I cannot die here, I am still afraid of it. I think that is just being human. No, it does not make me feel powerful, not really. I suppose it could, but you would be surprised by how quickly you no longer think about it."

"Aye, as am I, ye are right. Each battle terrifies me, but I push past it and fight for my life. Every time I stand there, across the field from the Hanover lines, I think I will nae return, and now ye have come to tell me I will nae. For all that I have feared it, it seems as though this time I dinnae fear it at all."

"If you could not die, what would you do?"

It was a powerful question, and he took a long moment to consider it. "I would make everything right for everyone I could."

"How?"

"Justice for those who did nae have it, rid the world of the tyrants who crave war and send others to die."

Rid the world of those who craved war. It was why Grace did what she did; to protect a future where that no longer existed. "But you are not afraid now."

"No. When I am with ye I find it hard to fear anything. I dinnae know why."

Grace rested her cheek against her knees. "You are safe with me, and it is my job to keep you alive. That is why."

"The one thing ye are meant to save me from is the one thing ye will nae."

"I still have time."

"Nae much. We are only here for a short time. We parted ways with the prince after Stirling as he continued north. Lochiel feared raids from the Fort William garrison, so we returned to make sure they did nae and laid siege to the garrison for a while before we gave up and came back here. The prince has now ordered us back. As strange as it is to say, I am glad that ye have come. I feel as though ye know who I am deep down, more than I do. There is something comforting in that. I dinnae need to pretend."

"No, you do not."

"I wish I understood this," he said in a near whisper.

"So do I," Grace replied.

"Ye are this secret I must keep, but I dinnae mind it, because it means I dinnae have to share yer time with anyone else, while at the same time I cannae figure out why such a thing matters to me."

"How often have you ever had anything truly be yours and yours alone?"

"Aside from my horse? Never," he admitted. "It is more than that though, but I cannae say what."

"You should get some rest."

"Is it strange to ye that I dinnae feel the need for it? For it is strange to me that I would prefer to be out here with ye instead of asleep in my own bed."

Grace's smile was faint in the darkness. "If it would not completely ruin you, I would say you are welcome to stay, but we both know you have a job to do and cannot do it if you fall asleep."

"Aye, that is true enough," Euan said as he rose. "Goodnight to ye, Grace."

"Goodnight, Euan," she replied as he went inside. When she was alone again, Grace buried her face in her knees. This hadn't helped.

CHAPTER 8

The following morning, Euan emerged to find that Grace had already fetched water. It was kind of her to do and he appreciated it a great deal. She came from the trees on the loch side and smiled when she saw him.

"Good morning. I hope you found at least a little sleep," she said.

"Aye, a bit," he replied as he returned her smile. "Thank ye for getting the water. It was good of ye."

Grace gave a gentle shrug. "I had to do something. I was feeling a bit useless."

"I am nae sure that is how I would ever describe ye. Would ye like to walk with me? I dinnae need to be at Achnacarry until the afternoon. I can show ye about."

"I think that sounds wonderful," Grace replied.

He held out his arm for her to take, a gesture that normally implied a sort of intimacy of connection, but it wasn't something he was thinking about. Grace took his arm and they headed into the woods, away from the loch. There was silence for a long time as they both searched for something to say.

"I know I will never see it, but could ye tell me about the future? Is that even allowed?"

"Not exactly, but I can tell you at least some things. You cannot speak of them to anyone though."

"Ye have my word."

"What is it you would like to know?

"I would nae even know where to start."

Grace laughed. "Excellent point. Hm, let me see. Well, we no longer use candles for light. We use something more complicated, but it can make it as bright as the daylight inside a room."

"Truly? That must be quite the luxury."

"No, everyone has it."

"Ye must all be rich then, in the future."

"No, we are not that either. Well, some are while many are not. Just like now."

"Some things never change, lass."

"Sometimes they do," Grace replied.

"Sometimes, ye are right, but slowly. What else?"

"Water is so clean we can drink it, so ale and wine become something had for enjoyment instead of something had all the time."

Euan raised an eyebrow at that. "Aye?"

Grace nodded. "Many things happen in the centuries to follow."

"It seems so. What do ye do to amuse yerselves?"

"There are so many options and I cannot tell you any of them but let us just say that we are spoilt for choice. There are the same things you do, of course. Music, dancing, walking, reading."

"What is the music like? Is it the same?"

"No, not at all, though a great many of us like the music that will soon be coming into the world and enjoy it immensely. It endures."

"I feel as though music is one of the things that always does."

"I agree."

"What of books? Ye mentioned reading."

"Books!"

The very word made Grace smile and Euan knew he'd touched upon something she was fond of.

"They are so inexpensive that everyone has them, all kinds of them, in their own homes," she said. "If they do not, they can buy them or go to a library and borrow them. I have shelves of books."

Euan stopped and turned to her. "Do ye? Shelves of them? What I would nae give to see such or even have such myself."

"I do. Books of every sort. Stories that are made up, stories that are true, books that teach. I wish you could see it, too."

Euan went quiet as he turned to continue walking. He said nothing further until they reached a spot where a small creek ran through, making its way to the larger river nearby. "This is one of my favorite places. It is quiet here; a good place to go when ye are troubled and need to think."

"Do you come here often?"

"At some points more than others," he replied as he turned to lean against a tree. "Where have ye been, Grace?"

"Been?"

"Aye, been. Ye must have gone all over in yer work."

"Oh. Yes, I suppose I have. England, France, Switzerland, Italy, Canada, Japan, the Americas," Grace said, trying to list at least some of them off.

"Christ, I have nae even heard of some of those."

Grace laughed. "There are more, and I promise you have not heard of those either."

"Is this yer first time to Scotland, then?"

"No, I have been here before."

"Oh aye? What was yer mission then?"

"It was the same time frame as this. I had to stop a night attack that —" but Grace froze, the color draining from her face. "No," she said, her voice tight.

Euan frowned and looked at her. "A night attack that what?"

"I ... no. Oh no. It is my fault," she said in a horrified whisper.

"What is?"

Grace looked at Euan, unable to check the tears that had welled in her eyes and looking as though she might be sick at any moment.

"Grace, what is wrong with ye?" Euan asked, her sudden change concerning him a great deal.

Grace sank to the ground to sit, burying her face in her hands as she began to cry. Euan made his way to where she sat and knelt in front of her. He didn't understand what was happening or why she was crying, but it made him uncomfortable to see the normally calm and confident Watcher become so emotional. Grace looked up at him and then sat up on her knees to throw her arms around him. It took Euan by surprise and he didn't embrace her at first, but he overcame that surprise and put his arms around her as she cried into his shoulder. It was clear she needed some sort of comfort and he wouldn't deny her. To do so would be a heartlessness he wasn't capable of.

"I am so sorry, Euan," she sobbed out.

"Sorry? For what?"

Grace couldn't seem to answer him through her tears, nor did she even try, her entire body shaking.

"Grace, shh it is all right," he said, his tone gentle as he tried his best to comfort her. Despite his initial reaction, it felt perfect now to have her there in his arms, it felt right to him somehow. There was, again, that feeling of having always known her; the feeling that he'd been waiting for her to come back from a long journey to see him again. Something that made him want to say, 'ah, there ye are at last.'

She looked up at him when he said her name, and Euan's breath caught as the movement brought her face so close to his, the pain in her features bringing an ache to his heart. It was an almost exquisite torture, this feeling of wanting her near but wanting to pull away from her. The torture of the in between. Euan reached out and stroked her cheek with the backs of his fingers, watching as she closed her eyes and feeling her shiver against him. He had a feeling they shouldn't be doing this but, at this moment, he didn't care. In this moment she was his entirely, and he found it was all he wanted.

The temptation he'd felt before came roaring back, once again threatening to overwhelm any sense he had. Why did he feel this way about a woman he barely knew? What was it that drew such feelings and thoughts from him whenever she was near? He'd felt it the other morning, too, when they'd sat upon that rock together. That urge, that need to touch her, to hold her, to find a way to keep her here forever.

"Please do not go," she whispered. "Please."

Euan sighed and rested his forehead against hers, closing his eyes. God help him, but he wanted to agree to not go. In this moment he felt as though he might agree to anything if it kept her here, but it wouldn't. Even his agreement wouldn't. She would be gone, and he would be here.

"I must," he whispered in return.

Grace turned her face away from him and tried to stifle another sob. "I cannot do this. Please, I cannot do this. Please choose someone else, you have to choose someone else," she whispered, the pain in her voice clear.

"What do ye mean?" he asked, though this time it was whispered in her ear. Who was she talking to?

"I mean the ones who sent me. They need to send someone else. It cannot be me. I want them to replace me."

A sense of panic seized Euan's heart. "No. Please ..."

"Why?"

"I dinnae know, I just ..." he trailed off as he struggled to find the words. "There is so little time left, and what time there is I want to spend with ye, nae some other. Please dinnae leave."

"There does not have to be. You can choose not to go," she replied, turning her face back to him. "That is all."

"And if I do? What then? What happens? Ye go on to yer next mission and I remain here to suffer the consequences of my decision."

"There would not be any because there would be no one left alive to mete them out. Euan, please, I cannot watch you die!"

"I am nae sure ye will have a choice, lass. I have already

made mine and it is what we shall both live with," he said as his voice dropped near to a whisper, unable to stop himself from brushing his lips across hers.

Grace's breath caught and she looked at him in confusion. Before she could wonder whether that had been accidental, he made sure to make it clear that it hadn't been, this time with an actual kiss. It was a moment of weakness for him, but right now he didn't regret it. Her lips were softer than he could've imagined they'd be, and the small sound she made against his lips caused a flare of desire he hadn't known he was capable of feeling.

When she finally met him in that kiss, he couldn't help but respond to it, and it only made that feeling stronger for him. It was something he'd never felt when he'd kissed others, and it was far deeper than that. It was as if he could now feel her in every bit of him, melting everything he'd been and replacing it with something made up of them both. What it left behind ensured that the very essence of her being would never leave him, no matter how much its presence might torture him, and every bit of him cried out for more. His hands flattened on her back, pressing her against his body. When she responded by gripping the arms of his coat, it pulled him back into reality and away from her, seizing him with the sudden panic of letting her in too close, this person who could change everything if he let her. She was his mirror, and the realization was more than he could take.

Euan stared at her for a long moment, surprised by what he'd done, by having allowed himself to do what he knew he shouldn't, while at the same time fighting himself not to do it again. "I have to go," he said before he stood and walked away from her.

"Euan wait ..." Grace said, reaching out a hand to him, but it was too late.

***

After Euan hurried from the clearing, Grace was left to wonder what he'd meant when he'd said he had to go. Did he mean to battle or to Achnacarry? Perhaps it was both. She rested her hand against her chest; the pain from everything she felt now was crushing. What was happening to her?

The horrible thought that had started all of this curled around her once more, and Grace felt like her heart might choke her. He'd wanted her to tell him what was wrong, but how could she tell him? How could she explain it? To answer him would've been to chance the alteration of history, and she couldn't take that chance. Her last mission here had been to make sure the night attack that would've given the Jacobites the upper hand at Culloden didn't happen, and she had. Now Grace realized that in doing so she'd sentenced Euan to death. She hadn't known him then, and it had been an entirely different timeline than this one, but he would've been there then, too, or a version of him. He would've died the next day because of what she'd done.

There was an agonizing pain in being forced to confront the consequences of her actions face to face. She'd never had to do so before, and while what had happened was supposed to happen, here was a casualty of that history. Not just a name but a face, a body, a personality, all gone because of what she'd done. What was The Council doing? How could they send her to both save him and kill him, and why hadn't she realized it before now? The answer, of course, was that the first mission hadn't been about him while this one was. But in that timeline, he'd died, and it was because of her. It still would be if she was unsuccessful in stopping him in this one. She would once again be the agent of his death and the thought broke her heart.

On the other side of that pain was what he'd just done. Being so close to him had made her crave it and fear it all at once, and it was the strangest feeling she'd ever known. It had inspired the desire for the intimacy of a type of touch she normally hated when he'd stroked her cheek, that specific touch being one she'd always pulled away from. This was dangerous. *He* was dangerous. She should've pulled away from him, taken a step back, but she couldn't. She hadn't wanted to. What he was stirring up in her were things she'd never encountered; not with any of her other targets, not with anyone in her own time. The kiss he'd given her had been slow, gentle, and overwhelming in its power. No one had kissed her that way before, and they'd never made her feel what he just had, that was for certain.

She had to stop him. She couldn't fail because failure meant that he would be gone from the world yet again. He would die and she would have as good as pulled the trigger.

CHAPTER 9

Euan hadn't joined Grace again that night, though she felt that was probably for the best. The two of them hadn't spoken when he'd returned from his duties at Achnacarry, and Grace had barely been able to look at him. She'd reached out to The Council again, and again gotten no response from them.

When she returned with water the following morning, Euan was already gone. Grace set the buckets down with a heavy heart. They needed to talk to each other, but she wasn't sure she wanted to or could. He made her feel too much and all she wanted was to run from it and from him; but she had a job to do. Grace let herself follow the feeling of him to where she already assumed he would be: back at the creek they had been at yesterday. He went there to think, and she was certain they were both doing a lot of that.

As Grace entered the small clearing, she found Euan leaning against a tree as he watched the water slide by, fidgeting with a small stick in his hands. He looked exhausted and torn, the same as she imagined she'd feel in her own body if it were here.

"Do ye nae wonder about it?"

"About what?" Grace replied without moving closer to him, not surprised he knew she was there.

"About what ye are doing?" he said as he tossed a piece of broken twig into the water.

"No. What is there to wonder about? I have known about this all my life."

"But what do ye really know, Grace? What do ye really know about the motivations of those who send ye to do what ye do. What makes ye so sure they are right?"

"I have seen what comes of this work. How much better the world can be."

"Better for who?"

"For everyone."

Euan scoffed. "Nae better for those of us ye stop from doing what we feel we must."

Grace frowned. "What does that mean?"

Euan looked at her, and where there had once been sadness there was now frustration and anger. "What I mean is how do ye and the others know that any one choice is better than another? How do ye know that the other choice would lead to anything worse? Ye dinnae. Ye cannae because ye dinnae let it happen."

"It is not like that, Euan."

"Then what is it like, Grace? Tell me."

"I cannot. You know that."

"Ach, there ye have it. More secrecy, more hiding. Ye have nae even the decency to tell me and it is *my* life ye are playing with!" he shouted at her.

Grace winced, the words hurting her more than she'd thought they could. His life. He had no idea how right he was. "It is against the rules. I would tell you if I could. Please, you have to trust me."

"Why should I? What have ye done but throw my life into chaos and turmoil?"

"I never meant to —"

"Dinnae bother, Grace," he said, her name almost spat as if it disgusted him to speak it when he cut her off. "I want ye to leave me be. Dinnae come near me, dinnae speak to me. I want ye to tell those who sent ye that I have no intention of abandoning my duty, and ye can leave as ye begged to do yesterday."

"Euan —"

"NO! I dinnae know what ye have done to me, but I want it to stop. I cannae feel this! Any of this! No matter my choice ye will go. Ye will be gone and I will be left wondering why I did any of it because none of it will keep ye with me!"

"I cannot stay," Grace whispered over the lump in her throat. "No matter how much I might want to."

"Aye, ye cannae, and that is exactly my point. Tell me, Grace, would ye abandon yer duty if ye knew coming here to me meant ye would die?"

Grace shook her head. "But I cannot."

"If ye could. If ye knew a mission would lead to yer death, would ye still do it?"

"Yes, I would have to."

"Yet ye are asking me nae to do the same."

"It is not the same."

"Oh, aye, it is the same. Dinnae lie to yerself, Grace."

"How?" she asked, feeling her own temper rising now.

Euan laughed; the sound darker than it should be, cold. "Ye are just another soldier in a different war, sent by those whose true purposes ye dinnae know, by those who cannae be bothered to do it themselves. Just like me. Ye can say whatever ye like but that is the truth of it and deep down ye know it."

"No, I know the motivations. I know why I do what I do. I am fighting for everyone who comes after this. I am fighting for centuries of people. What are you fighting for? Nothing. You are willing to sacrifice yourself, but for what? What is it really for? What will it mean to you? Do you think it will be better for you? It will not matter. None of it will matter. Your life will still be the same as it always was no matter what king you get, right? Is that not what you said? At least if I died it would be to save the rest of the world. If you die it will be for a cause that fails."

"Ye know naught about me, Grace!" he shouted in anger, her words clearly hitting too close for his comfort. "Dinnae act as though ye do!"

68

"Yes, I do! I know that you are better than this! You deserve better than this! You have shown me so much even though you did not mean to! Think about what you will be removing from the world if you do this!"

"It will remove naught! No one will care if I was here or if I died. No one will remember my name in a hundred years. The only one who will care is my mother. I mean naught to the greater game of things."

"I will care!" Grace shouted at him in something bordering on a scream before her voice again became choked by the emotion that threatened to overwhelm her.

Euan looked at her for a moment in stunned silence, allowing her to see the impact her inadvertently intense and unreserved declaration had made before his anger smothered it.

"Euan, I will care," Grace continued. "I will remember all of that and I will know I could have saved you and did not."

"Ye will be the only one then. Again, it does nae matter. Ye can stay if ye like. Ye can try to talk me out of this if ye like, but ye must know ye will fail. I will nae change it. Stay and be my company before I am gone if that is what pleases ye, but I will nae bend, Grace. I will nae."

Euan pushed himself away from the tree and stormed past her, shoving Grace's hand away from him when she reached out to try and stop him from leaving again. Grace squeezed her eyes shut and looked up for a moment, trying to force herself to be strong, to contain her emotion, and failing miserably. Giving up, she buried her face in her hands and wept.

***

As Euan stalked through the woods he didn't look back. He couldn't. He couldn't see her now, couldn't touch her. He felt helpless, and that feeling had turned to anger at all of this. The one thing he wanted most was the one thing he could never have, and worse was the knowledge that he'd be hurting her more than he'd ever want to. That someone else besides his mother cared so much for him was more than he could stand, and all it did was make him angrier.

When they saw each other later that day, he forced himself to act as though nothing had changed and she did the same, something that was far more painful to see than he'd expected. Over the next few days there was an uneasy peace between them. She tried to convince him to stay back at every opportunity she could find, and he did his best to counter or ignore her by changing the subject. A sort of routine was established where they took a long walk in the morning with Euan pointing out his favorite places, while Grace animatedly told him of books she'd read, art she'd seen, music she loved; all things to come that he'd never experience even if he didn't go to Drumossie as planned.

He found it intriguing to listen to and to learn from, even as he knew it was information he could never share and that she was likely not supposed to be giving him. It was a secret between them, and it surprised him how much he still liked the thought. She was his alone until the end came, something special, someone to carry with him. Even knowing he would die, Euan felt strangely at peace with it. Grace would remember even when everyone else who would was gone, just as she'd said that day. He tried to put all of it out of his mind and just enjoy her company.

In the afternoons he would head to Achnacarry to see to his duties there, though he found he missed her presence. She couldn't come there — she'd told him as much — as it would bring too much suspicion upon him. It was the same for anyone she worked with; if they had some sort of employment they were on their own until they returned home. When the time came for him to return, he found he walked faster, eager to have her attention once more and a chance at conversation. His extensive education had long isolated him from his peers, and to at last find someone he could really speak to was something he was unable and unwilling to resist.

One afternoon at the end of the week, Euan returned earlier than normal to find Grace helping Aileen with the washing, and it made him smile to see them working together. He knew that each day brought him closer to being parted from both of them forever, but he also knew they were aware of it, too. His mother pleaded with him, and her tears broke his heart, but he could not and would not give in to that and she knew it. She'd eventually stopped, and he knew she now could only pray for Grace's success. He was glad he wouldn't see his mother's grief when Grace inevitably failed.

"Grace," Euan called out as he entered the clearing. When she looked up at him and smiled, he felt nervous, which was new. "There is a party tonight at Achnacarry. Would ye like to attend with me?"

Aileen looked at him with a wary eye. "What kind of party?"

"A farewell party," Euan replied. Aileen's expression tightened, and she stood up before she turned and walked back inside. Euan shoved aside his desire to go after her and looked at Grace. "Will ye come?"

"I will."

Euan nodded and made his way back to the loch to bathe and he could hear Aileen weeping inside as he passed. By the time he returned, Grace was ready to go with him, having pulled a fresh dress from the bag she'd brought with her. It was a deep red, cut in a style meant for a more formal function, and trimmed with black lace.

Euan smiled in appreciation when she stepped out to meet him. "That color looks beautiful on ye."

"Thank you," she replied, her tone shy for the first time he'd ever heard.

Euan offered his arm to her and they walked together as he started to fill her in on who would be there, why they were important, and what was happening. As they arrived,

Grace stopped to look around her, and Euan remembered this was the first time she'd been here. Achnacarry was a beautiful place, and he remembered the first time he'd truly seen it. The castle itself was quite large, rising about three stories high and made of wood planks from ancient trees. The sun had not yet set behind the mountains, and it bathed the whole of it in a golden glow. Around it was a wall that was nestled into the surrounding hills. If Grace turned around, she'd see a large expanse of land leading to the river. Inside the castle yard people moved about freely, the large doors to the hall standing open and welcoming them with warm light, music, and laughter.

When they moved on to go inside, she was more reserved and stayed close to him. That she was a stranger showing up on Euan's arm earned her more than a few irritated stares, but she ignored them, and seemed to be observing everyone and everything around her with a keen gaze.

"Euan!"

His name called; Euan turned to find Lochiel beckoning to him. He approached his chief with Grace and bowed, while Grace gave an elegant curtsy. "Lochiel," he said.

"Good to see ye are still with us. Ye have been so distracted of late I was starting to worry about ye. Ye know how important yer leadership has been to the men, and how important ye have been to the prince and the rest of the chiefs. Who do ye have with ye?"

Grace looked at Euan, clearly finding Lochiel's words curious, but he ignored the questions there and didn't look at her.

"My cousin, Grace. She is visiting here from the colonies in the hopes of finding a proper Cameron husband."

Lochiel laughed and shook his head. "I cannae blame ye for that lass. I welcome ye, but I am sorry ye came at such a time, for we are all about to go to battle once more."

"I know," Grace said. "I suppose I shall have my pick of who returns."

Euan stiffened at her words because they felt pointed at him, a reminder that most of them wouldn't return.

"Ye are welcome to them, lass. Though from the looks of things, it may be ye, Euan, and the lasses of Achnacarry will wail with grief for it," he said with a smile and a wink.

Grace and Euan looked at each other and then looked away. They both knew it would never happen. Grace would soon be gone, and Euan would soon be dead.

"Come Euan, we all have much to discuss."

"Would you mind if I came, too? I find this sort of thing fascinating," Grace said.

Lochiel and Euan both looked at her, their expressions curious. "If ye wish."

Euan followed the man, along with Grace. "What are ye doing?" Euan hissed at her.

Grace ignored him as they stepped into a chamber where a map lay spread out upon a table. On the map were small figurines, which symbolized varying clan forces. Some of the Cameron officers stood around it, discussing the best place to gather and attack from, and Euan felt her release his arm as she stepped forward.

Grace studied the map and then spoke without looking up from it. "Perhaps if you simply lined up here," she said as she moved some of the pieces, "instead of here, you would have a chance of avoiding being caught in the marshy ground I have heard is there. If you go through it, it will skew your line toward the wall you have marked here and could trap you under fire with no way out."

Euan's heart felt like it had stopped as he realized what she'd done. She'd just warned them. She'd told them what their downfall would be, doing exactly what she'd told him she couldn't do, but why? Why would she risk everything just to stop him? He stepped up beside her to take note of what she'd set out, and he could see what she was saying, could see that she was right, even if they couldn't.

"How do ye know the ground there," one of the men asked her.

"We passed it on my way here," Grace said, shocking Euan with how easily the lie rolled off her tongue.

The other men looked at her movements on the map but said nothing.

"Thank ye for trying to help, lass, but ye should leave the battle strategy to the men. We are where the prince and Lord Murray will wish us to be," Lochiel said.

"But, if you just —"

"Euan, ye should see the lass out to a glass of wine and return," Lochiel said in a deliberate move to silence Grace.

"Lochiel, what if —" Euan began, but stopped as he saw the looks fixed on him. "Of course. Come Grace," he said as he took her arm.

"Euan, wait, please," she whispered as he led her out.

He could hear the panicked distress in her voice, but it did nothing to ease his temper. "What have ye done?" he asked her once they were clear of being heard, pulling her hard around by the arm he held to stand in front of him. "Ye fool woman! What are ye about?"

"You told me the only way to stop you was to help you win. I just told you how. Why will you not listen to me?"

"Ye said ye could nae do such and yet ye did. So ye were either lying to me before or ye are up to something else."

"I have *never* lied to you," Grace said, bristling at the accusation. "I do not want any of you to die."

"It is too late for that now."

"No, it is not. Please, just listen to me! The prince's forces, along with those of Murray, Stewart of Appin, Lochiel, and others, will try to mount a night attack at Nairn the day before the battle. It is not supposed to work, they get disoriented and turn back, they lose the element of surprise, but if you can just convince them to —"

"Grace, stop," he hissed through clenched teeth.

"You have to believe me! I am breaking every rule there is and I am doing it for *you*! How do you not understand!"

"I am nae sure what I believe now," he said as he released her arm and turned away from her to go back to the others.

"Euan," she called after him, but he didn't stop.

When he was released from the strategy meeting, Euan watched as Grace sat and talked with the other women in attendance, laughing and smiling as though she'd known them all her life. He couldn't help but wonder what she was like in her real life. Was she different? Was the person he'd gotten to know the real Grace, or was it the persona she put on as part of her duties? It surprised him that he even wanted to know. He'd spent these last days attempting to see her as a hindrance to his duty to Lochiel, but was she? What if she was right? What if this *was* all for nothing?

Euan took a long drink of wine to try and quell those thoughts. He knew his duty and would do it no matter what. He knew she must do hers, but all she could do now was try to warn him and convince him not to move forward. Those things he could ignore, the same way he had been for the last several days. He frowned into his cup as he watched one of the other men approach her and ask her to dance, his chest tightening as he saw her place her hand in his with a smile and agree. It made him want to go to her, pull her away, and punch the man in the face for even daring to speak to her. Euan shook his head and looked away. He couldn't let himself feel the things he had that day in the woods. To even think about those moments made everything in him ache with sadness. She wasn't his, and she never would be. That moment was ending.

Euan spent the rest of the evening avoiding her and in conversation with the other officers. They would ride out tomorrow at dawn to join the rest of the forces, and he'd be free of her at last because he'd made his choice. The self-doubt began to creep in once more before he shoved it away. There was no time for that now.

He felt a hand on his and looked over, finding himself almost disappointed when it wasn't Grace. Instead, it was Brenda, someone with whom he'd spent much time before the war.

"Hello," he said before Brenda drew him aside into one of the darkened corridors and wrapped her arms around him. As she tried to pull him into a kiss, he pulled back from her. "No."

She frowned at him. "What is wrong with ye? Ye have nae wanted to spend any time with me since ye returned, and now ye are about to leave again."

Brenda had been trying to tempt him back into her bed since they'd come back from Fort William, but he hadn't been interested then either, though that'd been for different reasons. "I told ye before I left for Glenfinnan that I did nae feel for ye the way ye wished me to. That has nae changed."

"Even if it has nae, we can still —"

"No." Euan said, his tone firm, cutting off her words. Where before she might have tempted him, she no longer did. There was someone else there now, even if he didn't want to admit it. "Brenda, please, dinnae do this."

"It is her is it nae?"

"Who?"

"That lass ye brought with ye tonight. For all yer swearing that ye did nae want anything serious, look at ye now."

"No, it is nae. I have no time now and we leave at dawn. I have no interest in anything until this is over. I cannae think of the future."

"I dinnae care what ye say, Euan, there is clearly something in yer way, and I can see how ye look at her."

"Then how do ye explain my nae wanting to bed ye when we got back? She was nae even here then."

"Ye were tired. Anyone with eyes could see that."

"And I still am." She didn't understand what war was really like. None of them did.

Brenda shook her head. "I wish I knew what to do for ye to get ye to my side again."

"There is naught ye can do. When the war is over, that is the time to think about this," Euan said as he stepped back and started to walk away from her.

"I will pray for ye, Euan. Pray for ye to come home to us. To me."

He stopped for a moment, his jaw tightening as he closed his eyes, thankful his back was to her. Pray for him to come home. They could pray all they wanted, but it would make no difference. Euan Cameron was a dead man in a matter of days. He shook his head and walked back out into the hall.

Once the party dispersed, he collected Grace and the two of them started the walk back together in complete silence. It was surprising to him, because she was usually talking to him, trying to convince him to stop what he was doing, but perhaps she realized now that it would do no good. Indeed, Grace seemed more subdued and withdrawn than he'd ever seen her.

"Ye are quiet tonight," Euan said, breaking the silence.

"There is not much to say," Grace replied.

"Ye have given up then?"

"No."

"Then should ye nae be even now trying to convince me nae to go tomorrow?"

"You will go tomorrow no matter what I say. That much is clear."

"Then ye *have* given up."

Grace looked at him, her expression curious. "Did you want me to keep trying? It sounds like you want me to convince you otherwise."

"Is that nae yer job?"

"It is, but there is nothing worth saying tonight. Our time together is not over tomorrow. I still have time."

Their time together. Euan looked over at her and, once again, very much wished she could just stay. If she could stay, he might be persuaded to listen to her pleas, but as it stood, she clearly couldn't. Euan stopped walking.

"If it goes as ye say, will ye mourn me? Or will ye simply go on to the next task?"

"Yes, I would mourn you. Very much." The reply escaped before she could stop it and Euan saw Grace bite her lip hard.

Euan looked at her, his expression softening. She would mourn him. If he died it would hurt her. Something about that hurt him, too, even as it surprised him. He'd worked so hard to believe it would mean nothing to her, that her words about remembering were just words but, here she was, telling him she would mourn him. There would be more than his mother to mourn his death, but Grace would be far from here and doing it alone. He reached out and stroked her cheek, finding it wet with tears he hadn't realized she'd shed.

"Grace," he whispered, "I really am sorry."

"If you were truly sorry you would stop this," she whispered back.

"I cannae. It is my duty, just as trying to stop me is yers, but ye will nae stop me. I know that hurts ye, and I am sorry for it."

"It is not just me you will hurt. It is not just your mother. It is whatever future depends on you not doing this. All of the people who will be affected by your choice."

"I cannae think of them. I dinnae know them and they dinnae know me. I am just one person and I need to play my part here."

"Then you will die," Grace replied, her voice thick with the emotion she was trying to hold back. "Make your peace with it."

"I have, long ago," Euan admitted. "And now so should ye."

Grace let out a small sob and stepped back from him, yanking her arm from his in a violent motion, before she started to walk ahead of him into the woods so fast that he had to run to catch up to her.

As Euan caught her hand in his, she turned and snatched it back as though he'd burned her. "Stop! Please!"

"Stop what?"

"This! What you are doing! Stop making this harder than it already is for the both of us!"

"I dinnae understand what ye mean, Grace."

"Yes, you do. You know *exactly* what you are doing," she replied angrily as she backed away from him and further into the darkness of the woods. "You go from ignoring me, to gentle and caring, and back again. Please go back to distrusting me and being distant. I cannot handle this otherwise."

In the darkness, Euan grabbed her arm, pulling her against him before pressing her back against a tree before she had a chance to free herself. "I cannae."

Grace gasped in surprise. "Euan …"

"Why do ye have to be this way, Grace?"

"What way?"

"Why do ye have to be so captivating? Why do ye have to make me crave yer attention? Why can ye nae just be easy to ignore? How do ye make me want ye so much that it feels like my heart is ripping itself apart?"

Grace shook her head, seemingly unable to speak. So close to her, Euan could smell the scent of her skin, and it was like nothing he'd experienced before. It was a scent he couldn't place, and it was as otherworldly as she was. He hadn't noticed it last time. He knew he shouldn't be doing this, knew he shouldn't be giving in again, but he couldn't help himself. If this was the last moment like this he was to have, he couldn't let it pass. He suddenly felt Grace's body tense against his.

"No," Grace sobbed. "Not yet. Please not yet," she whispered. "Euan —"

He turned his face toward hers and stopped her words with a kiss. It was even more overwhelming than the last time, but the desire for her had broken through the wall he'd put up, and he hadn't been able to stop himself. He needed this, needed her, and that feeling of her being inside of him ignited again, white hot and reckless, consuming him from within. He made a small, involuntary sound as her hands found his hair and she returned his affections. She was so soft, so warm, so willing here in this moment. Euan pulled his lips from hers to place a fevered kiss against her neck and felt her arch against him, heard her utter a soft, pleasured sound as her hands tightened in his hair. He went to kiss her lips again and there was nothing there. No Grace. His arms were empty except for the arasaid she'd been wearing; the only thing she'd not arrived with. She had vanished.

In confusion and panic he turned in a circle, trying to see her in the moonlight filtering through the trees. She wasn't there. He would've felt her move if she'd run from him. Where had she gone? Euan's heart sank as he realized what had happened. It was his fault. He'd made his choice and now she was gone. They'd taken her back now that they'd realized she wouldn't succeed. She was gone, sent back to wherever she'd come from, and he would never see her again. The pain that ripped through his heart at the realization made his knees weak.

"Grace!" Euan screamed her name into the darkness with a final hope that she was there somewhere. The only response was the sound of rustling leaves, and it hardened his heart once more. With her gone, there was no reason not to proceed. If he was to die, then it was time to get on with it.

Lochiel's regiment left at dawn the following morning, as planned. The trip north was long and arduous, leaving the men exhausted after they quick-marched for 50 miles over two days. They arrived only to find that the prince hadn't bothered to think of provisioning for the regiments he'd ordered north. From somewhere, biscuits had been scrounged, enough for each man to have only one. It had caused a great deal of bad feeling amongst the men and didn't help the morale. Euan and the other officers did their best to keep them together, but the discipline was tenuous at best.

The following day, instead of being allowed to rest, they were ordered to stand in formation and wait for Cumberland to arrive. When the duke and his forces never showed, Lochiel was furious that an entire day, which could've been devoted to finding food and resting, had been wasted instead. It hadn't helped his men's exhaustion and had certainly not helped their morale. It only got worse when there was nothing to eat that night.

In the darkness just before dawn, Euan rested beneath his plaid and tried to ignore the hunger that gnawed at him. In his hands he held the arasaid that Grace had worn, trying to find comfort in the scent of her. He'd brought it with him because at least it kept a part of her there, and it had indeed brought him comfort on the journey here. He wouldn't see her again and he couldn't put words to what he felt. It was pain, yes, but it was something more, too. It was as though a large part of him was missing, once again opening a void he'd never realized was there until it wasn't. It was fear, too, perhaps. Fear of what he knew was coming. He didn't have to be here. He could go, get a head start, they wouldn't chase him when there was a battle to fight. Euan shook his head to clear the idea from his mind. He couldn't abandon his men, his friends, his chief, his clan.

The night attack she'd warned him about had happened and had failed. Men had dropped to the ground during the march to Nairn, passing out from hunger and exhaustion, forcing them to turn back. There had still been four miles to go and they would have arrived just an hour before dawn, eliminating the element of surprise they'd hoped for, just as she'd said. He'd considered doing what she'd told him and trying to get them to go forward, to change everything, but had stopped himself. To do that would bring harm to her if her own actions hadn't already done so. She'd done what they'd said she couldn't, and she'd done it for him. If he'd used that information, what would've happened? How would it have changed the future in which she lived? Would she live or even be born if the world changed in such a way?

He closed his eyes and began to sing to himself, the only thing he could think of. The song she'd sung to him. Her song.

Chì mi ann coilltean, chì mi ann doireachan
Chì mi ann maghan bàna is toraiche
Chì mi na féidh air làr nan coireachan
Falaicht' an trusgan de chèo
Beanntaichean àrda is àillidh leacainnean
Sluagh ann an còmhnuidh is còire cleachdainnean
'S aotrom mo cheum a' leum g'am faicinn
Is fanaidh mi tacan le deòin.

"Is fanaidh mi tacan le deòin," he whispered.

And I will remain there a while willingly.

CHAPTER 10

Grace opened her eyes to an entirely different set of woods than the ones she'd just left, and it took her a moment to register the change. She'd been ripped out of a moment with Euan, a moment she'd wanted more than she cared to admit, and now she knew she faced watching his end. She buried her face in her hands and wept. Why did it have to be this way? Why couldn't he see? If he wasn't here, she wouldn't be here. He'd made his choice and had come to do his duty. He'd come to die.

Grace had tried her hardest, but nothing she'd said had swayed Euan from his course. What would happen to the timeline if he died? What would happen to her or to any of them? He didn't seem to understand what could happen, but then how could he? The concept of a future so far away being dependent on one's actions wasn't easy for anyone to grasp.

This was, by far, the most difficult mission she'd ever worked. She'd broken all the rules and still it had made no difference. She'd even told him how to thwart her previous mission at Nairn where she'd supported the English, and the defeat which would inevitably lead to his death, but he had *still* come here. She knew it wasn't the failure of her mission or the effect on the future she cried over, but the thought of such a person being forever lost to the world. He fascinated her, and she felt as though in the end she might be the only one who would ever know who he truly had been. He was more than a name on a muster roll in some dusty library, so much more, but that was all he was about to become. The frustration, and honest heartbreak at the thought that every moment she'd spent with him had brought them closer and closer to that moment she'd seen was crushing, that awful moment where he lay dead upon a moor just like the rest, and now that moment was here.

She wanted to go back to the moment she'd just been in, when his cheek was near hers and she could feel the tension in his body as he waged an internal battle she wasn't privy to. A moment that had been too perfect for thinking about any of this, and he'd sent a torrent of emotion rushing through her with the passion that was behind what might be his final kiss, before another feeling had distracted her, a feeling that had sent dread coursing through her veins. It was that heavy feeling that told her she was about to disappear and be moved to the last moment. His last moments. The last moments she had to save him. Grace's mind had fought desperately against the very thing she'd been asking for. She hadn't wanted to leave but she'd had no choice.

The sound of men, guns, and cannons in the near distance brought her head up, and she wiped her eyes on her sleeve. She still had time. She had to try. It was daylight now and easy to see even though it was raining. Grace moved toward the edge of the woods and stepped out into the light, surveying the battlefield. This place was about to become a mass grave and Euan was going to be in it.

In the distance, she could see the English forces mustered and looked away from them. Grace was aware that, by now, the Jacobite men had been under cannon fire for quite some time, suffering many casualties, but that parts of the lines had fallen back to escape it. His must have been one of them if she was here, and she had to find him.

Even as she scanned for him, she knew Euan might see her first. It was hard to miss her now. Gone was the blue wool dress, replaced with a dress of all white. Her hair was down around her shoulders, the rain not seeming to touch her. The choice had been made; the end was near. There was no need for pretense now, no need to hide what she was. An angel should appear as an angel, if that was what you believed they were, even if they are the harbinger of death.

Grace saw Euan at the same time he saw her, and he hurried toward her, momentarily leaving his men and causing Grace to retreat back into the woods when she saw him coming.

"Grace," he called out, breathless, as he stepped into the trees. "Grace, where are ye?"

"Here," she replied as she stepped into view.

"Thank God," he said as he rushed forward and wrapped her in his arms. "Where have ye been?"

Grace wrapped her arms around him, the embrace between them tight as each sought a moment of comfort from their reunion. He wasn't the same, didn't look the same. Instead, he looked exhausted almost to the point of illness. She wanted to beg him not to let go of her, because if he didn't let go, he couldn't follow them to his death.

"They moved me here to the end, to the last chance I have to save you," Grace replied. "I am sorry, I cannot control when it happens."

"Save me," he repeated as he released her. "Ye cannae save me."

"Yes, I can! We can leave here right now! Please, come with me."

"Grace, I cannae."

"Please," she whispered, her tone pleading. "Euan! Do not do this. You know how this ends! You can save yourself."

"No. I cannae abandon my men. How do ye know I would nae be the turning point? How do ye know I dinnae kill an officer and turn the tide?"

"Because if you did, I would not be here! If your contribution had done anything it would happen without interference! How do you not see? You are all going to die here!"

Euan looked down for a moment before a sudden thought seemed to occur to him. "Unless yer mission is to stop me so that someone else lives. Unless it is to keep history as it is written for that person. Perhaps they want ye to stop me so that I dinnae kill them."

"Euan, no, that is not how this works. If I was meant to save someone else, I would be with them, not with you! I am begging you —"

Euan cut her off by holding up a hand. "No more. I have made my choice and there is naught ye can do or say now. I am here and it is over. I am sorry ye failed in yer duty and I hope it does nae bring ye too much pain."

"Chlanna nan con thigibh a so's gheibh sibh feoil!" *Sons of the hounds, come hither and get flesh!*

The Cameron war cry echoed from behind him and Euan turned toward the sound of it before he looked back at her, his expression sad as he reached out to stroke her cheek once more. "I have to go now. Thank ye for that night. It is what I will remember," he whispered before he turned and walked away from her.

Grace stood for a moment in stunned silence. No. There was still time. Shaking it off, she hurried after him, and her emergence from the woods shocked many of the men, who looked surprised to see a woman there at all, let alone Grace. She didn't care anymore about rules or whether anyone saw her. As Euan strode into the line of his men, Grace grabbed his arm and pulled back.

"No! You cannot! Euan, please!"

"Grace," he said. "Please. Let me go."

Grace was in tears now, not bothering to hide her emotions. It was about more than a failed mission; she didn't care about that now. She couldn't let him die. "No!"

"Begone, ye wailin' woman! He has no need of yer distraction before battle," said an unfamiliar voice before he shoved her hard away from Euan. As Grace fell and lost her grip on Euan's arm, the man smirked. "There ye go, lad. That is how ye handle such a pest."

Euan's fist found the man's jaw and sent him sprawling to the ground; none of the men making a move to help the offender. He'd dared to cross a superior officer and thus got what was coming to him. Worse, he'd crossed Euan, something none of them would ever dare do.

"How dare ye lay a hand on her!" Euan shouted at him before knelt to help her up. "Grace."

Grace's hand shot out, grabbing the dirk from its sheath on his baldric, bringing it between them and placing the point against his chest, his back shielding the move from his men. "I will not let you do this!"

Euan gave a slight smile. "Dinnae make threats ye know ye cannae keep, Watcher. If ye kill me yerself ye still fail."

Grace faltered and Euan took the dirk from her hand, re-sheathing it on his baldric.

"It is over," he said again, cupping her cheek and placing a final kiss on her lips. "Goodbye, Grace. Remember me as ye said ye would. Soon enough ye will be the only one alive who does."

"No! Wait!" she cried out, grabbing at him as he stood but unable to keep a grip on him as he called the order to join up with the rest of the regiments and they ran up to the front line to mass with the rest of the men.

Grace stood up, frantic. The sound of yet another cannon blast jerked her head toward the action, the ground rumbling beneath her feet with the shockwave. She saw the English soldiers lined up and the Scots readying for their doom with the Camerons in the front line. They raised their swords and shouted together, a fearsome sound. She heard someone call the Cameron charge, watching as they ran forward en masse, and without another thought she ran toward the moor after them.

With the smoke so dense it was suffocating, Grace couldn't see him, but she could feel him. All around her, dead or injured men dropped to the ground in the acrid, yellow haze of smoke caused by the ignition of the powder in muskets, pistols, and cannons. The sounds of their screams rang in her ears as men collided in a mass of bodies and steel. The ground shook beneath her from cannon fire and the footfalls of thousands of charging Highlanders. For just a moment the smoke cleared as someone ran through it, and she finally spotted him. He was running straight toward the English lines. If she could just get to him and hold him down, he might be able to escape.

Grace sprinted toward him even as she heard musket balls, grapeshot, and shrapnel whiz past all around her. Some of it buried itself with a sickening, indescribable sound inside the bodies of the men she was weaving her way through, while other bits hit the ground, sending up sprays of earth. She wanted to scream in terror, to close her eyes and get away from all of it, but she shoved it away. Euan was her sole focus.

"EUAN!" she screamed, desperate to be heard above the ear-splitting sounds of the battlefield.

The smothering miasma of powder smoke again cleared for a moment to show both of them the muskets pointed right at Euan. His eyes widened and he stopped moving just as Grace grabbed hold of him. The crack of the muskets firing reached her ears at the same time the unexpected and searing pain that coursed through her did. She wasn't supposed to feel that, and this time her screams were real.

The two of them crumpled to the ground together, Grace landing on top of Euan. She couldn't tell if he'd been hit too and there was no time to check. Grace could taste the blood in her mouth and looked down to see her white dress turning crimson with it before she rolled onto the ground beside him. She felt weak and knew something had gone terribly wrong. She wasn't going to heal from this. She was going to die, but that didn't matter. All that mattered was him. He was her mission and he had to survive.

Grace sobbed in fear as she laid there, trying to force herself to get up even though the pain was excruciating. She had to move. Pushing herself up onto her hands and knees, she coughed up the blood that came into her mouth with the movement and choked her. Her breathing ragged, she stood and grabbed his arms to try and drag Euan away. If she could get him back to the woods, he'd be safe, and he could flee when he came to. No matter what happened to her, at least he would be there, hidden and safe.

There was another flash of pain, white hot, and this time in the center of her back. She suddenly felt as though she couldn't breathe, and her body wanted to fall but something was holding her up. Grace looked down to see the point of a bayonet protruding from her chest; the silver stained with red. It was yanked back from her torso, and in doing so it turned her body toward the person who held it, his face a mixture of fury and fear. Grace touched her chest, tears sliding down her cheeks. Pain, there was so much pain. Her knees gave out and she fell to the ground beside Euan.

CHAPTER 11

Euan gasped, taking in a great heaving breath before coughing. It felt as though he'd been holding his breath for too long. Gone were the sounds of battle, and in their place was a silence so loud it was deafening. Where was he? He must be dead. Yes, he remembered the muskets now, the ones pointed at him. He remembered that time had seemed to slow down with the realization that he'd been here before, heard this before. The vision. The vision when he'd first touched Grace. He'd seen his end. It had been a warning. There was the sound and the flash of the muskets firing at him, and he remembered someone screaming his name; he'd heard that before, too.

Screaming. Grace! They'd been a woman's screams, so it had to have been her. She'd seen him die; she'd seen the end she'd fought so hard to prevent. The mere thought of her brought tears from beneath his closed eyelids. What had he done? She'd been right. He'd changed nothing, and it had all been for nothing. His heart shattered for the pain in those screams, the pain he knew he'd caused her. The scream erupted from his mind, becoming his own and obliterating the silence. He screamed in a way he never had before, the sound primal as his back arched away from the surface beneath him, unable to stop the anger, fear, and grief from overwhelming him before he broke down in tears.

"Welcome back, Mr. Cameron," an unfamiliar female voice said.

Startled, Euan's eyes blinked open and he found himself staring at a white ceiling that was smooth and shone like marble. Turning his head toward the voice, he saw a woman standing there, and though her clothing was strange to him, her smile was pleasant.

"Where am I?"

"The future," she said, her tone nonchalant and her smile not fading.

"The future?" Euan asked, confused by the word in such a context as well as the suggestion. "Then why do ye welcome me back?"

"I welcome you back to consciousness, that is all. Here, let me help you sit up."

With the woman's help, Euan took his time to sit up and looked around him. Everything in this room seemed odd to him. So many small lights and strange instruments that he couldn't comprehend. He turned his attention to himself and found he was clean, as though he had just bathed. His clothing was spotless and fresh, no tears, no dirt, no blood. He looked up at the woman in bewilderment.

"All will be explained soon. The Council wishes to see you."

"The Council? Who are they?"

"Those who sent Grace."

"Grace? *My* Grace? Is she here?" Euan asked, an edge of excitement in his voice.

"No. Come," she said, helping him down from the table.

Euan's knees felt weak in that first moment, and he caught himself against the edge of the table before trying again when he felt steadier. As they reached the door, it slid open without a touch, and Euan jumped back.

With a chuckle, the woman looked back at him. "Nothing to be afraid of. Come on."

Euan made his way through the door with caution and continued to follow her. The halls were just as smooth and shining as everything else here, and no one seemed to notice him as they passed. There were varying doors and other corridors branching off from the one they were in. They eventually came to a set of doors so large they reminded him of the doors of the Great Hall at Achnacarry.

"What is this place?" he whispered to himself.

"The Council will see you now," the woman said as the doors opened. "Please go in."

Euan stepped forward through the doors and, once he was inside, they immediately shut behind him. There was no sound, which he found odd for doors so large. The room was a soft white, the floor glittering in hues of blues and purples he'd never known existed, and on one wall hung a massive tapestry. Before him was a long table with a group of women occupying the seats behind it, all of them looking at him in silence before the one sitting in the center spoke at last.

"Good morning to you, Mr. Cameron," she said.

"Good morning to ye, miss," Euan replied, unsure of how to address her.

"My name is Councilwoman Rochford, and I am the head of The Council," she said, her smile warm and genuine. "I welcome you to our world."

"Yer world? Where is that? Why am I here?"

Councilwoman Rochford chuckled. "You are in the future. The very, very, very distant future. As for why you are here? Well, that is more complicated."

"I am listening."

"You are here because of Grace, and you are with us because she died to bring you here."

The word hit him with a force he never would've expected. Dead. Grace was dead. She'd died for him. He'd asked her if she'd be willing to come to him if it meant her death, but he'd had no idea it would really happen. She'd proven, more than amply, that she would die for her duty. So had he.

"No," he choked out.

"She had to, or you could not have come."

"I was nae worth that trade and ye must undo it. Send me home and bring her back!"

"We cannot. That is not how it works."

"How it works? She is nae supposed to die on duty! That is what she said! Ye have traded someone who wanted to save people for someone who has spent the last nine months killing them! This is nae right!"

Euan felt like screaming in rage, in pain, in loss. He wanted to weep, but he was far too angry for it. This couldn't stand. She couldn't be dead. They had to fix this somehow.

Rochford held up a hand to try and calm him. "Please, listen. Grace did not come to you to save our future: she came to you to save her own."

"I dinnae understand."

"Every Watcher has a Companion, and it is someone she alone chooses. That Companion is her partner for the rest of her life. He will be at her side; he will help her complete her missions. He becomes integral to her success. More than that, he assures the continuation of the Watchers themselves. Their daughters and granddaughters become the next Watchers."

"What has that to do with me?"

"You are the Companion Grace chose, though she did not realize it. She had the opportunity to accept her failure to stop you or decide to act in order to save you. Had she accepted her failure, nothing would have happened. She would have come back here, and we would have briefed her on the unchanged timeline. Instead, she chose to save you. The mass of emotion and energy she felt in that moment made her as real as you were. She gave her life to save yours and, in doing so, made it possible for you to be transported here."

"What does any of it matter if she is dead?"

"She is not dead," Rochford replied. "She did die there, that is true, but she came back here as you did, and she will heal. She is with our medical staff even now."

"She is here? Please, let me see her!" Relief flooded Euan.

She was alive, and he offered a silent thanks to God for it. All he wanted was to see her, touch her, talk to her.

"Not yet. You have a choice to make, just as she did."

"What?"

"You must decide if this is the life you want. You can choose to stay or choose to go. If you choose to go, we will send you home. You have to choose her as much as she must choose you."

"My choice is to decide to return to my own time and all that I know, or be a stud to sire more Watchers for ye?"

"It is nothing so coarse as that, Mr. Cameron. If all goes well between you, it will eventually become what you, in your time, would call a marriage. If you choose to go, she will never know you were here, much less that you chose to leave. We will make sure she does not remember ever having met you, and she will go on doing her work. Perhaps, in time, she would find someone else to be her Companion."

"How can ye do this?"

"Do what?"

"Manipulate people this way?"

"We do nothing of the sort."

"Aye, ye do. Ye send people back in time to alter their own history to make sure it remains what ye want it to be. What if it would be better a different way? But all ye want is to pre-serve yerselves here."

"We are in a place of peace, Mr. Cameron. Hard won peace," Rochford explained, the tone of her voice taking on a firmer edge. "There are no more wars, no more suffering. We will not allow someone to change that, and that is why we do what we do. That is why Grace accepted her place in it. We do not alter history so much as prevent the alteration of it."

"But what of all the people that suffered before ye? What of them? What if ye could change their suffering by allowing a different outcome?"

"An excellent question," Rochford acknowledged before

pointing to the strange tapestry upon the wall. "Do you see this? This is human history. Every thread a different timeline. Every timeline filled with billions of points. Each point is a human life. Timelines repeat themselves in perpetuity, Mr. Cameron. We can see what such changes bring before they happen and decide to intervene or not. This," she said, pointing to a golden strand. "This is where we are now. If anything changes then its outcome is reflected here. Changes happen all the time. We only stop the ones that will bring harm to the future that is based upon those past choices. We cannot alleviate past suffering even though we would like to, because doing so would destroy everything that came after it."

"So, ye dinnae stop them all. Ye allow change."

"Yes. What we stop are the things that will bring back war, suffering, pain."

Euan stood quiet for a long moment. He could understand such a desire. A world free from of all of those things would certainly be a world most anyone would do anything to protect, and they did. Grace did.

"Your choice to die in war did not bring us harm. That is not why Grace was sent there, even though that is what she believed. Your choice to die changed her future. Had she not saved you, her future with you would not exist."

"Why did ye nae tell her that?"

"If we had, how would she have explained it to you? How would it not have been awkward for you both, and thus be much less likely to succeed?"

Euan gave a gentle nod, understanding her point. "We have a future? How do ye know?"

"If you choose it, yes." However, Rochford surveyed him with amusement at his second question. "We know because we are the future, Mr. Cameron. We have seen it. Grace's time is here," she explained as she pointed to a different thread.

In silence, Euan stood there studying the tapestry. It was quite a choice, indeed. Did he leave all he knew to be with

Grace in this new future? Was this the "greater thing" his mother had spoken of; helping the work of the Watchers? Being a father to those who would someday carry on the same work? But then, what was there to go back to besides his mother? If he went back, he would never see Grace again, and Rochford had just told him as much. She wouldn't remember meeting him, wouldn't remember their conversations. He would be just another stranger to her. The question was if he could live with that.

"What becomes of my mother if I stay?"

"I knew you would ask that," Rochford said, his clear attachment to his family seeming to please her. "We are prepared to offer you something we offer to all Companions in order to make their transition easier. You may bring one person with you if you choose."

"I can bring my mother?" Euan asked, incredulous.

"If you wish, yes. Most Companions choose to make a clean break, but you do not have to. But, before you make your choice, Mr. Cameron, it is best that you see what you would return to," Rochford said as she directed his attention to what looked like a large mirror.

Euan watched, startled at first, as it flickered to life with moving pictures, and he stared at it open-mouthed. Who would have thought such a thing could exist! He then realized he was seeing the battle he'd just been in. He watched as the Jacobites were cut down like so much grass and felt sick. She'd tried to caution him that they would all die there, and she'd been telling the truth. The ground had caused the line to skew, the forces to be pinned against the wall under fire, and the lines to break down. Just as she'd tried to warn them that they would that night at Achnacarry.

"My friends," he said, his voice quieted by the grief that thickened his throat.

"Have perished, I am afraid, as they were meant to. As you were meant to. As you all did in the past before we sent Grace."

Perished in the past. It had happened before. He'd died

before and there had been no Grace to save him. It was a difficult concept to wrestle with, to know he wasn't supposed to be here. Worse, Duncan and the others were gone. Most of the Cameron regiment, along with most of the Jacobite Army, were dead with the English soldiers now bayoneting the bodies to be sure.

The picture switched to a burning building as yet more English soldiers watched the flames and seemed pleased by them. He recognized it immediately: Achnacarry. They were burning Achnacarry. The sight filled him with anger even though he knew he shouldn't be surprised by it. They had quelled the rising and now they had to make sure there was nothing left to rebel for. The view lifted as if he were in the sky, floating over Cameron land, and he could see all of the cottages and homes being burnt, crops being destroyed, the land salted, women and children crying as they were cast without clothing into the snow, their livestock killed or stolen. Then his own home came into view. His mother was outside on her knees at the point of a bayonet, sobbing. Her son was dead, her home was burning. They tied her hands and hauled her up to take her away.

"She will be placed on a ship for transport to England," Rochford said before he could ask. "They are arresting her as a sympathizer because of your participation."

"And then?"

"She does not make it to England."

Euan's heart ached. Not only had he died, but his mother too. "What happens after this?"

"What is left of those clans who rebelled are quashed by laws made to ensure they cannot regain strength. Many of your countrymen flee and your leader flees to France with the prince. It will take generations for Scotland to recover from it."

He took a deep breath and released it. There was nothing left to go back for. Even if they sent him back alive, what would remain? He would be known as a Cameron, and it would mean suffering and death for him, anyone who knew

97

him, and anyone who assisted him. He couldn't run a one-man rising, and he was a prime target on the list of people the English explicitly wanted not only located but dead for the things he'd done over the course of the last nine months.

"How do I know what ye are showing me is the truth and ye are nae just manipulating things again?"

"We have no reason to lie. Whether you stay or go is of no concern to us, and Grace will continue on either way. As I said before, she would eventually find another."

Another. It was a thought he couldn't stomach. He couldn't lose her, couldn't let her go to someone who might not understand her the way he knew he'd begun to, the way she seemed to understand him. The realization that he had no choice but to trust them was frightening.

"If I agree, and then I go back and find out ye are nae telling me true, can I change my mind?"

"Yes. You will tell the person sent with you that you have changed your mind and that is that. We have no desire to trap anyone."

"Then I agree to stay, and I want to bring my mother. I dinnae want her to suffer and die for my actions."

"So be it. You will be assigned a Guardian to escort you. For now, you may go see Grace, but I warn you: you will not like what you see. She will not be awake and will not know you are there."

"Thank ye," Euan replied as the doors behind him opened once again. The woman who had earlier escorted him here was now waiting for him, and Euan went to join her.

"I will take you to see Grace. Come with me," she said, though the look on her face filled him with a deep sense of foreboding.

Euan followed her and wondered how anyone found their way around here when everything looked the same. They stopped before another door and she placed one of her hands against a flat mirror. The mirror turned green and the door opened. As they stepped inside and it shut behind them, the room was so dark it took a moment for his eyes to adjust. When they did, Euan gasped in horror.

Grace lay there on a table much like the one he'd found himself on earlier. She was still dressed as she had been when he last saw her, but the white dress was now red with her blood. It stained the skin of her hands, chest, and face, and she was so still and so pale as to look dead. The sob that rose from Euan choked him, and he almost couldn't see through his tears as he stumbled toward her. His hands shook as he reached out to touch her and, when he found her cold, he recoiled. He forced them back and stroked her face.

"What have ye wrought upon yerself for my sake, ye fool," Euan sobbed before he turned to look at the woman. "They told me she was nae dead!"

"She is not," the woman replied. "The table will mend her; it will just take time."

Turning his attention back to Grace, Euan could see the holes in her dress left by the balls of the muskets that had shot her. The ones meant for his own body. His fingers reached out and gingerly touched the wound on her chest: a bayonet. He would recognize anywhere the distinct triangular shape that particular weapon inflicted. He'd watched men die in agony from the wounds it could cause. The bastards had bayoneted a woman, and an unarmed woman at that. She'd suffered so much for him.

He gave her a gentle kiss and then rested his forehead against hers. "They say ye dinnae know I am here but, if ye do, thank ye. Thank ye for saving me, for caring enough to try. I am coming back for ye, Grace," he whispered before he kissed her again and stepped back. To see her this way made him physically ache in ways he'd never known he could. "I need hot water and a rag, please."

The woman looked at him, curious. "Why?"

"Because I cannae leave her this way. As with anyone

who has died, she deserves to be washed and respected."

"But she is not …"

"Please. I need to do this."

The woman nodded and left the room, returning a short time later with water and a clean cloth, as he'd requested. Someone else came with her, carrying a pitcher and a basin so that he might wash her hair, having anticipated the request before he'd made it. Once they had given him the items, they left him in silence.

This wasn't the first body he'd washed but it was, by far, the one that would hurt him the most to do. It was the most loving and respectful thing anyone could do for someone they'd once cared for. Euan began with her hair, washing it and rinsing it until the red of the blood was gone, and then spreading it out behind her so that it hung over the table and the excess water dripped into the basin. He then took the rag and began to clean her face of the dirt, blood, and gunpowder. From his boot he pulled a small knife, using it to cut the dress away from her. To see the wounds so plainly now brought his tears back and, through the fog of them, he paid no notice to how exposed she was to his gaze.

Euan took his time, smoothing the rag over her skin as though she might still feel it. He didn't know how long it took for him to finish and he didn't care. She deserved this from him, at least this. To leave her as she had been would have been shameful. He set the rag aside and made his way back to the top of the table, loosely plaiting her damp hair.

Stepping back to look at her, he wanted to make sure he'd missed nothing, and when he was satisfied, he pulled the pin holding his plaid at his shoulder and removed it. He shook it out and then spread it over her to cover her. She'd died a Cameron as far as he was concerned because she'd charged into battle alongside them, and thus should wear those colors. She'd more than earned them.

He heard the door slide open again. "Thank ye," he said to

the woman without looking at her. "I owed her that at the very least," he said as he reached out and stroked Grace's cheek.

"I understand. Your Guardian is ready. It is time to go."

Euan took a few moments to compose himself before he met with the person who would be escorting him back. "Hello," he said as he approached her.

"Hello Mr. Cameron," she replied, her voice gentle and her face kind. "I am here to take you back to get your mother, but I should explain a few things to you first. You are about to take part in what we call a transport. It is an ability that we Guardians have, and it allows us to take people from one place to another, no matter the time period or the place."

"How is such a thing done?"

"I cannot tell you that, as it is far beyond the period you will be joining. Even Grace does not have that information."

"That seems to be the answer to a great many questions here."

The young woman laughed. "The hazard of working in different time periods. I am sure you will get used to it eventually."

"What must I do?"

"Your part in this is just to take my hand and close your eyes. I will do the rest. I will warn you, however, that the sensation will be very strange, and you will likely be quite dizzy. Do not be alarmed, as that is normal. Wait for it to pass while you keep your eyes closed, and when you open them you will find yourself back in your own time."

Euan took her hand when she offered it and closed his eyes. The sensation was a strange one, just as she'd warned him, and it was as if someone had taken his hand and given him a sharp pull forward. Immediately afterward he felt a tap on his shoulder.

"Right, we are here," the woman said.

"When?"

"The day of the battle. You have time enough to explain, but the sooner you are away without anyone here to notice you, the better. Remember, you are supposed to be dying at

Drumossie with the others. Everyone here saw you leave."

Euan opened his eyes and shook off the lingering dizziness as he looked around him. They were in the woods and he knew where to go. "Come," he said as he turned and ran toward home without waiting to see if the Guardian was able to keep up. He knew she would find her way.

As he crested the hill, he was relieved to see the cottage still standing and not burning as he'd seen it. "Mam!" he called out to her, praying he was not somehow too late. As Aileen hurried out, Euan thought he might weep with relief.

"Euan!" She embraced him as he caught her up in his arms and she sobbed. "Ye are safe! Ye listened to her and turned back!"

Euan set her down with a gentle shake of his head as the Guardian crested the hill. "No."

Aileen looked at the Guardian in confusion. "Euan, what has happened? Where is Grace?"

"Come inside and I will tell ye all," he said as he took her hand and led her back inside.

"Ye tell me now! What has happened?"

Euan swallowed hard. "I did nae listen to Grace. She tried to warn me. She was there at the battle, she tried to stop me, but I went anyway. It is a battle they are fighting even now. I should be there now."

"Then why are ye nae?" A look of terror crept over her face. "Dear God above. Ye have died and the Lord has given ye leave to tell me farewell in a dream."

"We will all of us die there. All of us except for me."

"I dinnae understand!"

"Mam, she saved me. She ran out into the battle to try and stop me. She took the gunfire meant for me. She *died* for me."

Aileen's eyes filled with tears and she shook her head. "She is dead?"

"No, not exactly," the Guardian replied before Euan could. "Her sacrifice allowed Euan to live, because the emotional energy which also made her real enough to die, allowed them both to be removed back to us. I am Amy, a Guardian for the Watchers."

"Mam, I had the choice to stay there to be with Grace or come back here. They told me that in making the choice to save me she chose me as her Companion, the person to be with her always. I have decided to stay with her."

"Then why are ye here?" Aileen asked.

"Because ye can come with me and I have come to fetch ye. There is naught here to keep ye, Mam. The English soldiers will come, and they will burn everything before they transport everyone to England. I have seen it. Ye will nae survive it."

"Fetch me to where?"

"To the future, Mam, where ye will be with me and ye will be safe. Where yer grandchildren will someday be."

Aileen stared at him and Euan watched her struggle to comprehend what he was saying to her. "But what of Lochiel and the others?"

"The others are dead and Lochiel will flee to France with the prince to escape a traitor's death while the rest of the Camerons pay the price."

"Mrs. Cameron, this is a chance very few ever get. Every Companion is given the choice to bring one person with them, but few of them take it. Euan will become something very important to us. Companions are vital to the work of the Watchers; not only helping to carry on the lines of Watchers to come, but also accompanying the Watchers on their missions," Amy explained.

"Mam, ye said Grace being here could only mean I was intended for greater things. Ye were right, and this is it. Please, I am begging ye, come with me."

"We do not have much time," Amy said. "There is only a short window remaining before someone might see us."

Aileen looked between the two of them and then grabbed a box Euan recognized instantly: the box where she kept her most precious possessions. She also hurried to pick up several lengths of tartan she'd woven during the winter. "I am ready."

"Are ye sure, Mam?"

"I will nae stay to die for the man who sent my son to die, and I dinnae intend to miss seeing my grandchildren born."

Amy grinned. "That is the spirit, Mrs. Cameron. All right, Euan, you will feel the same thing. Mrs. Cameron, when you close your eyes you will feel a tug or a shift and when you open your eyes again you will be elsewhere and safe. You may feel dizzy but that is normal."

Euan heard someone call his mother's name. Someone was coming and they had to go now. He closed his eyes, the strange sensation came again, and by the time the person who had called out reached the cottage, they were gone.

CHAPTER 12

"**C**an ye believe such a place as this exists?" Aileen asked Euan as they sat together in a room, eating supper later.

Aileen had been to her own meeting with The Council, one Euan hadn't been part of. He'd been escorted to a different place to select a new wardrobe after being informed that he couldn't continue wearing what he was used to. Clothing styles had changed, and in order to blend in, he would need to do the same. In the end, he'd selected clothing from the 1940s, as the shirt and vest felt familiar to him, though the trousers and shoes would take a bit of getting used to.

"No," Euan murmured, picking at his food but not eating it.

"What is weighing on ye?"

"Naught," he replied, looking up. "Why would ye think so?"

"Because ye are here in body, but yer mind is elsewhere. I am sure ye must be starving, but ye have hardly touched yer food. It is venison stew, yer favorite."

The Council had informed him that, for now, they would keep the fare the same as what they would've had at home. Too much change so quickly could be traumatic, and they'd need to be worked into things slowly, especially after coming from so far back.

Euan let go of a heavy sigh and looked down at his plate. "I am thinking of everyone, that is all."

"Everyone?"

"All those left behind, those that are now dead."

"I understand now. I am sorry for the pain ye feel, truly I am, but ye cannae dwell on it. They made their choices, same as ye did."

"Aye, but it was nae truly a choice, and ye know that as well as anyone."

"Perhaps nae, but ye cannae change any of it."

"No, I cannae, and that does nae sit well with me."

"What would ye do, Euan? Save them all?"

"As many as I could, aye. Malcolm, Iain, Duncan ..."

"Aye, and what if ye could save only them and nae the rest begging ye for the same? Would ye feel such a weight for them?"

"I dinnae know."

"What of Malcom's wife and bairns?"

Euan paused and looked up at her.

"Aye, forgetting about them are ye nae? Ye would save him, but where would that leave them? Without a husband and father, for a start. Do ye think he would want that? To leave them behind and go on with his life as if they had never existed?"

"He could bring them, like I brought ye."

"Ye were allowed one person, and ye chose me. Even if they gave ye leave to bring those three with ye as well, I was nae given the chance to bring someone and they likely would nae be either. There would be impossible choices to be made."

"I wish it did nae have to be this way."

"Of course ye do, but that is nae the way of things. Ye said ye had the choice to go back, and that is the only way ye could spare yerself this. To go back and die with them. Ye chose to remain here with Grace."

Grace. Euan's wince was immediate and involuntary, the image of her from that first moment rising unbidden into his mind. "Aye," he whispered past the lump in his throat.

"Euan," Aileen said, not having missed his visceral reaction to the very mention of her name. "What happened to her that makes ye react the way ye just did?"

He wasn't sure he could make the words come, and when he

opened his mouth, none did. Closing it again, he shook his head.

Aileen reached out and covered one of his hands. "Love, ye should tell me so ye dinnae bear that knowledge alone. It may help lighten it for ye. I know ye have seen much, and there is much ye dinnae wish to say or cannae, but this should nae be one of those."

"She ..." he began, put paused to control himself. "They shot her, four times that I counted, and bayoneted her."

"Dear God in heaven," Aileen whispered.

"When I met with The Council, they told me she had died for me, and I could nae stomach it. I could nae think of her dead, this beautiful creature gone forever, killed in a place where no one knew her or even cared. Those eyes closed, her laughter silenced, the kindness and the knowledge gone. All of it gone."

"The same she felt about ye as she tried to persuade ye nae to go," Aileen reminded him.

"The difference is that I deserved it, Mam. I deserved my fate for the things I have done. She did nae."

"No one deserves it, Euan, nae even if ye feel ye are unworthy of anything else."

"They told me she would live, they let me see her," he continued, closing his eyes to try and stop the tears from coming, but failing.

"And?"

"She was covered in blood. It was everywhere. In her hair, on her face, her hands. Nae an inch of her was unstained by it. I have seen bodies like it and worse, but it was different because it was *her*. She looked dead, though they said she was nae, and I asked for hot water and a rag. I washed her body myself, as should be done, because they had left her the way she was. The wounds were horrific, Mam, and I know she must have suffered terribly."

Aileen wiped tears away with her free hand. "Aye, I am sure she did, but she made her choice, as ye did. Do ye nae see? Euan, she cared for ye so much she did nae bother to think about what might happen to her. What she did, she did to try to save ye, no matter the cost. She cares deeply for ye or was starting to."

Euan dropped his spoon and buried his face in his free hand, unable to stop himself from crying. Aileen moved her chair over and placed her hand on his back to try and comfort him. "It is this one which hurts ye the most, nae the others. To know she suffered for ye."

Nodding, Euan couldn't stop his tears now that he'd released them.

"What do ye feel for her?"

"I dinnae know," he whispered. "Ever since the moment I met her I felt drawn to her in ways I could nae understand, and it both excited and terrified me with the power it held. She was all I had wanted but she was nae mine to have. I have never known anyone like me, with the same education, the same mind, who could challenge me and make me think of things in new ways. I cannae tell ye how lonely that is, Mam, and when she arrived, she filled that space. It may be infatuation, that initial rush so strong because of how alone I had felt for so long, but I want to find out, need to find out. I could never say this to her, because to say so made it real, made her real, opened the door to her being able to stop me, and I could nae."

Aileen sighed and rubbed his back. "Euan, ye have such a deep heart, just as yer father did. If I told ye I had nae seen it between ye I would be lying."

"It happened so quickly that it did nae seem real, did nae seem right. At the same time, it felt like the most natural thing in the world that I should feel this for her, this woman I felt as though I had known for as long as I could remember. It was so strong that I shoved it away because I did nae know how to face it, because she was my mirror and it terrified me to feel such a pull to someone who knows me better than even I do."

"Sometimes it happens that way. Ye see someone and ye just know. The heart does what it will, and yer soul knew she was for ye the moment ye let yerself see her as more than just her task. Ye let her show ye she was just as real as ye were and, more, ye discovered someone ye could truly converse with, whose mind worked in the same way yers does. She was what ye needed, what ye craved, the only person who could have turned yer head so quickly. Someone different, someone who understood ye the way none of us could. Someone ye would never find at Achnacarry."

"I could nae leave her after all of this, could nae leave her and never see her again. I went through that once and I cannae do it again. It felt like my heart had been ripped out of me and I was left to walk the earth without it. I cannae be without her."

"Why would ye? Why leave her to go back to a place where ye are certain to die? Ye made the right choice, son."

"I know, and I feel that deep down. It is just difficult now."

"Aye, it will be difficult for everyone, I expect, even her. I am sure it will get better with time."

"She rests now under Cameron colors."

Aileen raised an eyebrow. "Does she?"

"Aye. I covered her with my plaid after I washed her. She deserved it; she died a Cameron as much as any of us."

"I think that is an honorable thing for ye to have done, and I agree. Then again, if it is as ye say, she will truly be a Cameron soon enough."

"She still has to agree."

"I dinnae know why ye think she would nae after everything."

"Dinnae know," Euan said. "I think I want to go for a walk. Would ye excuse me, Mam?"

"Of course."

Euan rose and left the room, stepping into the hallway and starting to walk. It didn't matter where he was going, he just needed to be moving because he was far too anxious to remain still. They weren't prisoners here and were free to go anywhere they liked in the massive building. The Councilwoman had explained that they couldn't go outside of it because it would expose them to things they couldn't see, and that even Grace hadn't gone out.

"Mr. Cameron?"

Pulled out of his thoughts, Euan turned to look at the Councilwoman. His eyes widening briefly with surprise, he bowed to her, as he had seen others do. "Good evening to ye, Councilwoman."

"Is everything well with you?"

"As much as they can be, aye. I just wanted to walk and clear my head. I dinnae suppose there is a place I could get some fresh air without breaking any rules?"

"There is, come with me," she replied, the look on her face telling him she quite understood his desire to be outdoors when agitated.

Euan followed her as she led him back toward The Council chambers and through the large doors. As they reached the other side of the room, she opened a door he hadn't noticed before, set into the wall so perfectly that you wouldn't notice it unless you knew it was there. They stepped out into a walled garden, moonlit and warm. The smell of flowers surrounded him, and the stillness of the night calmed him with near immediate effect as he sat down on a bench.

"You may sit out here as long as you need and are welcome to return in the evenings when we are not in session."

"Thank ye," Euan said. "Everything is so strange, but this is familiar."

"Yes, I like sitting outside when I am troubled as well," she replied as she sat down beside him. "I have heard your chief had a lovely garden."

"Aye, he did."

"I am sorry for all you went through, truly. You and all the others. Just know there is nothing else you could have done."

"What do ye mean?" Euan asked, finding her comment curious.

"For them," she said, turning her head to look at him.

"They had all of the information they needed to change history, but they chose to ignore it. There is nothing you could have done that would have changed it."

"I could have told them about Nairn."

"They would not have listened, and you know that. At the same time, you stuck to our most important rule, and that was not changing history even though you knew how to do it."

"Please, dinnae punish Grace for having done so, for having told us. She may have tried to change things, but it did nae work. She was doing all she could."

"Yes, she was. She was desperate to stop you, and we are fully aware that she never would have made such a choice lightly, or for anyone else but you. We have no intention of punishing her for it. We expect it on these missions, it always happens, and when it does it is always too late. It is the critical thing which pushes us all to our final choice. We have already crossed the biggest line, and it has failed, so we have nothing left to do but try to physically intervene. It is exactly what she did."

"She seemed to struggle a great deal in her time with me."

"You are different, as are all Companions. A Watcher is always thrown off when they meet their Companion, because everything is so disorienting as they try to make sense of the things they are feeling and what that is driving them to do, things they would never otherwise consider. Normally when she is working, Grace is quite the opposite. I will be honest: Grace is well on her way to becoming the best Watcher we have. She may be young and relatively new, but she has been training all her life for this job in ways no one else here or in our history has. Her grandmother made sure of it. More than that, she is a natural at it. She can see the puzzle pieces and fit them together to make sure she succeeds. There is a reason she is the only one who works the most difficult missions. No one else can work them quite as well as she can."

Euan was quiet, thinking of the young woman who was now lying so still and silent. The person Rochford had just described

111

seemed to be the opposite of the Watcher he'd met, but the knowledge that it wasn't the normal way of things for her was comforting. There was more to her than what he'd seen, and he was looking forward to discovering that side of her.

"What if she does nae agree to keeping me here?"

"She will. If she would not, she would never have made the choice she did. Please do not worry about that."

"What happens now that Mam and I are here?"

"You will learn all about the new world you are about to step into so that you are not overwhelmed and confused when you arrive. You will understand what things are, and their names; you will be given all you need."

"How long do ye think it will be until she wakes?"

"Hard to say," Rochford replied, her voice quieting. "There was a great deal of damage done. Weeks, perhaps. Only Dr. Fraser will know for sure."

"Fraser," Euan said, a small, amused smile appearing on his face.

"Indeed. He is Scottish, too."

"With a name like that how could he nae be?"

"You will meet him soon."

"What is yer name? Or is it just Councilwoman."

"My name is Alice, but do not tell anyone I told you," she said, before a sly smile crept across her lips.

"Alice. A pretty name."

"Thank you."

"There is nae a chance she cannae be healed is there?"

"No, not now. She is healing, it will just take time. If such a thing had been impossible, we would have sent you back without you ever knowing you had been here in order to spare you that grief."

"How well do ye know her?"

"Somewhat well, but probably not as well as Caia does."

"Who is she?"

"Caia is Grace's Guardian. You will meet her soon, too, and

I will let her answer those more personal questions for you."

"It is an odd thing to think about, this idea of multiple periods of time happening at once. I cannae imagine what such a thing would do to someone who was more religious. It would certainly shake their faith in any God."

"Perhaps, but those who truly wish to believe will always find a way to make it align with such things. Does it shake yours?"

"I am nae sure I had any to begin with, nae after all I have seen."

"I cannot say I do not understand."

"Thank ye for sending her," he said.

"It was not necessarily our choice. According to history and her timeline, she was meant to be with you, and we put her where she needed to be to accomplish that."

"History? Is that why I saw what I did when I touched her the first time?"

"What?" Rochford asked, confused.

"When I first met her, I took hold of her wrist to try to verify her mark, but the moment I touched her there came this vision. Guns, cannons, screaming. I felt hot and dizzy, I could nae think. It was frightening."

"I have never heard of anything like that happening."

"No? She felt it too. She tried to take my hand at another point and the same thing happened to her. She saw me dead, and then saw what I could have if I did nae go to Drumossie. Is it because it was meant to be our history together?"

Rochford was silent, looking at him as though he'd said something in a language she didn't understand. "No. As I said, that is not something that happens. I have never heard of it happening to anyone else."

"Hm," Euan said, moving his eyes forward. "Everything about this is strange and has been since the moment I met her. Ye say that she was thrown off, but there is something else to it, I know there is. I felt as though I had known her all my life; I still feel it. There is something I cannae reach, like those dreams ye remember having but cannae remember what was in them even just after ye wake. There is something more." His last words were a whisper, more to himself than to Rochford.

"How very strange," Rochford said, though there was something in her voice that told Euan there was information she was hiding. He knew, however, that he'd get no answers if he pressed her.

"I know she tried to ask ye to remove her," he said, switching the subject.

"She did, and though she thought we could not hear her, we could. It was what she had to go through, and we could not stop it. To hear her in such pain was difficult, but necessary."

"I am glad ye did nae. I dinnae know what I would have done."

"Exactly what you did do: go to war with a hardened heart."

"Someone once said to me that he was glad I did nae have a wife, for it meant I would fight all the harder with naught to go back to."

Alice frowned. "Only someone who did not understand the value of life would say such a thing. Someone who has never had to take the life of another but is content with others doing it for him."

"I cannae disagree. I thought I knew myself, but it turns out I dinnae after all."

"You do. You know what was there before, but this is a new door opened and you must explore it. Thankfully, you will not be alone when you do."

"I will be with her."

"Yes."

"I cannae fathom how any of ye do this, how ye can force yerselves to nae stop the suffering of others when ye know that ye have the power."

"You will find out soon enough, and soon enough you will be able to do the same."

"Must ye lose yer humanity?"

"Of course not. Did Grace seem to have lost her humanity

to you? I am not saying those choices are not amongst some of the hardest you will ever make. They absolutely are. You will want to help everyone, and it will break your heart that you cannot. All you can do is remember that what you are part of is something that has already happened, and it cannot be changed. All of the progress that comes after it will be lost if you change things, and we cannot have that either, because who knows what suffering you will cause that had not happened before."

"The one versus the many," Euan said. "Ye must always think about what is best for the greater group and nae just for one."

"Yes, precisely. Much as you would do in your army, is it not? You would not risk the deaths of many to save one, no matter how badly you wanted to."

"No, we would nae, that is true." Though Euan felt certain that, if it came down to it and Grace was the one he needed to save, he wouldn't hesitate to do so. He would get her back even if he had to do it alone, and there would be no army in history that would stop him from getting to her.

"You will be able to do this work and do it well. You will now save instead of kill."

"A way of repentance."

"Yes, if that is how you wish to see it. I must go now, I am afraid. I have some other things to attend to before I go home."

"Aye, of course. Thank ye for showing me this place."

She nodded with a smile and stood, making her way back inside and leaving him to the peaceful solitude of the garden. Euan closed his eyes and took a deep breath, letting the scent of the various flowers linger. How he wished Grace was here now, this moment, so he could talk to her. He wanted to hear her voice, see her smile at him. He had a feeling she would be able to ease him through all of this in a way the others could not, but for now he was on his own. When they returned home, wherever or whenever that might be, he was sure there would be plenty of other things for her to help him work through.

Standing, he left the garden to make his way back to their room. He knew his mother would worry if he was gone too long, and he felt a bit easier after talking to Alice, enough to be hungry. There was much to come, by the sound of it, and he'd need to be at his best to tackle it. It was something you couldn't do when hunger twisted you, and that was something he knew far too well.

CHAPTER 13

The following day, Euan and Aileen spent time with Council Specialists being instructed on things like running water, electricity, toilets, technology; all of the things people in Grace's time took for granted because they'd never known anything different. Aileen had been delighted with the water and the thought of never having to bring buckets from the loch again, as well as the flushing toilets to carry waste away, but the realization of the sheer amount of things to learn had been staggering and a little frightening. Unlike his mother, Euan was far more used to adapting to unfamiliar situations without showing any sort of reaction, though even he was a bit amazed by things. He was glad for this time, glad that they would be eased into the new world in such a way in order to soften the blow. There would be more to learn when they left here, far more, but at least they would have a foundation.

When those lessons were done for the day, they were free to do as they pleased. Euan had gotten permission from the Councilwoman to go and see Grace each day, and it was where he headed now. He put his hand on the screen as he'd seen the other woman do, and the door opened for him. Stepping inside, he heard the door slide shut behind him, but this time the lights were far dimmer, and his eyes didn't need to adjust much.

Grace lay upon the table, just as she'd been the previous day. He was happy to see they hadn't removed his plaid, and, for a moment, he could imagine she was just sleeping. He took a stool from nearby and put it down beside the table. As he sat down, he pulled her hand from beneath the plaid and held it in his own, stroking it with the other, before he lifted it to his lips to place a tender kiss on it.

"I am nae sure if ye can truly hear me, or if ye know I am here, but I am coming to visit ye anyway. Ye are all alone here, what if ye wake and there is no one here to see to ye? Cannae have that. I was given new clothing yesterday, and today we learned about lights, and water, and all sorts of other things. Ye told me about lights, remember? How it could make it as bright as daylight in a room."

There was no sign of any response from Grace, and he let go of a heavy sigh.

"I wish ye were awake. I need ye so badly, Grace, but at the same time I cannae help but feel it is my fault that ye are like this. I could have saved us both a great deal of pain if I had just listened to ye. I have chosen to stay here with ye, did ye know? We will be together, the pair of us, saving the world. It will be just as ye said. I will be defending the soul of history, the homeland of everyone. I will be doing things for good instead of war."

Euan pressed her hand to his cheek. "Wake up, Grace. Please wake up. I am begging ye. I am here, can ye nae feel me? I am here waiting for ye. Come back to me. Please."

When there was still no sign of life from her, Euan gave her hand a gentle squeeze, taking one of his hands away to stroke her hair as he began to sing to her. He started with the song she'd sung for him, but moved on to others, losing himself in it and in being near her in some way. Music had always eased him, and he was hoping it would help now.

"Excuse me, Mr. Cameron. I am very sorry to interrupt."

The soft voice of a young woman brought him back to the present, and he looked over at her. "Am I needed for something?"

"Yes, I was sent to bring you to Medical to see Dr. Fraser."

"Oh," Euan replied, reluctant to let of Grace's hand just yet.

"You need not go just now. You can take a bit longer if you are not yet ready to leave."

"I am nae sure I will ever be ready to leave until she is leaving with me."

"I am sure she will be glad to go home, too. I hate to see her this way."

Euan looked over at her with a questioning expression. "Ye know her at home?"

"Yes, of course. My name is Caia, and I am her Guardian."

Upon hearing her name, Euan took a closer look at her. Her height seemed average to him; her curly, light brown hair stopped at her shoulders. Her face was just a bit rounded, her complexion was smooth, her lips full. She was, in all, an attractive young woman. It was clear, however, that she wore her heart upon her sleeve, and was unable to hide her emotions. She looked sweet and kind, with an open and honest expression, and it was easy to see there wasn't a mean bone in her body.

"Councilwoman Rochford mentioned ye last night. It is good to meet ye," Euan said.

"And you," Caia said as she walked around the table to sit on the other side of it, taking Grace's other hand. "I was told you washed her body and put this over her. What is it?"

"It is a plaid, part of my uniform. The colors and pattern that make up the tartan identify me as being from Clan Cameron."

"It was nice of you to cover her."

"It was more than that. She wore the tartan when she was with me, and she died a Cameron, in battle alongside us, and she has earned the right to wear those colors, the same as anyone else."

"What a beautiful way to honor her."

"What is it ye do, Caia?" Euan said, wanting to change the subject, continuing to stroke Grace's hand.

"Take care of her. When she goes out on a mission, I am the one who protects her body. When she returns, I am there to help her re-adjust. She is my job, but more than that, she is my friend."

"It must hurt ye as much as it hurts me then, to see this," Euan said, gesturing to Grace.

"Yes, but in different ways. I love her dearly, but not in the same way you will hopefully do. She has been through so much, and we have been together since the day she became the next Evans Watcher."

"When her grandmother died."

"And her grandfather, too."

"Both!"

Caia nodded, her eyes reflecting the sadness she felt at the thought of it. "That is how it goes for the Watchers. The worst day of their lives is coupled with one of the most important. It seems to happen that way in a great many things when it comes to them. I am not sure anyone truly understands what they go through except for other Watchers and Guardians."

"How do ye mean?"

"The same day they died; she was here before The Council to accept her post. Her whole life had fallen apart, but she was still expected to do her duty, and she did. They all do. Can you imagine?"

"I actually can," Euan said in a quiet voice.

"Of course, I did not mean to imply otherwise."

"I understand," he replied, offering a smile to reassure her.

"She accepted and they sent her home with me. I stayed with her for the next week until the funeral, taking care of her, talking to her, doing whatever she needed to help get her through. I have been with her since then and will be with her for the rest of her life."

"Did ye know this was coming?"

"No," Caia said, her brow knitting. "But I understand why they could not tell me."

"When ye said no one really understands what they go through, what did ye mean?"

"It is a rather lonely existence. They are often gone for long stretches and are unable to tell anyone what they are or what they do. They must lie to everyone, except perhaps their immediate families who already know. For Grace, she has no real friends but me and another young lady. The rest are all acquaintances. She does not have time for it and does not want to lie to anyone. I think it also has much to do with how much she closes herself off from others to prevent being hurt by them."

Closed off? Euan hadn't seen that in Grace at all. "I can understand that. It is hard when ye have no one to truly confide in. It is a feeling I know well."

"Very much so. She can tell me, but then I think even I do not know everything."

"Councilwoman Rochford told me ye could tell me what she was like."

"Grace is …" Caia began, pausing to think about it. "Beautiful. She is a beautiful soul, full of kindness and empathy. Once she gets to know you, she is amazing to be around, one of those people who draws you to her, so you always want to be near her. She loves to laugh and is always ready with a smile for others even when she is hurting. Grace cannot abide others being hurt in her presence, and she will stand up for them, help them. She is also one of the smartest people I know."

"She has quite the quick wit," Euan said. "It is one of the things I enjoyed most."

"She does," Caia said with a quiet chuckle. "She is a master at insulting someone without them realizing she has, though if she wants them to know she has, then she is quite good at that, too. Her sarcasm can be pretty sharp as well when she wants it to be."

"Somehow that does nae surprise me," Euan said, the thought bringing a smile to his face.

"I am glad you have come at last. I knew someday she would have a Companion, as they all do, and I am glad her time has come."

"Thank ye," he replied. "I will nae hurt her, Caia, and ye need nae have any fear about her from me. I want to protect her as much as ye do."

"I know," Caia said. "But we should get to Dr. Fraser," she continued as she stood up. "Follow me, and you can come back here to her afterward if that is your wish."

Euan stood and kissed Grace's hand before tucking it back beneath the plaid and following Caia out. "Will ye be a Watcher yerself eventually?"

"Me? Goodness, no. Watchers are born to this from certain family lines, and I am not one of those. It is just as well, as I do not think I could do the things Grace does. I am happy here, being a caretaker and watching out for her. It is an honor."

"Family lines? How many?"

"Six at present, though there is always a possibility of starting another if it is needed. So far it has not been necessary. They represent a spectrum, making them specialized for certain parts of the world. For instance, if there is a mission in India or the Middle East, there is a Watcher for that area specifically. She is able to blend in where Grace would not."

"I see. And men?"

"Watchers are always women," Caia said before offering him the same sort of reassuring smile he'd given her.

"Smart, really. I have long believed that women are far more dangerous and clever than most would give them credit for."

"You are absolutely right," she said, her smile turning sly as she went through a set of doors. "And Grace is a prime example of it."

Euan followed her inside and then stopped, looking around him. It was a huge space, all white walls and natural light. Everything looked spotless and orderly, with people walking around wearing pristine white coats. A tall man emerged from another room and walked toward them with a friendly smile. His dark brown hair was cut short, his eyes were blue like Euan's, but his build was more slender.

"Ah! Companion Cameron! At last!"

"What?" Euan asked in confusion.

"That is your title, or it will be once Grace wakes up," he said, extending a hand. "Dr. Andrew Fraser, but ye can call me Andy like everyone else does."

Euan shook his hand. "Hello, Andy."

"Nice to meet a fellow Scot for once. I will nae keep ye long, there are just some points we need to take care of in order to get things started for ye."

"I will be waiting right here," Caia said.

"Right," Euan replied before following Andy, who led him into a room and shut the door behind them.

"Up on the table if ye please."

Euan did as asked, lying down and staring up at a dark ceiling. "I have nae seen any place like this before."

"Aye, I expect nae," Andy said as he walked over to a panel filled with varying things. "A bit overwhelming?"

"Very."

"I can only imagine. Let me explain what I am going to do," he said as he turned around and came up to the table Euan was on. His expression was open, honest, and kind, as though he understood exactly what Euan was going through. "I am going to do what is called a scan," he continued. "It will be a light that passes over your body, and ye need to remain perfectly still. The light cannae harm ye, so there is nothing to worry about. This will put an image of your body up on that screen there. With that, we can start preparing your mission body."

"My what?"

"It is what we call the form ye are in when ye go on a mission. It allows ye to be there without actually being there and makes ye invincible."

"Oh!" Euan said, recognizing it now. "Grace told me about that. I was wondering how ye did it."

"Did she? Well, the how I cannae tell ye, only that ye will have one now so that when ye work ye are the same as she is. No need

123

to worry about what happened to her happening again, that is a one-time thing and nae something ye will ever face."

That she wouldn't have to go through that again was a relief to him. "That is good to know."

"It will take a bit, as it will be rather detailed. I was going to ask ye, would ye like those scars erased? We can do that for ye, if ye wish."

"No but thank ye. I would prefer they be there to remind me of what came before."

"I understand. Once this is finished, ye will be given inoculations, which will protect ye from getting ill from all sorts of diseases. We have all had them, they are perfectly safe, and will ensure ye live a long life. Your mother will have them as well. Are ye ready?"

"Aye, ready."

"Then let us get started, Companion Cameron."

"Am I allowed to speak?"

"Aye, ye just cannae move," Andy chuckled.

"I am so confused by all of this."

"Aye, I would imagine ye are. It is a bit much, and ye are nae given a whole lot of time to decide."

"It makes me wonder what I have agreed to. I am nae sure I can adjust to all of this."

Andy pulled up a chair to sit beside Euan, whose eyes widened as the light came on at his feet. "Remember, it cannae hurt ye. Just try to relax, I am right here."

"Thank ye," Euan said, releasing a breath he didn't realize he was holding.

"As for what ye have agreed to, well, that is a bit more complicated. To boil it down to its simplest, ye are working with Grace. Your job will be to help her on missions, play whatever part is needed. It will be up to the two of ye to figure out what that will look like, as everyone works differently."

"Aye, but the differences, the advances in everything ..."

"There is that, aye. I think ye will surprise yourself with

how quickly ye are able to adjust, because ye really have no other choice. That does nae mean it will nae be a bit too much at times, it will be, but ye will get past it and Grace will help ye. Ye will make mistakes, but try to relax, to take things in stride and keep your mind open. Watch Grace's reactions and ye will know if something is to be feared or nae. Let her show ye and guide ye, let her take care of ye, and she will. She is good at that."

"Ye sound as though ye know her well."

"I do," Andy said, his voice softening. "She is one of my closest friends."

"Caia said she did nae have any but her and another lass."

"Aye, and that is because they dinnae know about our friendship. Nae yet."

"Were ye —"

"Absolutely nae," Andy said quickly, not letting him finish. "Friends. Only friends."

"Tell me about her from yer perspective."

"She is one of the kindest people I know. A good listener, a good storyteller, a good friend. She is always there for me when I need her, if I have had a rough day and just need to talk to someone, and I am there for her in the same way. She wants people to be happy and does her best to make them so. If ye can get her to trust ye, to open up, there is such a depth of feeling there, such empathy and love, such strength. At the same time, she is fragile, afraid, and broken. She has been hurt so much in her life that she does nae trust, does nae love, and is extremely guarded."

"Aye," Euan replied. "Her strength is something I saw, something I loved. She was nae afraid of me, nae afraid to challenge me, and unwilling to back down when she knew she was right. She spoke her mind. All of that drew me to her in ways I cannae even describe, ways that scared the hell out of me, if I am honest, and still do. The depth of feeling I saw as well in every interaction she had with me. Ye are the second person who told me she could be closed off, but I never saw that."

"Really?" Andy said, his expression becoming curious as he continued monitoring the light making its creeping way up to Euan's shins. "That surprises me, but I suppose it should nae. If ye were to be her Companion, it makes sense that she would be different with ye than any of us have seen her. May I ask ye something?"

"Of course. I have asked ye plenty."

"Are ye in love with her?"

Euan blinked, taken aback by the question. "I dinnae know. I care for her very much, and though it may nae be love yet, it feels as though that is the only word I have for it. I cannae help but feel there is so much between us that neither of us can yet understand, but I know it is there. I look forward to discovering what that is."

Andy gave a slight nod. "That is different than what others say, but that does nae surprise me."

"What?"

"Other Companions come in and will actively say they dinnae love the Watcher who came for them, but they want to take it slow and see what happens, as in a normal relationship. Nae ye, though. Ye may nae say ye are in love, but ye feel some love for her or are beginning to."

"Aye, that is a good way to say it. If they dinnae love them, why do they agree to stay?"

"A lot of times I think it is because they feel a sense of obligation to this person who gave their life for them. Sometimes it is because they are fascinated and want to learn more. Love comes eventually."

"Have any decided nae to stay?"

"No," Andy said, smiling. "As I said, it always comes eventually. Ye just seem to be starting out a bit deeper emotionally than they have. Unless ye have stayed out of obligation."

"No," Euan replied. "I have nae. I stayed because, in the end,

I did nae want to be without her. I could nae conceive of going back to my old life where this beautiful, fascinating creature did nae exist. I had to know her, to be part of her life somehow."

"That makes me glad to hear," Andy said. "If anyone deserves to be loved, truly loved, it is Grace. All anyone wants is for her to be happy after everything. It sounds as though ye have already gotten closer to her than any of us have."

"It did nae hurt that I really had naught to go back to."

Andy laughed. "Aye, there is that."

"I just hope that whatever mistakes I make are nae mistakes that will drive her from me or put us in danger."

"I would nae worry too much about that. Grace is far too good at what she does to let ye fail that way. Trust me."

"How do ye mean?"

"She has only been here two years and they already have her training others, have others watching her missions for pointers. Ye are in the best possible hands, and she will guide ye so expertly through the missions that ye will nae even have a moment to doubt yourself. She can still amaze me with what she is able to do."

"That sounds intriguing."

"Ye have no idea," Andy said before he grinned. "Just wait."

CHAPTER 14

Grace opened her eyes slowly, trying to adjust to the bright light over her head compared to the darkness of the surrounding area. The room spun and she groaned, her eyes forced closed again. What had happened? Where was she now? Euan. The battle. She'd failed and he was dead. As the realization swept over her, she broke down into sobs that wracked her body.

"Easy, Grace," a familiar voice said.

"Caia?"

"Yes, it is me," Caia said as she stepped up next to her Watcher.

"What happened? Where am I? I failed ... I couldn't ..."

"Shhh," Caia said, trying to soothe her. "You are at The Council. You did not fail."

"I did! He died!"

"He did not."

"But I saw ..."

Caia gave a gentle shake of her head. "Here, let me sit you up," she said as she held Grace's hands and pulled her up. "There you go."

Grace closed her eyes again to let the dizziness and nausea from the movement pass. "Caia, I saw him die. He wasn't supposed to join them." Grace then noticed the plaid that had been covering her like a blanket and looked at it in confusion before realizing she was undressed and wrapping it around herself.

"Your mission was not that simple," another voice said.

Caia bowed as the woman who had spoken came into view.

Grace's eyes went wide. "Councilwoman Rochford. I —"

She held up a hand to silence Grace. "Your mission was successful, Grace. You went to save your future, and you did."

"My future? Don't you mean *our* future? I don't understand."

"Do you not wonder why you are here right now and not waking up in your own bed? Or why you feel so ill?"

"Yes, but …" Grace began, even though it hadn't truly occurred to her before that moment.

"Grace, you died. You sacrificed yourself for Euan. He lived because of you."

The words brought Grace to tears once again. She'd died. Yes, she remembered now. The pain, the blood, the bayonet.

The Councilwoman rubbed Grace's arm. "Your sacrifice brought you both here. He had a choice to remain or to return; he chose to remain."

"What?" Grace gasped through her tears.

"You were sent to save your Companion, Grace. You had to choose him, you had to choose to save him instead of accepting defeat. You did that."

"Companion?"

"Yes. The person who will be with you for the rest of your life. The one who will assist you on missions, the one who will father the future Watcher from your family line."

"Future … I haven't heard about this before."

"We do not tell you about it for a reason. If we did, you might always be searching for them, wondering if each contact might be them, and that would distract you from your mission. We can see who they might be and send you when the time is right. The same way your grandmother chose her Companion, and the same way all the other Watchers before you did."

"That is how my grandparents managed to make it work." Grace replied, the realization starting to dawn on her. It all made sense now. "They did it together."

"Exactly. He knew what she was and what she did because

she had saved him. He joined her in that work, just as Euan has chosen to join you. So, you see, you were successful after all."

"He would've died anyway?" Grace asked before a memory came back to her like a punch in the gut. "I told them how to change the outcome. I broke the rules. I'm so sorry."

"Do not worry about that. They did not listen to you, did they? You knew they would not, but you had to try anyway. For anyone but him you never would have done so. We are well aware of it, and it happens to everyone in these cases, almost without fail." Rochford smiled, assuring Grace that she meant what she'd said. "As for dying, yes, he would have. Just as he had before and has, again and again. It is a cycle that repeats. The battle repeats, they continue to die. He continues to die. But, no longer. You have pulled him out of it. He is here, waiting for you."

Euan was here. Grace felt as though her heart was pounding so hard she couldn't breathe. She placed her hand to her chest and saw that the wound the bayonet had left was gone, which meant the others were too. "How did I die? I'm not supposed to die."

"When you made the choice to save him, the mass of emotional energy you expended to do so made you as real as he was in that moment. The rush of energy from your death brought you both back. I am sorry you had to experience such pain, but that is often the way of it."

"Is he all right?"

"More than," Rochford replied. "In these last few weeks he has been here learning about his new role and the new world he will be living in. We made sure he was inoculated against any illnesses which might do him harm, just as you were when you began. As he cannot walk about in his traditional dress, he had a rather grand time selecting a new look, I am told."

Grace couldn't help but laugh and Caia smiled at her. "Come on, Gracie. Let us get you dressed so he can see you again. He has been on tenterhooks waiting for you to wake up."

"What would happen if I did not like men, or anyone at all?" Grace asked, aware that there were Watchers who didn't line up with past convention. Caia paused.

"They choose a Companion of their preference or not at all. There are ways to have children that do not involve traditional methods. We would not force anyone to do anything that was against who and what they are," Rochford replied, shrugging.

"And those who do not wish to be parents?"

"We have ways for that, too. Given that you fall into none of those categories it does not matter."

It was then that the horrible realization that she'd been responsible for his death returned to the front of her mind. "How could you send me there," she whispered.

"What?"

"How could you send me to make sure the attack at Nairn didn't happen? The attack that would ensure Euan died the next day. How could you send me there and then send me to save him?"

"Grace, that was a different timeline."

"It doesn't matter!" Grace shouted, though the Councilwoman looked unfazed. "He was in that timeline, too. I made sure it happened. I made sure he died."

Rochford looked at her, curious. "What would have happened if you had failed, Grace? Sure, he and the others would have lived, but what of the other men who would die in their place? There are no winners in this. You cannot have it both ways."

"You should have sent someone else to do it. You knew this was coming. You knew I would go to him. You should have sent someone else."

Rochford sighed. "You are right, we should have, but you are our best asset. We know you will get the job done every time and, as you said in debrief when you returned, that mission was complicated. You were the only one who could do it, and we had no choice. It was not ideal and not something we wanted to do but needs must. Whatever you did, you did not kill him. You were not even there."

"I did. I made sure it went wrong and the failure of that attack helped lead to the loss the next day."

"You made sure history remained as it was written. That is your *job*, Grace. You met his friends, why are you not sad about their deaths? It is just his that hurts you. They were all meant to die, and you cannot change that no matter how much you want to."

"How did I end up with this?" Grace asked, holding out the plaid. She didn't want to talk about Euan dying anymore.

"He did it," Caia replied. "I was not here to see it, but I was told he insisted on washing your body like they did in his time when people died. He did not want to leave you that way and he did it out of respect. He took that off of himself and covered you with it. When I asked him later what it was and why he had put it on you, he said it was the colors they wore, the colors you had worn with him. He said you had died as one of them and so you should be covered by it."

Grace lowered her head and cried, understanding perfectly well what he'd done and what it meant. What all of it meant. It was a form of the highest respect and he'd given it to her.

Caia gave Grace a gentle hug to bring her back around. "Let us get you looking like yourself again. I will make sure this gets back with his things."

After a long, hot soak in a tub to ease her back into the world, Grace slipped into clean versions of her linens and followed Caia to where Euan was. Remaining silent, she stepped into a library where he sat at a table, reading. He hadn't cut his hair; it was tied neatly back against his neck. He wore a vest, a long-sleeved dress shirt, and trousers, and it made Grace smile to see him dressed in that style. It reminded her of her grandfather and how meticulous he'd always been with his appearance. She saw Euan look up, as though he could sense someone was watching him, and he turned around in the chair. When he saw her, he stood up and hurried toward her. Grace met him halfway, and he caught her in a tight embrace even as she burst into tears against his shoulder.

"Shhh lass, there now," he said as he held her and stroked her hair. "Dinnae cry, please."

"I thought —"

"I know, but I am nae. I am as real here as ye are." He smiled when she looked up at him and brushed her tears away with his thumbs. "Ye, on other hand, were quite dead."

Grace laughed through her tears and shook her head.

"Thank ye for saving me, Grace."

"I couldn't let you die. I just ... I don't know why ..."

"Because ye might be starting to feel something for me?"

"That might have been it, yes." For Grace, it was an odd thing to admit. She'd worked so hard to stay distant from everyone, but he'd somehow gotten past all those defenses.

Euan smiled at her admission. "I cannae say I object to such a reason. Ye were nae the only one, or the only one who refused to admit to yerself that ye felt something deeper, something intense and frightening."

"Really? You ... I mean ..." she stammered.

"Aye, really."

The confession shocked her, and she changed the subject rather than delve any further into emotions she feared. "You agreed to stay?"

"Aye. Naught to go back to but suffering and death. So, suffering and death or a life with ye. Hm. Nae a difficult decision."

Grace laughed. "I would have missed this sarcasm."

"Aye, but now ye are stuck with it for life."

"Good."

Euan smiled and stroked her cheek. "I cannae tell ye what I felt when I saw ye lying there so wounded for my sake. I dinnae think I have ever wept so hard in my life. All because I was too stubborn to listen to ye."

"I think you had to be for any of this to happen."

"That is what they say, but I cannae believe there was nae

an easier way than ye dying. That I could have saved ye from it only made it worse."

"Let's not talk about it. It happened and it's over now," she whispered as she hugged him again.

Euan embraced her and held her close. "The things I feel for ye terrify me. I have never met anyone like ye, and the draw I feel is like naught I have ever experienced. There is so much between us, so much there is nae words for, dinnae ye feel it?"

"Yes," Grace whispered in his ear. "I feel the same way."

Euan sighed, still holding her. "I am glad I am alive to find out what those things are."

Grace pulled back to look at him, surprised to find he was teary-eyed, and it was now her turn to wipe them away. "Don't cry."

"I cannae help it. Ye have given me a new life, how can I nae be grateful for it? Ye have given my mother a new life."

"Your mother?"

"She is here. The Council said all of us are given the chance to bring one person, and she is the only one I would have considered. If I had nae, or if she had nae agreed, she would have been dead. They burned our house and transported her to London, but she died along the way. Ye saved her from that."

Grace looked momentarily horrified. "I'm glad I could."

"So am I."

"Everything will be different from what you knew, Euan. Everything. I'm not sure any amount of study will prepare you for that."

"Probably nae, but we will manage. It is good to know the woman I met is the woman ye truly are."

"Not sure I could be otherwise, really, at least not around you."

"Then there is only one thing left to do."

"Oh?"

"Aye. Kiss me already, ye foolish lass," he whispered, grinning.

Grace smiled, happy to oblige him, though there was something more to it now, a bond between them created by shared experience. The feeling was just as intense as before, and Euan walked her backward to slide her into sitting on a desk. As he wrapped his arms around her and pulled her close to him, Grace reveled in all of the feelings it stirred in her because she'd thought she'd never feel them again.

The sound of someone clearing their throat interrupted them, and Euan looked over Grace's shoulder even as Grace glanced back to see Caia standing there, looking sheepish. "Sorry to interrupt, but you are both needed before The Council."

"Duty calls," Euan said with a wink and Grace smothered a giggle in his shoulder, which only made him laugh. "Come," he said to her, taking her by the hand and helping her off the table.

Euan didn't release her hand as they walked behind Caia, and Grace was thankful for it. She wanted the contact with him, the feeling of knowing he was there and alive. It was going to be strange at first, but she found comfort in the fact that Euan would now always be there.

"I must say, you look very dapper in your new clothes, Euan."

"Aye? Thank ye. The Councilwoman said I could nae go about in my old clothes because I would stand out too much now, so I had to pick something else. These seemed a good blend of what I was used to and the new, though as time goes on, I am sure I will adjust to the new as well."

"It was a good choice. I've always liked the style and lamented over how few men wear it now."

"Well, lament no longer for I am wearing it," he said.

"Men do still wear kilts, though."

"They do?"

"Yes, but mostly for dress events to express pride in their heritage."

"Good to know. I will have to bring mine with me; it will be authentic." Grace laughed and Euan smiled at her. "It is odd for me to see ye dressed so differently than I have known ye. I will get used to it though. My mam has quite taken to the idea of wearing trousers."

"Pants can be pretty comfortable, certainly," Grace replied as they arrived at Council chambers.

The doors opened and they walked inside together. It wasn't often that Grace came here, and each time she did so filled her with the same sense of humility she'd felt the first time. Aileen was also present and waved to Grace when their eyes met.

"Hello Grace. Mr. Cameron," Councilwoman Rochford said.

"Councilwoman," Grace replied with a small bow that Euan also went into.

"Now that you have been reunited, there are some things to be discussed."

"Could have done with a wee bit longer on the reunion," Euan muttered, and Grace nudged him with an elbow, even though his words brought an amused little smile to her face.

"First, we need affirmation from both of you that you understand what has happened and agree to it. Grace, you understand that it is your choice to save his life that brought him here and placed him in the position to become your Companion?"

"Yes, I understand."

"You understand that, in taking him as your Companion, he remains with you and accompanies you on assigned tasks? You also understand that, with him, you will continue your Watcher line in the birth of a child?"

"Yes," Grace said, though her voice was quiet. She understood it must be done, but it was a strange thought just now.

"Very well. With that understanding Grace, do you affirm your choice?"

Grace glanced over at Euan, who looked panicked. It was as if he thought she might say no, and she wondered what would happen if she did. "Yes," Grace replied, and Euan visibly relaxed.

"Euan Cameron," The Councilwoman continued. "Do you understand that Grace's choice to save your life is what brought you here and that said choice tied you together?"

"Aye," Euan said.

"And you also understand that becoming her Companion means you join her and us in this work? That you will produce a child who continues the work after you have gone?"

"Aye."

"Further, you understand that you are able to leave at any time. You are not trapped forever; you need only tell us of your decision, and you will be released. You can ask to be returned to your own time or remain in the new one."

He could just leave? Grace's heart lurched at the thought.

"Aye, I understand."

"Do you affirm your choice to stay with Grace?"

"Aye," Euan replied without a hint of hesitation as he gave her hand a gentle squeeze, and Grace knew then that he'd seen her anxious expression.

"Then it is done," Councilwoman Rochford said.

"Done?" Grace asked.

"It is recorded here officially," she replied. "He is now your Companion, will get the mark that identifies him as such to others, and will be treated accordingly. We no longer have marriage in the way you do, but it is close to that."

A marriage. Of course. Why hadn't she thought of that? "I see."

"Grace, your income will be expanded accordingly. Euan will also get one so that his mother may be taken care of with it. Yours will be enough to more than comfortably take care of both of you. When you have a child, it will expand again to accommodate. I suggest, however, you see to finding larger housing."

"Yes, Councilwoman."

"Euan, you will have all you need to step into life alongside your Watcher. There are documents that are required there, and we have made sure records are there for you as if you were born there." Councilwoman Rochford approached him and handed him a large envelope. "Inside you will find identification, birth records, travel documents, immigration documents, and anything else you might need. We have them for your mother as well."

"Thank ye, Councilwoman," Euan replied as he accepted the envelope.

Grace looked over at Aileen and, for the first time, realized that she had her own packet tucked under her arm.

"With that, you are dismissed. Caia will brief you on the new protocol for assignments. Good luck."

"Thank you," Grace said as both she and Euan bowed and made their way out.

Aileen was not far behind them. "Grace!" she called out, hugging Grace when she turned around. "Oh, lass, it is so good to see ye. Euan told me about the way ye had been left and it broke my heart for ye."

Grace smiled and returned the embrace. "It's all in the past now. No need to worry."

"I am thankful for this. Ye have done as ye promised and he is alive."

"So are you," Grace said. "And I'm glad for that."

Aileen smiled and patted her cheek gently.

"Time to go home, Grace," Caia said as she stood waiting with the bags containing the clothes and other things belonging to Aileen and Euan. "We can talk more there. You ready?"

"As I'll ever be," Grace replied. Her hand still in Euan's, she reached out her other hand to take one of Caia's. Aileen took the other and then Euan's. Grace closed her eyes, waited for the tug, then opened her eyes.

Euan and Aileen opened theirs, too, and Grace saw both of their mouths fall open with shock as they looked around Grace's apartment. The two rooms they could see, the living room and the kitchen, were bigger than their entire home. It was clean and bright, the floors made of shining wood, the marble countertops gleaming. Aileen walked over to one of the windows and touched the glass, something Grace knew would have always been far too expensive for her to even dream of having.

Euan followed his mother, but not to touch the glass. Outside of the windows a massive vista stretched before him of buildings, buildings as far as he could see, and Grace watched him take it in. In the distance were mountains, but they weren't green or craggy as he would be used to seeing. Instead they were a golden brown. He looked to his left and saw the sea, stretching shining and blue to the horizon, and she saw him smile.

Grace understood what they must be feeling now, because it was similar to what she felt anytime she went someplace new. There was nothing familiar to them here and it wouldn't be getting easier any time soon. Even as quiet as her apartment might be, it could still be loud to them. The sounds of modern life would intrude: the forced air cooling the space, the compressor of the refrigerator, the hum of electricity. They didn't seem to notice it now, but she had a feeling they would soon enough.

"This is an absolutely beautiful set of rooms, lass." Aileen said in quiet wonder. "How fortunate ye are to live so finely."

"There is more," Grace replied.

"More!"

Grace nodded and then smiled. "There are the bedrooms and the bathroom."

"Ye have rooms just for sleeping and bathing?"

Grace laughed, not having thought about what a novelty that might be for Aileen. The wealthy of her time had it, of course, but she hadn't. "Yes. There will be much to get used to here."

"I am nae sure I ever will."

"Ye will, Mam. We all will," Euan replied.

"Let us talk about logistics so I can leave everyone to settle in," Caia said. Euan pulled himself away from the window and returned to where Caia and Grace stood. "From now on, you will both get the alert that you are needed. I will show up as normal to prepare you and stand watch. Instead of it just being you, Grace, you will both go together. Sometimes you will have the same objective, sometimes different targets that

139

are pieces of the same puzzle. For those you will need to work together but cannot be seen to be connected."

Grace knew this would be harder than it sounded. Especially the closer they got to each other. To hide that affection would be the hardest part of all of it. "Information will still come the same way?"

"Yes," Caia said. "Though, I will tell you now, there will be missions you will take on your own, Grace. Euan will not be there."

"Why nae?" Euan asked, frowning.

"Because you cannot be. There are so many reasons why that might happen, such as a mission falling during your former lifetime, but none of them are personal."

"So, I just sit here for weeks and wait for her to come back?"

"No. It is a matter of days at most. Often it is only one or two, and her body will be here with you. You can help me watch her."

Grace felt Euan draw her closer to him in an unconscious display of protectiveness.

"When you have a child, your missions will cease for the duration of the pregnancy and for some time after. When they resume, I will be here to care for the child while you are busy."

"I was going to ask about that," Grace said.

"I think you have a while yet," Caia said, winking, and Grace realized Caia knew her timeline. The Guardian was giving her a hint. "For now, though? Aileen, you and I are going to go enjoy ourselves at a fancy inn."

"Wait …" Euan began.

"Ye need some time to yerselves," Aileen said. "Ye have been through much and ye need to talk through all of it."

"Precisely. See you two in a few days," Caia said as she walked over and took Aileen's hand. In the next moment they were gone, leaving Euan and Grace standing there alone.

CHAPTER 15

"Would you like something to drink?" Grace asked after they'd stood in awkward silence for a time, both searching for something to say.

"Aye, thank ye."

"Something of the whisky variety?"

"Ye read my mind. Naught better for nervousness," Euan said, chuckling.

Grace walked over to a cabinet, and when she returned, she set the bottle and two glasses on the table before she gestured for him to sit. Euan took a seat as Grace poured him a glass before sliding into a seat beside him and pouring her own. "What are you nervous about?"

"Everything. Being alone with ye for the first time since it all happened for a start." Euan lifted the glass and looked at it in the sunlight, the angle sending glints of sunlight from the cut crystal across the walls. "I have nae ever seen anything like this."

"I feel like you're going to be saying that a lot for a while."

"Probably. *Slàinte mhath,*" he replied, smiling before he took a drink and then nodded in appreciation. "Excellent whisky."

"Ought to be for what I paid for it."

"Ye paid for it? How much?"

Grace thought for a moment. "About £80, I would say."

Euan choked on his next sip. "That is more than a lifetime of money! Why would ye spend so much on this?" he coughed out as Grace laughed at him.

"It's not even close to that now. You'll learn that soon enough, though."

"I still have a hard time believing any of this. Part of me wonders if this is all a dream, if I have died and gone to heaven and this is what it is showing me."

"It's real," Grace said, her voice soft. "I'm real."

Euan looked over at her. "Aye, to me ye finally are, and if ye are nae I hope I never learn otherwise."

Grace reached over and gently undid the cufflink at his left wrist. As she parted the cuff, the mark on his wrist was now clearly seen, just like hers, but one of the figures was male.

"When did that get there?"

"It appears when you are dismissed. Mine happened the same way," Grace explained as she reached out and smoothed her fingertips across it, an action that made Euan shiver, before she leaned down and placed a kiss on it.

His hand tightened around the glass and he closed his eyes as her lips touched his skin. "Grace," he whispered.

She pulled back from him, looking sheepish. "Sorry. I just —"

"No, I was nae asking ye to stop. Nae exactly anyway. That just made me want to abandon talk altogether, but I dinnae think that is how we ought to proceed."

"Probably wise."

"Did ye want to marry me?"

"Wait, what?" Grace asked, looking at him in confusion at such an abrupt change.

"What we did there at The Council, that cannae be what ye imagined yer wedding to be like. It certainly was nae for me. They may nae have marriage there, but clearly ye still do here."

"I think they already set up the paperwork and records to say we are."

"That does nae mean we cannae find a church somewhere and have a priest do it properly."

Properly. To them that would and did mean different things. Grace didn't really believe in any of it, but she knew

142

Euan would. To have any marriage sealed in this way would be, to him, the only right way. "If that's what you want, we can. I'm not sure I ever imagined getting married."

"When I find what I want to give ye for a ring then we shall do it. For now, I guess ye are just suddenly a Cameron to everyone."

"I suppose I am. What an odd thing."

"What will ye tell yer parents? Do they still live?"

"My mother does, and I'm pretty sure she'll understand. My grandmother was a Watcher after all."

"Yer mam did nae want to do it? Or does she?"

"No. By the time my grandmother died, my mom was too old to step into the job, and she wouldn't have wanted to anyway."

"Why would she nae wish to?"

"She has always said it was because she was happy with a normal life. One where she didn't spend as much time in the past as she did the present. I understand, but I have no such qualms."

"I will do my best to make ye happy, Grace."

"I know," she replied, smiling. "And I'll do the same with you. It's the only thing anyone can do. Marriage is a gamble for anyone, no matter how they start out."

"I will nae leave ye unless ye ask me to," he said. "I saw ye today when they asked if I understood I could leave and realized they had nae told ye that part. That Companions are always able to leave is part of the deal, they told me, for if we are unhappy together it would jeopardize the work and make us unreliable. Nae that I feel I would ever have cause to leave ye. I am going to make a life with ye and do all that I can to make sure both of us are happy in it."

Grace looked down to hide the emotion in her face but squeezed his hand. "Thank you for that."

"My life would be with ye. My child would be with ye. How could I leave any of that to go back to a past where I would die without ye?"

"You could if you were unhappy enough."

143

"Then I will just have to make sure I am nae, as I said. It will all work out, Grace, I promise ye. I will never forget what ye did for me."

"I never want you to remain simply because you feel obligated. That wouldn't be fair to either of us. Though, you know, getting shot is rather painful when you can actually feel it."

Euan couldn't help but laugh. "I imagine it is, aye."

"A bayonet? Also not nice."

"Aye," he said, still laughing. "But I must admit, when ye pulled my dirk on me I rather liked it. I may have to get ye to do it again."

Grace's eyes widened and she choked on her sip of whisky, which only made Euan laugh more. "I was trying to stop you!" she said, the words wheezed out between coughs.

"Aye, ye were. For a moment ye almost did, because all I could think about was taking ye somewhere away from that moor so that ye could do it again in a much more … relaxed … setting. Had I allowed that thought to continue …"

"You should've so that I didn't have to die."

"If I had, we would nae be here now," Euan replied. "At least that is what ye are all saying."

Grace made a small sound of agreement and took another drink.

"Have ye ever kissed someone on a mission before?"

"No."

"Has anyone ever tried to kiss ye?"

"No, not once. Why?"

"I was just curious. That no one else has tried surprises me."

"I suppose none of them have ever considered it something they could do."

"I am glad I was the one who did then," he said before he reached out for the packet the Councilwoman had given him and pulled it across the table. "Let us see what is here shall we?" Euan said as he opened the envelope and dumped the contents onto the table. Reaching out, he picked up the driver's license, looking at it and then holding it out to her. "What is this?"

"A driver's license. It says you can drive, and we use it for identification."

"Drive what? Cattle? I can and I have, but this does nae seem the place and —" he stopped when Grace started laughing. "What?"

"Not cattle. Drive a car. It's the way we get around. Think of it like a carriage without horses."

"Then how does it move if it has nae got horses to pull it?"

"It has what's called an engine. I'll explain how that works another time."

Euan shrugged and looked at the license again. "How did they get my image here?"

"It is a photograph. It takes an image of your likeness and preserves it. This tells the person looking at it that you are who you say you are because they can match your picture to your face."

"Oh."

"The numbers here are the license number. Here's your birthdate, and the date that this expires and you have to get a new one." Grace looked at him. "Wait, how old are you, Euan?"

"Five and twenty," Euan replied. "Just turned this past winter. What about ye?"

"Same," Grace said. "My birthday is in the winter too."

"How can I have something that says I can drive whatever ye call it when I cannae actually do that?"

"I'll teach you."

Euan looked at the small card again. "What is this word at the top?"

"California."

"California," he repeated. "What in the hell is that?"

"It is the name of the state we're in. You see, the colonies fought a war for independence from England. When they won, they became the United States of America. Over the next century or so they expanded from one end to the other and there are now 50 states instead of 13. California is one of them. The city we're in is Los Angeles," Grace replied, trying not to laugh but failing.

"Good Lord," Euan said. "I have a lot of reading to do."

"Yes, and I'll help you, don't worry."

Euan set the license aside and picked up a piece of paper. "Record of birth," he said aloud as his eyes scanned the page. "They have got all this right, but the dates are different. Have to be I suppose," he said as he set it aside.

As they flipped through the documents, there were immigration records showing he had legally immigrated from Scotland. There were passports from both the United States and European Union, a checkbook and check cards. Grace explained each and every piece to him, doing her best to make it understandable. The last thing he picked up was a marriage certificate.

They both stared at the document in disbelief. Here was a piece of paper declaring their marriage, dated a year ago. A marriage they'd never undergone. Clipped to it was another envelope with Grace's name on it. Euan handed it to her, and Grace opened it to find a new license, new checkbook and cards, and a new passport – though now she also had an EU passport reflecting her dual citizenship as the wife of a citizen of the United Kingdom. On all of them she was now listed as Grace Cameron.

Grace put them down and stood up in one swift motion, her heart pounding, feeling overwhelmed by all of it.

Euan followed her to slip his arms around her and pull her close. "I understand how ye feel right now because I feel it, too. My whole life has been changed and distilled, but for ye? This is yer time, yer life, a place ye are used to. It is a place where ye have friends and family, people who know ye well, and ye have been thrust back into it with a husband and a new name and no time to adjust, nae even the amount of time Mam and I had."

Grace took a few deep breaths to try and calm her heart. It would all work out. He'd told her so and she needed to have faith in that. The Council had sent her to him because that was where she'd been meant to be and she needed to have faith in that, too. She closed her eyes as Euan placed a gentle kiss on her cheek.

"We should go downstairs to the office and see about getting on a list for a larger space," Grace said.

"We would need larger than this?"

"Your mother needs a room."

"She has never had a room, Grace."

Grace blinked a bit but then realized he was right. Their cottage had been just one room. "Well, she should have one now. Come on."

She stepped back out of his arms and took his hand instead. Grace pulled her set of keys and fob from the hook on the wall and opened the door, stepping out into the hallway with him and heading for the elevator. When the doors opened, she led him inside and pressed the button without thinking.

"Christ!" he shouted as he grabbed the rail the moment the elevator moved. "What is happening?"

Grace looked at him in alarm before realizing how it must feel to someone who had never been in one before. "No, no. You're safe, it's okay. This is an elevator. It's taking us from our floor down to where the office is. I know it probably feels like we're falling, but we aren't. Just give it a moment and the feeling will go away."

Euan released the rail and stood up. "This is a strange place."

"We should have taken the stairs. I'm sorry, I wasn't thinking about it and how different this is from what's at The Council."

"No, I need to get used to this. This is my life now."

When the doors opened again, Grace walked out and Euan went with her, crossing the lobby and walking through an open door where she was greeted by a young man at the counter.

"Hello, Grace! I haven't seen you in a while. What can I do for you?"

"Peter, I wanted to introduce you to my husband, Euan."

Grace wondered if it was as strange for Euan to hear it as it was for her to say it.

"Good day to ye," Euan said.

"Oh! Well, congrats! I had no idea you were even engaged!"

"Thanks," Grace replied. "I need to get him a set of keys if you would, and a set for his mother who is coming to live with us. I also need to put their names on the lease."

"Sure, give me a moment and let me pull all that up."

"I also wanted to see if there were any larger units coming up anytime soon?"

"How much larger?" Peter queried.

"I know there are some four beds on the higher floors. Maybe one of those?"

"You're in luck. Someone just put in their notice on one of those today. It'll be a month before they're out and then we'll need some time to freshen it up. It's a good one too. On the ocean side."

"Perfect," Grace said, smiling. "We'll take it. Let me know how much you need in a deposit and paperwork."

"I'll put you down for a transfer. You're one of our best tenants, so we'll just do it for the difference in rent and transfer your deposits. Did you change your name?"

"Yes, sorry I should have told you that."

"No problem, just write it down next to your old one and I'll change it," he said as he pulled the paperwork from the printer.

Grace wrote down her name, and the names of Aileen and Euan, and handed it back to Peter.

"Are you from Scotland, Mr. Cameron?" Peter asked after looking at the paper and starting to type the new information.

"Aye, I am. From the Highlands."

"I've heard it's beautiful there," Peter said.

"It was," Euan replied, his voice becoming quiet and causing Grace to look at him sadly.

"Been a long time since you've been back huh?"

"Aye," Euan said quickly in order to cover up his mistake. "A very long time, indeed."

CHAPTER 16

After the new arrangements were made; Euan followed Grace back into the lobby. This time, he took a moment and walked over to the huge windows facing onto the street. Things streaked by, and he assumed these were the cars she'd spoken of earlier. There were people milling about everywhere and buildings all along the street. He stepped back from the windows, returning to the elevator with Grace.

Once they got back upstairs, Grace showed him around the apartment. He noticed new noises now, ones that were so different from anything he'd heard at home, and different from the ones he'd gotten used to at The Council. When he'd requested a bath, Grace took him to the bathroom attached to her bedroom and demonstrated how to work the controls on this shower so he could use it, before leaving him alone so that he might do so.

The hot water felt good and helped to loosen up his shoulders, which ached from the tension he hadn't realized he'd been holding. Now that they were here, now that she'd come back to him, he felt as though he could finally let himself relax a bit. He could let go of the fear that she'd not wake up, the worry that she wouldn't accept him; those things had passed. He thought back to that moment in the library, how she'd shied away from talking about what had happened, and Euan fully understood that desire. There were a great many things in his past he felt the same way about, things he couldn't speak of because the words would open the door to things he didn't want to remember. Then there was what he'd just witnessed in the office, the ease with which she'd not only adapted to the story about having a husband, but the smoothness in her manner and voice when she told it, showing him that she was more than what she seemed.

Euan shoved those thoughts aside and focused on relaxing himself. He had to admit he loved that there was instantly hot water to bathe with that didn't require fetching from the loch and heating over a fire, and this certainly beat bathing in a cold loch. Taking a moment, he smelled the different soaps and found one that smelled like her, that scent on her skin that had intrigued him in a moment that seemed so far away now. All the scents were pleasant, and he found himself very much wishing they'd had these soaps back in his Scotland; more than a few men he knew could've used them.

Once he'd finished, he dried off and stepped back into the room, having wrapped the towel around his waist the same way he would have done his kilt at home, and found Grace sitting on a bench seat in front of one of the windows. Before her, the city stretched out, vast and darkening with the setting sun, twinkling with lights as they came on to greet the night. She looked unreal to him then, much as she had that night in the woods with the buck. She looked like what she was: a different being, human but not, a Watcher. He could see that she'd changed into a sort of shift he'd never seen before. It left her shoulders and back exposed to him and he crossed the room to take advantage of it.

When he reached her, he knelt behind her and kissed her shoulder with the barest of touches, placing his hands over hers where they rested on the bench. He heard her soft gasp and felt her jump before she turned her head ever so slightly toward him. What she didn't ask him to do was stop. Euan dragged his lips across her back to her other shoulder and placed another tender kiss there. He could feel the goosebumps rise on her arms beneath his fingertips as he dragged them slowly up her arms and over her shoulder to push her hair away from the back of her neck, placing another kiss there before he slid his arms around her from behind and drew her back against his chest.

Grace's head dropped back against his shoulder as she closed her eyes, and Euan dragged the back of his hand down the center of her body, nuzzling her neck before he kissed his way up to her ear. He could smell her perfume, something she hadn't worn before, but it smelled wonderful and only made him want to kiss her skin even more.

"I will stop if ye wish me to," he whispered.

"No," she whispered in reply. "I don't want you to stop."

Euan placed a kiss against her ear and then slid his lips along her jawline before one hand cupped her cheek and turned her face toward him. The kiss he gave her then was the same as the one he'd first given her that day in the woods, but there was nothing to stop them now. No battle to fight, no mission to complete, no rules. It was just them. It felt as it had then, intense, and all-consuming, but the sensation of being able to feel her in every bit of him was so much stronger this time. She was part of him now, he could feel it, and it set both his mind and his heart racing, everything but her and this moment drowned out. His anxiety, his fears about this new world and his place in it, all of it gone with the feel of her lips on his and all that she was now intertwined with his soul.

Grace turned herself to fully face him, putting her arms around him to draw him in and against her. The material of the nightgown she'd put on slid across his skin and made him shiver. He pulled his lips from hers and kissed her collarbone, his fingers pushing the straps away from her shoulders. He could feel her breathing quicken, but he left her no time for nervousness as he made sure to lavish attention upon the newly exposed skin. She was perfection to him, and he needed her, wanted her, more than he'd ever needed or wanted anyone in his life. He craved her, every bit of him demanding her in the ways he'd never let himself admit he'd wanted.

As Euan kissed his way down her body, his hands moved to her legs and he slid his fingertips along her calves. Catching the fabric of the gown on his way up, he pooled it around her hips, the tips of his fingers digging into the tender skin for just a moment as he fought his nearly overwhelming desire to simply take her right that moment. That sort of interaction was for another time. When he was steady again, he pulled back from her and lifted one of her legs, kissing his way up it. The smoothness of every part of her was driving him mad with desire. He'd never encountered such a thing before, as women in his time were as men were and thus their limbs were unshaven, but he now very much wished he had.

Grace found she could hardly think as his lips and hands made free to roam every part of her. Not that she wanted to think. She wanted to surrender to this, to him, to everything she'd felt in her time with him. There was no defense against him or the emotions he stirred in her, the need to be near him, the strange desire to have him want her in ways she'd never cared about before. She could feel the tension in his body, in his touch, could feel him holding back, though she understood why. His hands were surprisingly soft and gentle, proving just how much control he had over himself. She jumped when he placed a feverish kiss against her inner thigh, but when he went further, she cried out and let her head drop back, her back arching for a moment. She had no idea this was something they even did then, much less that he'd do it. She also wouldn't complain because he was doing it extremely well. As he reached up and applied gentle pressure to one of her shoulders to push her upper body down, she went with it and found herself gripping the edges of the bench as he continued.

There was no need to stop when her enjoyment of this was quite clear, but he wouldn't and couldn't let her down that easily. Her reaction, however, was making it even harder to focus, and while part of him wanted to finish her this way, the urge to possess her entirely was smothering it into submission. Euan took her to the point where she was skating the edge and then pulled away from her. A small, involuntary sound of disappointment emanated from Grace, but he smiled and kissed the inside of her other thigh.

"Dinnae fret, I will nae leave ye disappointed," he said, his grin wicked, before he stood and brought her with him.

He felt the shift slide to the floor, and Euan pulled the towel away from his waist, tossing it aside. Pulling her fully into his arms now that there was nothing between them, he kissed her hard, much more like the kiss he'd given her the night she'd disappeared. They fell onto her bed together, though they turned so that she was now over the top of him. The collapse made Grace laugh a little and Euan joined her in it, but it didn't last long before Grace silenced it with another kiss.

Euan was more than happy when she didn't let the leverage she now had go to waste and set to exploring his body as he'd done hers. Her teeth just barely grazed his ear before she returned those kisses to the neck. Two could play at this game, and she heard his sharp inhale as she kissed his chest and dragged a fingertip along his side. She didn't miss the way his hands clutched the blanket as she proceeded to kiss each scar she found on his torso, or the way he shivered as she placed a line of kisses down the inside of one of his arms. Kisses to his hips made him moan and almost want to move away, but he didn't. Grace wanted to drive him to distraction as he'd done to her, and it wasn't long before she had him writhing beneath her with each kiss she placed upon him.

Euan had no idea what she'd done to him, but whatever it was, other women hadn't done it before. He felt hot and cold all at once, and he knew he didn't want her to stop. Every kiss she placed on his skin set it to tingling, to anticipating where she might go next. When Grace then dragged her fingernails across the insides of his thighs so faintly it drove him mad and made him want to scream, he couldn't think at all; and the sound he made when she finally took her mouth to him was foreign even to him. Christ, where had this woman been all his life? Though he certainly didn't want to, Euan forced himself to stop her and brought her up to his level to kiss her again. Moving so that she was now beneath him, he finally gave in to the deep desire for her that had been with him since the moment he'd first dared to kiss her. The feeling of that first moment was so intense it made him dizzy, and the loud moan from her didn't help matters. He paused a moment, gripping the blankets tight in his hands, because he had to get control of himself or this would be over far too soon. Euan took a deep breath to steady himself before he continued, though neither of them were quiet about the pleasure they were finding in this or in each other. Grace hooked one of her legs around his hip and he gripped her thigh hard to hold it there as he swore under his breath. When Grace suddenly clutched his shoulders and smothered a cry against one of them, he knew he could let himself go and did.

They held each other, unmoving, trying to breathe and process all of it. Had they done this that final night he never would've left. What would've happened then? All that mattered was that he was here with her now and had no reason to leave her again.

"Christ, lass, I dinnae think anyone has ever made me feel that way," he said, still feeling a bit breathless before giving her a gentle kiss.

"Good," she said, her smile just as wicked as his had been not long ago. "It means no one else ever will."

"Thank Christ for that," he said, chuckling as he moved away from her. "I am nae sure I would like more than one person having that sort of power over me."

Grace laughed, turning on her side to allow herself to look at him. "I would ask you where you learned any of that, but I'm not sure I want to know."

"I could say the same for ye," he replied, amused by her reticence to even ask such a question. "It seems perhaps the lasses really can get up to the same as a man here without fear of retribution."

"Not exactly, but certainly more so than in your time."

"My time. I dinnae think that exists anymore. My time is now this one."

"A good point. I should probably stop saying that."

Euan gave a gentle shrug in response. "I think, when we are alone, it is sometimes the only way to make the needed distinction."

"As time goes on, I think it will become less relevant all on its own."

"Aye, I agree with ye. It has nae been that long since it all happened." Euan drew a fingertip from her shoulder down along her arm and watched her shiver, which made him smile. "Tell me, have ye been to the Highlands in this time?"

"Oh, yes. It's still beautiful. It's one of my favorite places in all of the places I've been."

"So at least the war did nae destroy it. I wonder what became of my home. I know they burned it, but what became of what was left?"

"I don't think any war could destroy such a place. Not beauty like that," Grace said before falling quiet for a second. "Would you like to go there and find out?"

"Ye would be willing?" Euan asked, surprised by the offer.

"Of course I would," she said.

"How long would it take to reach it? A few months?"

Grace looked confused for a moment before seeming to realize what he meant. "Oh! Goodness no. We could be there in a matter of hours. There are other, faster methods of travel now. Even if we took a ship it would only be a couple of weeks."

Euan's eyes widened. "Hours? What do ye do, fly?"

Grace couldn't help but laugh. "Actually, yes."

"Ye are lying to me now."

"No, I'm not, I swear," Grace said, still laughing. "It's called an airplane."

"Well, no matter how we get there, I would like to go. Do ye think The Council would spare ye for a time?"

"I'm sure they would if I asked. It isn't like they wouldn't understand, and I have a feeling they'll leave me be for a while anyway and give us time to adjust to life here. Besides, I'm quite certain they already know we'll be going."

"Good point. Thank ye, lass, I look forward to it. Ye know, this is the most comfortable bed I think I have ever had the pleasure of spending time on. There are a good many things to like about the future."

"I'm sure you'll find more. Are you hungry?"

"Famished," he replied. "I dinnae think I have eaten yet today, but my bearings are off, so it is hard to say."

"Come on then, I'll make us something to eat," Grace said as she moved to sit up and leave the bed.

Euan, however, was quick to grab her and pull her back. "I am nae sure if I want to eat if it means letting ye leave this bed. Unless my dinner is ye. From the scent of yer perfume I can say it is a tempting thought."

Grace gasped and then blushed, which made him laugh at her. "You're terrible."

"I did nae hear ye complain just a short time ago. And what is that scent, now that I am thinking about it?"

"And you won't either, but we can come back. It's honey-suckle and apple."

"I hope ye wear it again. It smells wonderful on ye," he said before he released her.

"I will, for you."

Grace got out of the bed and crossed the room to grab a robe from a hook on the wall. Euan took the opportunity to look at her and he gave his head a small shake to keep himself from telling her to forget the food and dragging her back to bed, getting up to follow her instead. She handed him another robe, this one made of blue terry, while she slipped into one made of the same fabric as the nightgown she'd worn earlier.

Euan pulled it on and tied it around himself before following her out to the kitchen. Grace was already busy, pulling things out of cabinets and drawers, and he walked over to the counter to lean against it. He then noticed something in the open pantry and picked it up, turning around in alarm.

"Grace, what is this? Campbell's? It says it is soup, but what sort of container is this? How does it nae spoil just sitting here this way? I would nae eat it. The Campbells are right bastards and might be trying to poison ye, especially if ye are a Cameron," Euan said.

Grace was laughing so hard it left her trying to catch her breath in between. "No, Euan," she managed to get out between laughs. "I don't think it's the same people. It's called a can, and it doesn't spoil because it's sealed against the outside air."

"I still would nae trust it," Euan muttered as he put it back on the shelf. The hatred of the Campbells was something every member of Clan Cameron was born with as part of a feud that had lasted for centuries.

"It's good that's not what I'm making you then."

"What *are* ye making?" he asked as he walked over to where she stood. "And where is the hearth?"

"Something called spaghetti. It's from Italy. And we don't need a hearth for a cooking fire anymore. It's right here," she replied as she pointed to the stove and turned the knob to ignite the gas burner.

Euan jumped back and then came closer to peer at it. "Where does the fire come from?"

"It creates a spark, which ignites the gas. Gas comes from the earth and is piped around," she said as she placed a large pot of water on the burner.

"Amazing. So many things have been created in all of this time."

"Progress can be an amazing thing, but it can also be a terrible thing, too. We often use it to create ever greater instruments of war and do harm instead of good. That's why The Council does what they do. They've stopped that and why go back?"

"I agree. Why would ye if ye have managed to end it for good? Other than being with ye, it is why I agreed to stay. I have never known a time without some sort of war. I want there to be a time when people dinnae know the same."

"I'm glad you decided to stay."

"I could nae live with the idea of nae seeing ye again. Nae after everything." He reached out and took her hand in his before he lifted it to his lips and kissed it. "That night, when ye disappeared, I felt as though there was a hole in my heart where ye had been. If ye were gone I would be fine to die, for I would nae be seeing ye again."

"Even if that had been true, Euan, you shouldn't have wanted to die."

"I was going to die anyway, was I nae? Ye being gone that way just made me more resolute to get on with it."

"Euan —"

"No one has ever made me feel for them the way ye did, Grace, and ye were a stranger to me even though I felt I had always known ye somehow. There was just something in ye that called to me, something that drew me to ye. I knew I could love ye so easily, I had already started to. I feared it and feared what ye made me feel, feared the power it gave ye over me. I had always avoided such feelings, always felt as though I was waiting for the person they were truly meant for. Then ye showed up, and ye were this being I wanted but could nae have. To know ye made me feel what I had wanted to feel but that ye were out of my reach was maddening. It was why I did what ye accused me of. I would catch myself getting too close to ye, letting ye into my heart, and I would push ye away because I could nae stand the hurt I felt at the thought of what was to come. Ye would leave me and I would die."

"I felt the same, and that made it very hard to do what I had to."

"Is that why ye broke the rules?"

Grace nodded without looking at him. "I cared for you, a lot, even though I couldn't say it and didn't even really understand it. I didn't want to lose you, but I knew I would no matter what happened. You would live and I would come home, or you would die and still be lost to me. If I was away from you forever, at least I'd know you hadn't died horribly in that battle. I had to do what I could. You told me the only way to save you was to help you win, and I tried. I wanted to protect you no matter what trouble it might cause me."

"Ye were right about the battle," he said. "I saw it. I saw what happened. If they had listened to ye ..."

"If they had listened to me, the Jacobites might have won at Drumossie and history would have been forever changed. To what, I don't know."

"I was so angry with ye for doing it. I knew ye had just put yerself in peril for me. Ye had ignored yer duty for me. At the same time, it made me want ye more, which also made me angry. Ye were willing to risk everything for me, and every moment it made it harder for me to do what I had vowed I would. When we argued that morning ... Grace, I knew."

"Knew?"

"I knew ye had the same sort of feelings for me that I did for ye. Ye did nae have to say it; I knew, and I could nae take the knowledge that someone other than my mother cared so much for me. I had to go, and it was going to hurt the one person I would nae wish to. I hated myself for it, hated myself for doing it to ye, but at the same time I was furious that ye were beyond my reach. Ye were the one thing, the only thing, which could have made me stay and I knew it, but it did nae matter because ye were nae mine to have. The look on yer face and the sound of yer voice when yer control slipped and ye told me ye would care if I died ..." Euan paused and shook his head. "I will never forget it. I am so sorry."

Grace looked at him, speechless for a moment. "Euan, I ..." she began before she closed her eyes to force the words past the emotion tightening her throat. "I forgive you, if that's what you need to hear, but I don't hold it against you. We were both angry over the same things; you because you were conflicted, and me because I was scared."

"Scared? Of what?"

"Scared to lose you. Scared because I knew you would die frightened and in pain and I could've stopped it if only I'd tried harder. We're so alike, and neither of us could handle that. It's like fighting with yourself."

"Aye, that is true," he admitted. "We are alike in so many ways it is honestly frightening. I told my mother that ye were my mirror, and ye are."

Grace took his hand in hers. "I don't disagree. You're mine, too. As for the disappearing, I'm so sorry it happened that way. I had no control over leaving."

"I know that now. Had ye nae, things might have turned out very differently. One moment ye were there, and the next all I had was the arasaid ye had been wearing. I took it with me because it smelled of ye and it was all I had. I wanted ye near me."

Grace's lip trembled, clearly touched when he told her he'd carried a token with him, something to keep her with him. "I was. In the end I was. I was always going to be."

"I did nae know that."

"I know."

"Tell me what happened. What do ye remember?"

"They didn't tell you?"

Euan shook his head. "I did nae want them to."

Grace took a deep breath and released it. "I ran after you because I thought if I could pull you down and keep you there, we could get out. I caught you just as they fired on you, I was pulling you down and the shots hit me instead. I remember that it hurt more than I could imagine it would've. I was confused by the pain, but I knew I had to get you out. I knew something was wrong, that I wasn't going to heal, and I was going to die; but I couldn't stop. There was so much blood." Grace paused, her expression seeming far away. "I could taste it, I coughed and choked on it when I got up. I didn't have time to think about it though. I went to drag you to the woods because I thought you'd be safe there; you could run when you came to. Then I couldn't breathe, and I looked down to see the point of the bayonet sticking out of my chest. The man who did it looked angry and scared. That's all I remember until I woke up with Caia."

Euan reached up and wiped his eyes on the sleeve of the robe. He could still very vividly see Grace on that table, mortally wounded and crimson with her own blood. It was a sight he knew he'd never be rid of. The knowledge that she'd been aware of what had happened, aware that she was going to die, broke his heart. He could only imagine how scared she must have been. He knew he would've been terrified. In fact, he had been.

"Christ, lass, it never should have happened. Nae like that."

"We can't change it, Euan. What happened was what needed to happen. We're here together now and that was the reward."

"Aye, love, it is. A reward I will forever be thankful for."

Euan heard Grace's breath catch when he called her "love," and he realized in that moment that no one had ever called her that before. How in the world that was possible he didn't know, but it would never happen again as long as he was with her.

She reached up and stroked his cheek. "You are a beautiful man, Euan. That you were lost to the world was a tragedy. You could've done and been so much."

"I am no longer lost," he replied, his voice soft.

"No, you aren't. I remember when I first truly saw you, when you were bathing, I felt as though there was just something there you were hiding, and I wanted to know what it was. I know now."

"What do ye mean?"

"Your mind, your depth of feeling, your passion, your empathy. The things that make you truly the man you are. There is the fire, the darkness, the rebel and warrior that you are. That's what everyone sees. I feel as though I'm the only one who has had the privilege of seeing the rest."

"Aye, ye are. Aside from my mother, perhaps. None of those things were useful for the man I was expected to be."

"You don't have to hide it now."

"I am nae sure it is a habit I can break. Besides, it is something I would prefer to keep just for my bride: ye."

"Thank you," she said, that shy tone he'd heard in her voice the night of the party returning. "I want to love you," she continued, her voice now a near whisper.

Euan's face registered his surprise before the expression softened to one she would recognize. It was the same expression that had been on his face that last night when he'd told her he was sorry for hurting her.

"And I want to love ye," he replied, drawing her into his arms to kiss her. "I am sure I will love ye, and I dinnae think it will take all that long for either of us."

Grace rested her head against his chest and closed her eyes for a moment before she placed a kiss on his chest, and then looked up to find her water boiling. She moved from his arms to put the pasta in as he watched her with curiosity. Grace grabbed the jar of sauce she'd pulled from her pantry and put it in another pan to warm. As it heated, Euan breathed in the scent of it, and his stomach wasted no time in reminding him that it was empty.

"That smells delicious. I dinnae know what it is, but it smells good."

"I'm sorry it's from a jar, but with the time we have it's the best I can do. I promise to make it properly by hand next time."

"I dinnae think I care at the moment," he said with a chuckle. "My mother could only dream of having this much food available whenever she wished it."

"This is less than I normally have. I haven't gone to the grocery store yet."

"The what?"

"The place you go to buy food. As you can see, we have no place to grow it here, so we go to the market to buy food there."

"I think my mam will faint when she sees it."

"Possibly," Grace replied, laughing, before she busied herself with stirring the sauce.

Euan watched as she drained the pasta and then mixed the two together. She placed only a mouthful on the dish and handed it to him. "Just a little bit at first. You may not like it," she said as she lifted it to his lips.

Euan took the bite but didn't know what to make of it at first. It was like nothing he'd ever tasted. There were so many different flavors in it, so many he didn't recognize, but it was delicious.

"If this is what all the food is like, I shall be a great, fat man before long," Euan said when he finished that first bite.

"I take it that means you liked it."

"Very much, thank ye."

Grace placed more on his plate before getting some for herself. She went to the fridge and pulled out parmesan cheese, letting him taste hers first. "Did you want some, too?"

"Aye, thank ye," he said.

"There's more than just food, you know."

"I am fine with food for now."

"I'll show you even more of your new world tomorrow."

"Ye are assuming I will let ye rise tomorrow," he replied.

"Promises, promises," Grace said, grinning.

"Promises I intend to keep, believe me. I have nae had my fill of ye yet."

"Hopefully you never will."

"I dinnae think ye need to worry about that."

"There are some things we ought to do, but we can deal with those tomorrow," Grace said, changing the subject.

"Aye, the real world can wait awhile. We have a lot of talking to do."

CHAPTER 17

When they woke the next morning, it was nearly 10. They'd spent much of the evening talking and spending time together. Grace had opened a bottle of wine for them to enjoy with their supper and, afterward, they'd returned to bed just as she'd promised. That she wanted to love him and be loved by him was something harder to admit than she'd imagined. To admit it made it real, made it so he could hurt her. In the end, she'd fallen asleep with her head on his chest, listening to the sound of his heartbeat, a heart that should no longer be beating. A heart that was over two centuries old. A heart that was now hers.

It had been a strange sensation to wake up beside another person, but it was a pleasant thing all the same, and Grace couldn't remember having slept so well in a long time. As Euan showered, she made breakfast, introducing him to eggs, pancakes, bacon, and orange juice: the staples of an American breakfast. He'd found the juice strange and almost too sweet, but he'd adjusted to it by the end of the meal. The rest was quickly and happily eaten, though she was certain that most things here would beat a bowl of oats.

"Euan," Grace said when she emerged showered and dressed after breakfast. "We should set up your bank account access and an email address for you."

"Ye would know best when it comes to that," he said as Grace brought her laptop over to him.

"You'll access all of your accounts on the internet," she said before pausing. "Wait, did they teach you how use a computer?"

"Aye, a wee bit. Mam did nae take to it, but I did well enough. It was strange at first, and typing was stranger still, but I can manage it. I do like the idea of being able to look up anything I wish in a matter of moments."

"Oh, good! At least we won't have to start so far back as how to turn on the computer."

"No," Euan said, laughing. "Someone did that for ye."

"I'll have to send them flowers," Grace said, handing him the laptop. "We'll have to get you one of your own, and then I can teach you some of the more complicated stuff."

After helping him set up an email address, she talked him through setting up the online accounts to access his banking information. A bank was a foreign concept to him, as everyone handled their own money, but he caught on quickly. Money by itself wasn't a surprise; he was used to handling larger sums when he assisted Lochiel in the carrying, delivering, or collecting of it, as well as at varying other times. When he saw the balance in his account, however, he'd sworn there was a mistake, but she managed to eventually convince him otherwise.

Once he was finished, she worked on booking the flights for them to Scotland, leaving in a week, while Euan stood transfixed, examining the entire contents of her bookcases. This was a luxury he could never have dreamed of, and he'd very much wanted to see it when she'd first mentioned it. Now he could.

"These all belong to ye?"

"Yes, though my grandparents' collection is bigger. This is only what could fit here," Grace said, getting up and making her way over to stand beside him.

"Ye have more books than can fit here?" Euan asked, incredulous.

"I do. These are just the ones I like the most."

Euan reached out and tentatively touched the spine of one of the books, as if to test whether it was actually there or not.

"Go ahead. You can pull out and look at anything you want."

"Ye are sure?"

"It isn't like you're going to ruin them, Euan. Besides, if you're my husband then these are also your books now. Everything I have is also yours."

Euan smiled at her and then turned toward the shelves, looking for all the world like a giddy child. Pulling out the first book he touched, he smoothed his hand over the hard cover and admired the decoration.

"Ooo, John Keats. An excellent choice. He's a poet."

"Aye? This book is all poetry?"

"Yes, all of it. He was very prolific for such a short life lived."

"Have ye a favorite?"

Grace took the book, opening it and moving to the page she sought, before she began to read to him.

> *"I cannot see what flowers are at my feet,*
> *Nor what soft incense hangs upon the boughs,*
> *But, in embalmed darkness, guess each sweet*
> *Wherewith the seasonable month endows*
> *The grass, the thicket, and the fruit-tree wild;*
> *White hawthorn, and the pastoral eglantine;*
> *Fast-fading violets covered up in leaves;*
> *And mid-May's eldest child,*
> *The coming musk-rose, full of dewy wine,*
> *The murmurous haunt of flies on summer eves."*

Euan closed his eyes to listen. "Ye read as beautifully as ye sing. There is a gentle cadence to poetry that is so soothing, dinnae ye think? What a beautiful scene he paints."

"Thank you, and yes he's quite good at that. He has a couple of poems about Ben Nevis."

"If ye are a poet I cannae see how Ben Nevis would nae inspire ye to create," Euan said as he turned back to the shelves. "Ye have Shakespeare!"

"Yes," Grace said, chuckling.

"Ach, I did love that. I got to read a bit when I was in lessons."

"The plays?"

"No, the sonnets, but the tutor would let me stay longer to read from his book," Euan replied, smiling at the memory.

"Did you have a favorite?"

"To ask me such a question is like asking me to choose a favorite memory or song. I cannae pick just one. I did always like the line, 'love alters not with his brief hours and weeks, but bears it out even to the edge of doom.'"

"Sonnet 116," Grace said. "I like that one, too."

"It amazes me that ye have such a collection in yer own home. I dreamt of having one book, maybe two, and ye have all of these."

"I take it so much for granted," she admitted. "These things that are great luxuries to you are commonplace to me. It's nice to be reminded of how lucky I am to have access to the things I do."

"It is nae as if ye do it purposefully. Everyone does it in their own way, and why would it nae be so for ye? Ye live in a time where such things are easy to come by, why would ye think about it as a luxury? Even I took things for granted."

"Like what?"

"The peace and the beauty of home; a place I saw every day. I took all of it for granted, so much that I hardly noticed it anymore. Then ye came and I saw it again through yer eyes while we were on our walks. I realized how much I had stopped seeing, but all of it is gone now."

"It isn't," Grace said. "The beauty and the peace have recovered, you'll see."

"I also took life for granted. I believed everything would stay the same as it was, forever. Life would go on at Achnacarry in the same way it always had. All of those moments ye think so trivial at the time suddenly become more when they are gone."

"I'm sorry," she said, reaching out and taking his hand.

"Dinnae be. Ye did nae do it, and now I have the chance to nae make the same mistake. I will gladly take it."

"I can still be sorry they're gone, and I am."

"I know ye are," Euan said as he stepped closer to her and smoothed a hand over her hair. "Ye would have saved us all if ye could have, and I know that. Hell, ye even tried. Dinnae fret about it."

Grace slipped her arms around his waist and rested her head against his chest, closing her eyes. "I'm happy you're here. Happy we can do this instead of fighting each other."

"So am I. Very much so," he said as he kissed the top of her head and put his arms around her. "I prefer getting to know ye this way."

"I prefer it, too," Grace said, amused. "We'd better get moving, though, or we'll never get anything done today. Did they teach you about mobile phones?"

"Aye. They showed me what they were like and what they did. I am still amazed by them. Ye have the whole of the world at yer fingertips."

"That's true," Grace conceded. "We should get you one of your own. Probably one for your mother too."

"If ye think we need them."

"It's always a good idea to have them. If anything happens, you're able to reach help. Come on, let's go."

***

"What is this place?" he asked as they stepped out of the elevator, stopping to look around the rather large space filled with gleaming vehicles in every color imaginable.

"The garage. This is where everyone parks their cars."

"These are the things ye spoke of? There are so many colors and shapes."

"Yes, there are. One for every kind of taste you can think of."

"Which one is yours?" Euan asked as they made their way through the garage.

"This one," Grace replied as they stopped in front of a car which was a shining shade of dark green.

Euan ran his fingers over the hood and studied it with an awestruck look. The beep when Grace unlocked the car made him jump back, but he laughed when Grace did. She opened the door for him, and he slid into the passenger seat as she shut it behind him. What immediately struck him was the scent of the leather, a beautiful golden color. His body sank into the seat, and he could only imagine how comfortable such a thing must be on a long journey. In front of him there were all sorts of black surfaces and knobs.

Grace opened the door on the other side and got in, shutting the door, and setting the remote key down in the dash. The ignition light turned green and she pressed the button. The car roared to life, all the black surfaces coming alive with numbers and other information. When she reached out and squeezed his hand in reassurance, he realized he must have looked as momentarily terrified as he'd felt.

"It's all right. It's supposed to sound that way," she said.

Euan nodded, trusting her. Once she'd shown him the seatbelt and given him a set of sunglasses, Grace shifted into reverse. Once out of her space, she started forward and Euan gasped, grabbing onto the armrest of the door. As they pulled out of the garage and into the sunlight, Euan suddenly understood the purpose of the glasses. It was exceedingly bright outside, and these were another thing he wished they'd had. They were already travelling faster than he ever had before, and it almost felt too fast. However, looking at Grace, he knew it wasn't. It was normal. This was how they travelled here, and he did his best to relax. He needed to get used to it, and he knew Grace was doing her best to make it easier for him.

As they got to the end of the road, the sea lay before

them. "Would you like to see what fast is really like?" Grace asked him, her look becoming mischievous.

"What do ye mean? Ye can go faster than this?"

"Oh absolutely. Aston Martins are made for it."

"Faster," Euan said to himself before he looked over at her. His curiosity and his love for adventure won out over his hesitation and caution. "Show me," he said as a grin spread across his lips.

"Hold on."

When the light changed, Grace swung right and punched it, the car surging forward with a smoothness that belied the work it was doing. It brought a shout from Euan and pinned him to the seat as the landscape outside became a blur. When he got past his initial shock, he started laughing uproariously. It felt as though they were flying, and it was an incredible thrill.

Grace, laughing with him, slowed the car considerably so they didn't get a ticket. "Told you."

"Christ, that was incredible! How far do ye reckon ye could go when ye go that fast?" His heart was pounding, the rush of it all making him nearly giddy.

"At the speed I was going? If you didn't slow down and kept steady, you would go a hundred miles in an hour."

"Jesus!"

"It goes faster."

"I believe ye." Euan smoothed his hands over the leather. "I can see why ye would want one."

"Once you learn to drive, you can get one."

"Like this one?"

"If you want."

"Oh, I do. I definitely do."

Grace shook her head and laughed, driving on at a much more normal speed now. Euan settled in and watched everything go by from the window. If he ever had to go back for good, he wasn't sure he'd want to. This place was far superior in many ways. As they drove, she explained the rules of the road. The lights, the signs, all of it.

It didn't take them long to handle the business of picking out a laptop for Euan and adding him and Aileen to the phone account while picking up devices for them. They'd opted for something simpler for Aileen unless she decided she wanted otherwise. Euan picked one just like Grace's, the latest with all the bells and whistles. He was eager to learn how to use it, but not so eager that he already had it in his hands to study. Once it had been activated at the store, he'd turned it off. That was for later. Time with Grace was now.

"Grace!" someone called out as they started to walk away from the store.

Grace turned her head toward the voice and smiled at a young woman coming toward them.

"Hi, Van!" Grace replied.

"I thought it was you!" she replied as she reached Grace.

"Sorry I've been out of communication, but work has been a bit crazy. You know how it is."

Euan couldn't help the small smile that crossed his lips at the mention of Grace's work. This young lady surely had no idea how true that was.

"Eh. Typical Grace, really," she replied, chuckling. "You go on and off the map all the time. I'm used to it."

"Vanessa, this is Euan. My husband."

"A pleasure to meet ye, Vanessa," Euan replied, putting on his most charming smile.

"I'm sorry … what?" Vanessa stared and held up her hands. "Hang on. You go radio silent for like, three weeks, and suddenly you've married some hot Scottish dude?"

Euan raised an eyebrow, not sure what she meant.

Grace laughed. "Yeah, something like that."

"Girl, we have some serious catching up to do. Sorry, Euan, nice to meet you," Vanessa said, extending her hand to Euan to shake. Euan, instead, took her hand and kissed it with a small bow. "Hoooooly hell," she squeaked.

Grace smothered a laugh in her hand and Euan looked at her, wondering if he'd done something wrong. She gave him a small shake of her head to reassure him.

"We were just picking up a phone for him that will work here."

Vanessa cleared her throat and fanned herself. "Yeah. Good idea. Also, good idea for snapping that up in a hurry 'cause, damn."

"I am sorry, did I offend ye, lass?"

"Oh hell no. You can do that all you want, sir."

Euan smiled, liking this woman already, and he recalled Caia mentioning her as Grace's only other true friend. She was animated and plain spoken; it didn't surprise him in the slightest that she was a friend of Grace's. Her dark brown hair and eyes stood in stark contrast to Grace's fair coloring, though they were nearly the same height. Vanessa was bright and cheery, and seemed to be one of those people who would always be ready with a smile when you needed it.

"Thank ye for understanding. I am still learning what is acceptable here."

"Where in Scotland are you from that it would be any different?" Vanessa queried.

"The Highlands. We do everything differently there."

"Maybe I should follow your lead and go there, Grace," she said while still looking at Euan.

"Once you're done undressing my husband in your mind, would you like to have some lunch?"

Both Euan and Vanessa laughed. "I'd love to. Like I said, catching up and all that."

Euan gathered Grace's hand in his as they walked, and they made their way to a place where people were sitting out in the open air, eating. The smell of the food made Euan's stomach rumble. The two women seemed to know the place well, and they took a seat at a table outside. Euan studied the menu when it was handed to him, but he very quickly realized he had no idea what any of it was.

"Margaritas, Gracie?"

"Not this time. I'm driving."

"Booooooo."

"Euan, did you want one?" Grace asked him. "It's a drink with spirits, fruit, and ice. They put it all together. It's really good."

"No, thank ye." While he was tempted, he thought better of trying any sort of spirits outside of their home for now.

The young man serving them set a basket of something on the table, along with a small bowl of what looked to be something like the sauce she'd served last night. Euan picked up one of the thin pieces from the basket and ate it, taking a moment to appreciate the flavor of it before he grabbed another. This time he dipped it into the sauce in the bowl.

"No, Euan, wait!" Grace said, but it was too late.

The taste was strange. It wasn't sweet like yesterday, but it was good in its own way. Then his mouth suddenly felt hot. His eyes widened and he looked at Grace before he grabbed the cup of water just put down and drank it.

"What is that!" he asked with a cough.

Vanessa looked at him in shock, and Grace was struggling not to laugh. "Salsa," she said, clearing her throat. "It's supposed to be a bit spicy. It has peppers in it."

"I dinnae know what those are, but it is strange to be burned by food that is cold."

Vanessa looked at Euan in curiosity. "Dude, wow. I thought everyone everywhere had tried salsa. Are peppers called something different in Scotland?"

"They don't grow there," Grace said quickly. "They'd have to go to a specialty place to get them where he lives."

"Oh, gotcha," Vanessa replied as she took a chip and dipped it into the salsa.

"You don't have to eat it," Grace said to Euan.

"No, it was actually quite good, I just was nae expecting it."

"Here, have some more chips but go easy on the salsa this time," she replied. "I'll order a bunch of different food for you to try, and you can see what you like. Does that work?"

"Aye, thank ye," he replied

Grace smiled as he pulled the sunglasses back down over his eyes and relaxed back in the chair. It was lovely to be out with her and doing something so normal as sharing a meal with a friend. He was, however, having a difficult time reconciling this moment with everything that had come before it. It was all so surreal, but here they were. The sun was shining, a cool breeze from the ocean just across the street helped cut the heat, and he was alive.

"What do you do, Euan?" Vanessa asked.

"Do?"

"Yeah, for a job."

"I work for the same people Grace does," Euan replied. Not a lie, just not entirely the truth.

"Ah, so I should expect double the secrecy," Vanessa quipped. "I swear to God, I truly believe Grace is a spy."

"Nope," Grace said.

"You wouldn't admit it if you were anyway," Vanessa shot back.

"Nae the first time she has been accused of such," Euan said, remembering that morning at the loch.

"That's definitely true," Grace said.

"So, is that how you met? At work?"

Euan couldn't help but laugh at the question. "Aye. They sent Grace to rescue me from a poor choice. It was hard going, but she managed."

"Intriguing," Vanessa said. "What choice was that?"

"That I cannae tell ye."

"Ugh. The good stuff is always classified." Vanessa said as Grace chuckled. "How long ago was this?"

"About a year ago," Grace said quickly, though it was a question neither of them had been prepared for. "We kept in touch after that and things just happened."

"You never mentioned him."

"I don't mention anyone."

175

"You usually tell me if you're seeing someone, though."

Those words set Euan on edge even though he knew they shouldn't. Grace had a life before him, of course she had, but there was something about hearing it — in that way — that didn't sit well with him. It was something he'd have to get past, because it was her life he'd walked into now, not the other way around. She'd of course had relationships with other men, otherwise things yesterday would have gone far differently.

"It was complicated, so I just decided not to."

"What do your parents think? I mean, they were there right?"

Grace gave her head a gentle shake.

"You didn't tell your parents!"

"It all happened really quickly."

"I'll say," Vanessa muttered. "Not that you're not awesome, Euan."

Euan inclined his head in a slight nod to acknowledge her comment before a scream made everyone jump. Both Euan and Grace turned in their chairs to see a woman chasing after a man holding a bag.

"Hey! He stole my purse!" the woman screamed.

Euan stood and, without thinking, grabbed the chair he'd been sitting in. He held it out, right in the path of the running man, who collided with it full force. The man's body snapped back, his legs yanked out from under him, and he hit the ground with a loud thud. The loud gasps from everyone who saw it were the only sound. Euan set the chair down and took the woman's bag, handing it back to her as she caught up.

"Whoa!" Vanessa cried out.

"Euan! Knife!" Grace suddenly called out.

Euan jumped back and the blade very nearly missed making contact with him. The man scrambled up and tried to bring it down, but Euan stepped aside, grabbed his wrist, and twisted it up and behind his back. The man screamed in pain and Euan wrenched the blade from his hand, placing it against his throat.

"That was nae wise, lad. Nae wise at all. I swear to ye, if

ye move ye die," Euan hissed into his ear. This man was far too close to Grace and Vanessa for his taste, and there was no way he was letting the man get any closer to them and do them harm.

The man went still as he felt the blade against his throat. His face was already bloodied from his collision with the chair, but he had no desire to die, that much was clear. The sirens came then, loud, and unrelenting. They were painful to Euan's ears, but he held fast.

"Both of you! Hands up!" an officer shouted.

Euan immediately complied, but the other man tried to run as soon as Euan released him. He heard the man scream and saw him drop to the ground, writhing in agony, as little pops and sizzles sounded from curling strings that seemed to have attached themselves to his skin. Euan's eyes widened and he didn't dare move. He didn't know what that thing was and had no desire to find out.

"You with the knife! Drop it!" Euan let it fall from his hands and an officer approached him slowly, kicking it away, where another officer picked it up with a gloved hand.

"He helped me, officer!" the woman whose purse had been stolen interceded immediately. "That guy stole my purse and this man here stopped him. Then the other guy pulled the knife and tried to stab him."

Several of the other patrons shouted their agreement. They'd all been witnesses to it. Euan was nothing but compliant as they searched him for other weapons and, finding none, let him relax. They took his ID and his information, as well as his statement and the statements of everyone else.

"Good job, Mr. Cameron," one of the officers said. "Glad you stopped him. Not many people would stop someone hopped up on drugs like that. Have a nice day," he said before he turned and walked off, the officers departing with the man and the woman whose purse he'd attempted to steal.

Euan's demeanor was calm as he returned to his seat as

everyone else did, all murmuring about what had happened.

Vanessa stared at him in utter shock. "Where did you learn to do that?"

"Practice," Euan said as he looked at Grace, whose face was pale. "It is all right, love. I am fine."

"But ..."

"I am fine," he said, a bit more firmly this time. They could discuss this later when there was less of a chance of saying something wrong.

Grace nodded, having gotten his meaning. She'd never seen him do anything like that, and he knew it. He'd gone to battle, she'd been there, but she hadn't seen him attack anyone, and he watched her face as the realization that there was still much to learn about the man beside her set in.

From inside the restaurant, the server brought out a glass of tequila and put it in front of Euan. "On the house. In fact, your whole party's order is on the house. Least we could do," the young man said.

The other patrons applauded, and Euan smiled in appreciation. "Thank ye," he said as he picked up the glass and sniffed the clear liquid inside before taking a sip.

As things settled back down, the food was brought out. Euan laughed to see the array of dishes Grace had ordered, and he tried all of them. Some were hotter than others, but he liked most of them. He was quiet as Grace and Vanessa caught up, listening to them to get a better idea of what Grace's life was like here. Eventually, they went their own ways with Grace promising to have Vanessa over for dinner soon.

The two of them made their way back to the car in silence and, when they were underway, Euan took Grace's hand and lifted it to his lips. Grace said nothing, but she didn't need to. Her silence and her inability to look at him said enough.

When they reached the apartment, Euan waited for the door to close before he spoke. "Ye are angry with me."

"No," Grace said, her voice tight. "I just ..."

"What."

"What if he'd hurt you? Or worse? You only just got here; you need to be careful!"

"Love, I understand ye. But what was I to do? Let him go?"

"You didn't see anyone else jumping in," she argued. "Things are different here! What if he'd had a gun?"

"That does nae mean I should nae, whether he had a weapon or no," Euan countered. "I was nae thinking, I simply acted. In the end, I was nae worried about me, but about the two of ye sitting there unarmed while he had a blade. I was nae about to let him near ye."

"I've never seen you that way."

"Ye have."

"No. It isn't the same. You were just marching, you didn't —"

"I did before ye got to me, the same as I did in every other battle I fought." He wasn't going to lie about it.

He'd killed people, he knew there was no way she wasn't very aware of that fact, but hearing it from him in so direct a manner had thrown her.

"But, what if …" Grace began before she sank into a chair.

"Dinnae ask that question. It never helps."

"I can't lose you, Euan, not now. Please, you have to be careful."

Euan sighed and knelt in front of her, taking her hands in his. "I will try, I promise ye, but I cannae change what is in me. I cannae stop that training from taking over. Ye of all people have to understand that."

Grace nodded but slid from the chair to be on her knees in front of him. She slipped her arms around his shoulders and buried her face in his neck. Euan embraced her and could feel her shaking. Kissing her cheek, he rubbed her back.

"There is so much I don't know about you," she said.

Euan looked down at her. She had no idea how right she was. She didn't even know a fraction of the things he'd done or seen, and he hoped she never would. That man would be a complete stranger to her. He was a stranger even to Euan himself at times.

"I can say the same about ye," he replied.

"I don't think that will change any time soon."

"Nae likely."

"I saw your face when Vanessa mentioned people I'd dated."

"It was strange to hear it. Deep down I knew ye had to have had at least one man before, but hearing it was strange."

"It's different for you, I know. Women weren't supposed to do that."

"Nae exactly. It happened often, but it was usually someone ye already knew, so ye knew exactly who she had been with if she had and why."

Grace was quiet for a moment. "The people Vanessa referenced were one date, maybe three or four. I walked away from them because I simply didn't have the time or the desire to explain my life. The only real boyfriend I had was at university, but that was over when school was."

Euan smoothed her hair back from her face. "I would nae have thought less of ye if it were otherwise. What ye did before ye met me is nae something I have any right to hold against ye."

"It was so different with you."

"I felt the same," he replied before he kissed her. "We will get through this. We will adjust. It will take time, but we will get the story we tell down. I know ye were nae ready for it today, but ye handled it admirably."

"So did you," Grace admitted. "I have considerably more practice."

"Though, I will admit I did nae understand some things said."

"Such as?"

"What did she mean when she said ye had married a hot Scottish guy? I did nae feel overheated. And what does 'dude' mean?"

Grace laughed. "When someone says hot that way, they mean someone really attractive. It was a compliment. Dude is sort of a multi-use word. A bit like an exclamation."

"Oh, that makes more sense then. What are ye going to tell yer parents?"

"The truth," she said. "At least my mother. I'm not sure about my stepfather, but likely the same thing we told Vanessa."

"Does yer stepfather nae know what ye do?"

"No. He wouldn't understand."

"Do ye still know how to speak Gaelic?"

"No, that left me as soon as I left your time."

"Oh, right, I forgot. I can teach ye if ye would like. I rather liked that ye could."

"I would love that," she said, smiling.

"Thank ye for the introduction to the food today, too. It was all wonderful."

"I'm glad you liked it."

"Even the salsa was good once I got used to it," he said with a laugh that Grace joined him in. "Now, ye should show me how to use the phone we bought so I can keep up with ye."

"Oh! Right!" Grace said, thankful for the change in subject. "It may take a while, so we'll sit at the table. Come on, let's get started."

CHAPTER 18

"**K**nock, knock!" Caia called out as she came into the apartment with Aileen after the third day.

"Hello, Mam!" Euan said, standing up from the couch where he'd been relaxing with Grace.

"Ach, love!" Aileen said, hurrying over to him and hugging him. "Ye do look well. Some time alone seems to have agreed with ye."

"Aye, but so has time nae being at war and the knowledge I will nae be going back to it," he said, smiling. "Did ye enjoy yerself?"

"Oh, aye! Caia is such a dear. We tried all sorts of foods, oh, Euan, if I could have cooked with half the things here we would have feasted like kings!"

Euan laughed. "Aye, I certainly believe that. What else?"

"I had a … a … what is it called, Caia, love?"

"A massage," Caia said, looking quite pleased.

"Aye! A massage! Oh, it was grand, son, and ye should have one too. I dinnae think I have ever felt more relaxed in all my life."

"There's a lot to be said about a good massage," Grace said from the couch.

"And then, then we went to the movies! Big walls where there are moving pictures the size of buildings! And ye sit in a darkened room with others and watch while ye eat small foods. I did nae wish to leave!"

"Ye sound like ye had a grand time, Mam," Euan said, her enthusiasm infectious and bringing a grin from him.

"Oh! I almost forgot! I rode in a thing called a car! What a thrill that was! Ye can go so fast!"

"I did as well," Euan said. "In Grace's car. I went so fast that if we had kept on, we could have covered 100 miles in an hour!"

"No!" Aileen said, looking at Grace in shock. "Truly?"

Grace nodded. "It can go faster, but that was enough."

"Heaven help us! Well, I will leave that part to ye. I dinnae need to get anywhere that quickly."

Caia laughed, as did Euan and Grace.

"What are ye watching there?" Aileen asked, pointing to the television.

"Oh, that is a television, Mam. It is like what ye saw but smaller and with different choices."

Aileen came closer and then sat down in a chair near the couch, watching it with a sort of fascination. "It even looks different."

"It was shot live instead of on film like a movie. Oh, Caia! Here! You wanted to watch this anyway right?" Grace said.

"Is it that show you mentioned before?"

"The very one."

"Yes, please!" Caia said, excited as she hurried to sit down in another chair.

Euan shook his head with amusement before he returned to the couch, where Grace snuggled up against him. "People are strange."

That's the entire point," Grace said. "You're watching for the strangeness."

"If ye say so."

The room went silent but for the sounds of the squabbling on the show, with interjections from the women about varying things being done or said, which made Euan laugh.

"Ach, he is a bad one, look at him," Aileen said, pointing to one of the guests.

"Agree," Grace said.

"What is a lie detector test?" Aileen asked.

"It's a test where they hook you up to this machine and

they can see if you're lying or not by the way your body reacts to the questions."

"Christ, why would ye even bother lying then?"

"I would tend to agree," Caia said. "What is the point if they know you are lying?"

"People think they can beat it."

Caia rolled her eyes but went back to watching all the same. When the results were read and proved the man was lying, the reactions of all three women had Euan in hysterics.

"I knew it!" Aileen crowed. "I dinnae need a thing to tell me he was lying!"

"Busted," Grace said, laughing.

"Oh look! He is running now!" Caia said, pointing at the television.

"Ach, get him lass!" Aileen cheered as the woman chased after the fleeing man. "He deserves yer wrath!"

Euan was struggling to breathe because he was laughing so hard, and Grace was holding her sides. "Mam!" Euan got out between gasps for air.

"Well, he does!"

"I dinnae disagree," Euan said as he wiped his eyes and the show ended.

"Goodness, I can see why that is a guilty pleasure, Grace," Caia said. "You do rather get sucked into it."

"Right?" Grace said. "Besides, as someone who deals with human behavior constantly, it's interesting to watch the falseness and see how it manifests. I can use it to my advantage later."

Euan glanced over at Grace, finding her statement interesting. He hadn't thought of that while watching it, and he was surprised she had, but it was a good point.

"I should be off," Caia said as she stood. "Before I go, I have a message for you Grace."

"Oh?" Grace asked. "Is everything okay?"

"Perfectly fine. The message is that the time off you requested is approved, and the Councilwoman wishes everyone a pleasant journey."

"I knew I wouldn't have to ask," Grace said, her lips curling into a wry smile.

"Never. Right, that is me off then," Caia replied. "Goodbye Aileen!"

"Ach, goodbye Caia dear," Aileen said, giving her a hug. "Thank ye for a lovely time."

"Will not be the last, I am sure," Caia replied. "Goodbye, Euan."

"Good journey home," Euan replied. "Thank ye for taking care of Mam so well."

"My pleasure. Have fun!" Caia said as she left.

"I suppose there is only one thing left to do," Grace said, looking to Euan and Aileen.

"Aye?" Euan said.

"Show your mother where she will be sleeping."

"I just assumed here," Aileen said, gesturing to the couch.

"Not while I live and breathe," Grace said, echoing Aileen's own words back to her. "Come on."

Grace got up off of the couch and Aileen followed Grace down the hallway with Euan behind her, looking around. She hadn't come this far into the apartment when she was first here. "Ach, but it is lovely."

"I'm glad you like it. You have your own bathroom, here," Grace said, pointing to it. "And I've put everything you'll need in it for you: soap, shampoo, that kind of thing. Right across from it is your room."

Grace opened the door to what had been the mission room. The bed was still there to be used by Aileen, but the curtains that had once surrounded it were gone. There were fresh and colorful sheets and blankets instead of the plain white that had been there, and Grace had added decorative lamps and hung some art on the walls.

Aileen gasped, covering her mouth with her hands. "What have ye done?"

"Nothing special," Grace said. "I had it rather plain before because it was where I stayed when I was down for missions. Now it's your room."

"All for myself? But, where will ye go?"

"We'll be moving to a bigger apartment soon, and I won't work again before then. I'll set up the room there. I tried to make it pretty for you; I hope you like it."

Aileen walked into the room, looking around her at the art and the furniture. "Ach, what a sweet thing!" she said as she saw a small fountain sitting upon the dresser, bubbling with the sound of running water.

"I figured the sound of water might help you sleep since you lived so close to the loch before."

"What a lovely thing for ye to consider. Velvet!" Aileen exclaimed as she ran her hand over the top of a jewel toned blanket. "I have never ..." she began before she turned and hugged Grace. "Ye are the kindest, sweetest lass I could ever have wished for my boy. Thank ye for all ye have done, Grace, and all I know ye will still do. Ye are his wife, and I will love ye as I love him."

Her reaction seemed to take Grace by surprise, but she returned Aileen's hug. "You're welcome. I want you to be happy here. If there's anything else you want, we can get it, this should be your space." Grace said as she stepped back, her smile shy. "And I'm not his wife, not really."

"Ach, aye ye are. By law, by what The Council says, and in his heart. Caia told me all yer new documents have ye listed as Cameron, but to me the most important part is what he feels, and I know full well that to him, he is yer husband and will behave as such. That is what matters."

"Aye, it is," Euan said in a soft voice from the doorway, where he'd remained in order to let Aileen examine the first bedroom that had ever been her own. "We may nae have done it in front of a priest yet, but in my heart ye are my wife unless ye tell me otherwise."

Grace wiped a stray tear from her cheek. "Well, I'll let you get settled in, shall I? Euan will teach you how to use the phone we got for you while I make dinner," she said before she turned and hurried out of the room.

"I hope I did nae offend her somehow?" Aileen said, staring in confusion at the direction Grace had gone.

"No, ye did nae. I think she does nae know how to accept such things. Caia told me Grace keeps herself closed off from others so they cannae hurt her. I have nae yet asked Grace about it, but I will when the time is right."

"Poor wee lamb. Deserving of love but nae allowing people to love her."

"She has allowed me to try, and I am grateful for it."

"It is good to see ye so happy, Euan," Aileen said.

"It is good to be this happy again."

Aileen patted his cheek. "Ah, but the last time I saw *this* Euan was when ye were 16. Ye have nae been anywhere near this happy since, and I thought that lad was gone forever, but it seems I was wrong. No matter what ye may think, ye are just as deserving of love and life as she is. I want ye to remember that."

"Harder than it sounds, but I will try."

"Try is all I can ask of ye."

"Dinnae get too comfortable here, however."

"Why?"

"We are back to Scotland in a week. Grace is taking us home to see how it looks now," Euan said, grinning.

"Oh! That is the journey Caia just mentioned? How exciting! Oh, I cannae wait to see it and what has changed! Such a long journey though!"

"Apparently nae. We can be there in 12 hours."

"What? How!"

"We fly."

"Ye should nae lie to yer mother, Euan Cameron."

"I am nae!" Euan protested, though his eyes betrayed his amusement at the accusation. "We do. It is a thing called an airplane, and I will tell ye about that later. Come, let me help ye get settled in and show ye how things work."

***

Over the course of the week, Grace watched as the two became more accustomed to life in the future. The gadgets that had seemed so shocking became accepted and normal, though there had certainly been a steep learning curve and the hilarious moments that went with it. Aileen loved to watch television — Grace couldn't blame her — and was happy with the film channels. Euan would either read or spend time on the internet learning more about all that had happened between Culloden and now or researching things he'd seen or heard, while growing more proficient in the use of the technology he was using to do so. He would often ask Grace for clarification or, if he was particularly bothered by what he'd read — as he had been when he reached World War II — would discuss it with her.

They'd gone grocery shopping with Grace, and both had been astounded at the size of the market. The number of offerings was staggering, and they'd spent a great deal of time there just looking at everything. The three of them had then gone shopping for clothing for Euan and Aileen, both for their normal lives in California and for the trip to Scotland. Aileen had been shocked at how much clothing she could now afford to own, amusing Grace when she said it made her feel like a high-born lady.

Vanessa came over for dinner one night and decided to accompany them on their first trip to the beach the following day. As they lounged under an umbrella, towels spread out on the sand, the three women surveyed the other beach goers while Euan went into the water. Aileen stayed covered up, but in much thinner material, and Grace knew she still felt

nearly naked in it. Vanessa and Grace, however, donned biki-
nis. Euan hadn't been quiet about just how much he enjoyed
seeing it on Grace, and she'd had to resist his playful attempts
to send the other two on without them.

Grace got a good laugh out of the reaction drawn by Euan
walking out of the surf in swim trunks. He looked much as
she had seen him at the loch, but it still made her heart skip,
and she was glad she'd forced herself to turn around and not
let herself look too much at him when he'd been bathing. Had
she done so, she had a feeling he would've been much harder
to resist and who knew what would've happened. She watched
as other women, including Vanessa, lowered sunglasses to
watch him walk by. His muscular frame combined with his
looks made it hard not to notice him.

"Damn, dude," Vanessa whispered to Grace. "Please tell
me he isn't just a pretty face."

"Oh, he isn't. He's brilliant."

"Not what I meant."

"I know. My original statement still applies to both mean-
ings."

Vanessa laughed, throwing her head back. "Yassss."

"Ye are wicked girls, both of ye," Aileen said, teasing them,
which made all three of them laugh together.

In the run up to their departure, Grace did her best to get
them ready for the experience. She showed them videos of
planes taking off and landing, movie clips of people on flights,
did her best to explain turbulence and how loud it would be.
She walked them through the security process and all that
would happen at the airport. The advance preparation did
well in alleviating stress as the check-in, security, and boarding
stages went smoothly. She'd booked them into first class to
make them as comfortable as possible on the overnight flight
to London, but Grace could tell both were nervous as they
waited for the plane to board and the doors to shut.

She held their hands as the plane taxied down the runway

and the jet engines kicked in to shoot them forward and up into the sky. Aileen let out a loud gasp, gripping Grace's hand but holding the armrest in a vice grip on the other side of her. Euan, however, was grinning and looking out of the window as the ground grew smaller beneath them. Aileen leaned over Grace to look out and then sat back, crossing herself and muttering a small prayer.

CHAPTER 19

As they descended into Inverness after the short flight from London, Euan watched his homeland come more and more into view. Seeing the green stretched out beneath him sent a sense of calm familiarity throughout his body. He was home. That feeling only grew stronger once they'd collected their bags and rental car and were on the road.

A sign caught his attention and he placed his hand on Grace's arm. "Love, stop the car."

"What? Why?" Grace asked as she pulled over to the side of the road.

Euan got out of the car and walked slowly toward the sign reading "Culloden Battlefield," with an arrow pointing the way. He'd learned from his reading that the place was no longer called Drumossie, and he stared at it for a moment before he turned and looked back at the car. He could see Grace's face and knew she understood. She gave him a small nod and he returned. When traffic was clear, she got back onto the road and took the turn directed by the sign.

Euan felt anxious as Grace turned into the car park and pulled into a space, but he got out and walked toward the battlefield, Grace and Aileen following him in silence. Euan could smell the powder, the smoke, the blood, as if they were there even now. He could hear the screams, and when he looked at Grace, he knew she was the same. Following the path that took them from behind the government lines toward the Jacobite lines where he'd once stood, he noticed the stones with the names of the clans who had perished there, and he scanned the familiar names until he found what he was looking for.

Clan Cameron. The sight of it made his heart seize, and he made his way toward it with slow steps. His friends were here. His clan. His chest was heaving with sobs as he reached it and he knelt before the stone marker, letting his forehead rest against the grass of the moor. He should be there even now, mouldering in the earth alongside them, but he was here, and they weren't. Perhaps in some other timeline he was, but in this one he could only struggle with the immense guilt he felt. He could've saved them, and he hadn't.

"Son," Aileen said as she placed a gentle hand on his back. "It is all right, Euan. All right. I understand yer grief. Ye should count yerself lucky to be on this side of the world and nae on theirs. They would have wanted this for ye, wanted ye to live. Ye were given another chance, and ye will save many with what ye are to do with it."

Something in him broke through the grief, sharp and alarming. *Danger. She is in danger.* His tears ceased as he looked up with a start, only to see some strange, spectral version of himself, blood staining his uniform, hand outstretched toward Grace.

"Mam," Euan said, his voice quiet with fear. "Mam, do ye see that?"

"See what?" Aileen asked.

Euan looked at her in shock. She couldn't see it? His head whipped back around to see Grace reach out her hand, trance-like, and start to walk toward it. *"It will pull her down. It will take her with it and away from you. Stop her. Stop!"* The words were so loud they reverberated through his head, as though he were there, screaming at himself.

Euan scrambled up from the ground and sprinted toward Grace, watching her move ever closer to it. The warnings in his head became louder, more frantic, and he felt as though he was moving too slowly. With growing horror, he saw her hand lowering into the still outstretched hand of that figure. Lunging forward, he seized her wrist and yanked her hand back even as she was millimeters from having made contact. Holding her wrist, he spun her around, pressing her back against his chest and putting himself between her and whatever it was.

"No," Euan whispered in her ear as he kept her wrapped in his arms, his back blocking the view of the ghostly figure. "I see it, too. Dinnae touch it. That is nae me. Stay with me. I am right here."

Grace burst into tears and turned toward him, hugging him tightly as they both sank to the ground and the spirit dissipated. "I have to help! I failed! I have to help you! This is my fault! All of it is my fault," she sobbed.

"No, ye did nae fail. I am here. Grace, look at me."

"I can feel it!" she said, the panic and fear in her voice painful for him to hear.

"Feel what?"

"The ..." but she couldn't get the word out, pressing her hand to her chest.

"It is nae there, I swear it to ye. Grace —"

"There is so much blood, so much. I can taste it and smell it. They're screaming! Euan, please! Help me! Make them stop! Please!"

The last word to leave her lips was nearly a scream and it brought him to tears even as she covered her ears and buried her face against her knees. He knew this reaction, he understood it. He'd seen it so many times, been through it himself.

"Love. Grace," he whispered to her as he reached out to stroke her hair. She screamed and jumped when he touched her, her head snapping up as she looked at him in abject fear. "Shhh it is me; I swear it to ye. It is gone now. All of it gone. No one is here but us. Dinnae fear."

"Euan, what's happening to me!"

"I know, *leannan*. I know ye are frightened. I know ye are there again but ye must listen to me. Listen to my voice and try to breathe. The wounds are nae there. There is no one here to harm ye, no one dying now. It is just ye and me."

Euan watched Grace struggle to get control of herself, struggled to take the deep breaths he was urging her to take. It was hard, he knew that, so hard to fight through that terror once it had its talons sunk into your mind and body. Slowly her breathing became deeper, less erratic, and she looked up at him.

"Aye, there ye are. Let us leave this place. There is naught left for us here. Naught at all," Euan said as he scooped her up into his arms and carried her back toward where Aileen stood. He had to get her off this ground, this ground where her own blood had mixed with the blood of men she never should've known.

As he walked, Euan fought to get control of himself. He couldn't ever remember feeling so emotionally out of control as he did now. The graves beneath those stones held men he'd once known so well, men he'd fought beside and lived beside, and they were nothing now. Did anyone even remember their names? Surely no one knew what they'd even looked like anymore, but he did. He was the only one left to remember them, and the weight of that seemed too immense. They'd died for nothing; for a king that never came, for a cause not truly their own. It had done nothing, earned nothing; nothing but a marker on a moor to say there had once been living, breathing men here who had wanted to believe in something greater than themselves.

Grace's past words rang in his ears. *It is for nothing, Euan. Nothing comes of it except the destruction of the Highlanders. The Stuarts do not come back and there is so much lost.*

Why hadn't he listened? Why hadn't they listened that night? Why hadn't he listened to her in that moment and tried to convince the Camerons to back away? Had he been successful everything would've been different. Duncan and the others would've lived, but for how long? The Camerons had already committed treason by fighting for the prince from the beginning. The government would've hunted all of them down and it was foolish of him to believe otherwise. They may have had a little longer, but not much.

How many times had this battle replayed? How many times had they died? There were so many questions that would forever remain unanswered. The Council had told him he'd died before, many times, until Grace came to rescue him from it. It never would've changed no matter what he'd done. Nothing would ever change. She'd tried, she'd given them the keys to victory, and it had still happened just the same as it always had and it always would, because there were some things too deeply etched into the earth to ever change them. She'd saved him from an eternity of walking this moor while his body rotted beneath it; saved him from an eternity of dying amidst horror and fear.

He'd come here to try and make his peace with all of this and, though he hadn't told her so, he knew she'd been aware of it. His Grace. The angel who had tricked Death by giving her own life for his, a life that Death couldn't truly possess in that world. He couldn't say what had triggered inside of him to let him see that spectre, to know he had to pull her back from it, not let her touch it. It would've dragged her down, taken her from him. He wasn't sure what that meant, but he hadn't wanted to find out.

***

Grace felt some of the weight lift as they got farther from that spot, and it felt as though she could breathe more easily. Her eyes fell on the woods where she'd spoken to him again before he'd marched off to join the charge, and she could see the moment so clearly. How gaunt he'd looked, exhausted, torn. She knew how conflicted he'd been, though had she asked him he would've denied it. He'd had a chance to walk away, a chance at self-preservation, yet he'd resisted it in order to do what he felt was right. Grace felt that was him all over, that instinct to protect others no matter the cost to himself, and in the end, it was what made him perfectly suited for the role that very decision had opened for him.

"I have to go now. Thank ye for that night. It is what I will remember."

The words reverberated through her mind, sending out ripples of pain that made her heart ache. Grace buried her face in his neck to get away from the sight of those woods and the grievous memories they contained.

"Mam let us leave. There is no reason to remain and it is still dangerous."

"What do ye mean, Euan? Grace, are ye all right?"

"The spirits here are restless and dinnae take kindly to losing one of their own, nor do they appreciate the one who pulled him out. They will claim us both if we stay. We can never come here again."

It took them only an hour and twenty minutes to go from Culloden to their lodgings near Achnacarry. Grace had booked a self-catering holiday cottage on the loch that hadn't been there when Euan and Aileen lived here, having come some 70 years later. It was charming, just off the road, with the back facing onto the loch itself.

Later that evening, after they'd unpacked and had supper, Grace stood in the yard, looking at the loch. Just as it had done on the night she'd left him, the full moon reflected off of its surface. She heard Euan's footsteps approaching her before he wrapped something around her shoulders.

"Ye forgot yer arasaid in the house, lass," he whispered.

"My what?" Grace was brought out of her thoughts by the repetition of the once customary warning and looked down to find the familiar pattern and soft wool before she looked back up at him.

"Aye, the very same. I had it with me, tucked away, so it came with me to the future and is now back with its rightful owner. I could nae let ye come to Cameron land without it."

Grace smoothed her hands over it and closed her eyes. So many memories attached to such a small thing. She pulled it around herself as Euan wrapped his arms around her. "Is it strange to be here? So close?"

"Aye. Strange and yet familiar. I know it is nae the same place even if it looks it, but I am home. I can feel it in my bones. More so, I am home with ye."

"You seem lighter now."

"I am, I think. I had to say goodbye, had to try and let them go so they could no longer haunt me. I cannae tell ye what it feels like to imagine ye could have saved those ye loved if ye had only been brave enough to stand up and say something. I know now that it was nae so and it would nae have mattered what I did. Even if we had left that day, we would have been caught up by Cumberland afterward."

"Likely so," Grace replied, surprised she hadn't thought about such an outcome even as she'd tried to stop him.

"Could ye be happy here, do ye think?"

"How do you mean?"

"What if we stayed? Perhaps go back during the winter but stay the rest of the time here. Somewhere we could live in peace."

"I don't know. What about my family? The logistics are a bit difficult."

Grace looked up and saw him staring out across the water. He needed this. He'd adapt to the city, of course, but his soul needed what he found here, or he would forever be restless. The Highlands were a part of him, and she wasn't sure the occasional visit would give him what he wanted. Despite everything that had happened during the mission, she'd come to love it here in Achnacarry, and had even then been sad at the thought of leaving it. The beauty, the peace, the solitude. To stay would mean having all those things in abundance, and she knew she'd miss them when they returned to California. He'd lost everything he'd known, and she now had the opportunity to give something back to him.

"Okay," she whispered.

Euan blinked in surprise and looked down at her. "Truly?"

"Yes. I have quite a bit of money stored up, my pay from The Council that I never used because it was only me. I didn't spend a lot of it. We should be able to buy something here and they might help us. Then, with the continuing income between the both of us, we should be able to afford to keep up the rent on the apartment, too, so we have a place to go back to."

"But what about yer family, as ye said?"

Grace shrugged. "Planes go both ways. Watchers in the past used to live remotely in places like this, so why shouldn't I? Besides, you need this. You need to be here. I may not be able to give you back everything, but I *can* do this."

"I feel as though ye have given so much already."

"No more than you have."

Euan rested his cheek against the top of her head for a moment. "As long as ye will be happy."

"I'll be fine. I don't have many ties even though I've lived there all my life. I keep myself distant for a reason."

"That sounds a lonely existence."

"Sometimes."

Euan turned her around to face him and looked down at her. He placed a soft kiss on both of her cheeks as the moonlight gave her skin a faint glow. "I remember I kissed ye on a night like this," he whispered.

"I do think I recall that a young man named Euan kissed me 270 or so years ago."

Euan chuckled. "Perhaps he should kiss ye again."

"Perhaps."

Euan moved his lips to hers and gave her a kiss that was gentler and slower than the one he'd given her that night and she melted against him. When he pulled back from her, he rested his forehead against hers.

"Ye should know that I fully intend on picking up where we left off once we are in my own woods," he murmured.

Grace shivered at the promise that lay in his words. "Good."

Chapter 20

The next morning, they made their way around the loch to Achnacarry proper. There was a small museum for Clan Cameron now, though it seemed you couldn't get to the castle itself any longer. They parked at the museum and stepped out.

"Did you want to go in?" Grace asked, gesturing to the museum.

"Nae yet," Euan said, "and it does nae seem open just now. Come with me."

Euan started out in the direction he knew better than the back of his own hand. He'd walked this land from the time he was old enough to wear breeches and there wasn't a bit of it that wasn't familiar to him in its own way. Coming to a sudden stop, he stared at the place where the castle he'd known had once been. There was nothing left but a chimney now.

"I cannae believe it is gone," Aileen said in a quiet voice.

"Nor I. I knew they burned it, but I did nae expect it to be all gone." There were so many memories here, bound up in the rooms and corridors he'd always known; all of them gone, blown away in the ashes left behind by Cumberland's retribution.

"The new castle is there," Grace said, pointing behind them.

Euan turned around and walked toward the gate, looking through it to see the castle at the end of a long, tree-lined drive. It looked far different than the one he'd known, smaller in scale and made of gray stone, but more modern in appearance. The Cameron flag flew above it, but it was a private home now. Backing away, he took Grace's hand and continued onward.

His heart beat faster as they neared the woods, and he walked into them as if in a trance, drawn by the pull of a place still the same though it had been 270 years since he'd last set foot there. Euan took a deep breath, letting the familiar scent of the woods wash over him before he made his way forward. As they crested the top of the hill, he stopped. Here was the clearing where his home had once been, but there was nothing left of the cottage except some of the stones that had once been walls.

Aileen made a sad sound and took Euan's arm to steady herself. She'd been a wife here, raised a son here, and it was gone. He covered her hand on his arm with his own before releasing her and watched as she walked forward and touched the remaining stones.

"Can I help ye?" a voice called out as an older man stepped into the clearing and surveyed them.

"Aye, we were just seeking out the home of our ancestors," Euan replied.

The man smiled at the sound of Euan's voice, recognizing a fellow Highlander instantly. He nodded toward Grace, who was wearing the arasaid around her shoulders. "Camerons, are ye?"

"Aye," Euan said. "My name is Euan Cameron."

The man's eyebrows raised. "Is that so? Ye know, a young man named Euan Cameron used to live in just this spot. Is that the ancestor ye are looking for?"

Euan nodded and the man went on.

"A sad tale. Young Euan was an officer in Lochiel's regiment who marched off to war at Culloden with the other men and never came home again. He is likely buried with the rest beneath that hallowed ground."

"What of his mother," Euan asked, seeing Aileen stiffen near him.

"No one knows for sure. Some stories said she was gone when Cornwallis and the Munros arrived because she'd known her son was dead and had gone to seek him, perishing on the way. Others assumed she'd been taken up with the rest and transported. There are no records of her after 1746. They burned the cottage anyway, just the same as the others."

Euan shook his head. "Are there records of Euan dying at Culloden?"

"No, but he was counted with the men who left, so it's safe to assume he both went and died, for there is no record of him returning and no record of his execution as a traitor afterward as there would've been if he'd lived. The lad had a bounty on his head, so if the English *had* caught him, they certainly would've made record of it. There's also no record of him in France with the exiled Lochiel. In a way he was lucky, for a traitor's death is nae a pleasant one. We've tried to trace the fates of all who lived here at the time."

"We?" Euan asked, deliberately ignoring the surprised expressions on the faces of the women at the mention of his having had a bounty on him.

"Aye, the Lochiels and the researchers."

"There is a Lochiel?" Euan asked, his surprise clear.

"Aye, lad, has been since the lands were restored." The man looked at him curiously. "Ye are a Cameron, and clearly a Highlander, but ye have nae been here and have no idea of your own history?"

"I have only just begun to study it," Euan said. "I suppose I am just surprised he is still named such."

The look the man gave him made it clear he wasn't entirely sure if Euan was to be believed. "Who do ye have with ye, lad?"

"This is my mother, Margaret, and my wife, Grace." Euan didn't know how much this man knew about his family and calling his mother by her true name might be too close. Her middle name would have to do.

"A pleasure to meet ye, ladies. My name is Malcolm, and I'm one of the caretakers here on the Achnacarry estate."

"Did they truly burn everything?" Aileen asked.

"Oh, aye, everything. Every cottage and the castle too. When Lochiel arrived ahead of the government forces, he gave warning that they were coming. Many of the most priceless things were removed and hidden before Cornwallis arrived, but much was still lost. Lochiel and his remaining men fled into the hills. He eventually made his way to France, and the others were rounded up and executed."

Grace saw Euan's jaw tighten. He'd been right last night when he'd said that even if she'd managed to get them to turn back, they all would've died anyway.

"Is the castle open for tours?" she asked.

"No, it is a private residence and Lochiel does live here. It does nae look anywhere near as it did when your forebears were here. That's all long gone."

"But this is the same," Euan said, his voice soft. "This has nae changed."

Malcolm looked at him in curiosity. "Aye, the lands have nae changed much, though they have seen much change."

Euan looked around him. He still knew this place, every bit of it. He knew he could still find his way even in the dark. "Is there any property for sale near here?"

"Aye, there is. It does nae come up often, but one is about to be put up. Are ye looking to come back to your ancestral home, lad?"

"Aye," Euan replied. "My wife and I would like to spend most of the year here, and the winter in her home in California."

Malcolm laughed. "Cannae say I blame ye for fleeing a Highland winter if ye can manage it. There is an old hunting lodge about to go up. It was built when the lands were restored in 1784. Lochiel has no need of it and thought to perhaps sell it to someone who would be interested in making it a home. Sounds like that may be ye."

"Would I need to see him about it?"

"No, ye would see me. He has given me the leave to act for him. Would ye like to see it?"

"Aye, I would, thank ye."

"Come with me, then. I shall give ye a ride up to it."

The three of them followed Malcolm out of the woods, with Euan casting a glance back at the place he'd called home for so long. They made their way back toward the road, where Malcolm's Range Rover sat. It had been parked in the trees and he'd likely seen them make their way toward the woods.

Once they got in, they drove across the loch on a private bridge, then turned right down a single-track road, the same road their rented cottage was on, but in the opposite direction. Euan knew this section of the road well. *Mile Dorcha* — the Dark Mile. It was about three quarters of a mile before they turned onto a dirt road, which immediately went into the trees. About half a mile later, they came over a small rise and the lodge appeared. It was a large, two story, stone building with the hills behind it and a view of both the estate and Loch Lochy.

As they got out of the car, Euan walked to the edge of the hill and looked out over the view with a small smile. He knew this place. His Lochiel had liked to hunt here and there had been a lodge here then, too. It had, however, been smaller and simpler than this one, more like a single room cabin.

"This way," Malcolm said as he approached the large door and unlocked it. The old lock turned heavily, and Malcolm pushed the door open.

Immediately in front of them was the staircase, made with old, dark wood, illuminated by the light streaming in from a large window at the top of the landing. To their left was a massive fireplace and hearth in a large open space, the Cameron crest carved into the back of it as well as into the stone of the mantlepiece. To their right was what looked to be a sort of parlor.

"It has been updated a wee bit with some of the conveniences. Running water, water closets, a working kitchen and stove, electricity, but it needs more work."

"How many bedrooms are there?" Grace asked.

"Five above stairs, two below. The second floor are all

sleeping quarters. There is the room for Lochiel, which is the largest, and then the others. If ye go past the stairs, ye will find where it was set up with a dining area and the kitchen beyond that. To the other side is a study with built in shelves for books and the like."

"Who lived here to add all of these things?" Euan queried.

"Varying Camerons throughout the years, usually members of Lochiel's family. It has been sitting empty for years now, though."

Grace took the stairs up, followed by Euan. Aileen explored the kitchen while Malcolm stood back, allowing them to look. What greeted them at the top of the stairs was a long hallway, the doors all standing open. Each room had a window that faced the drive and was generally spacious and bright. To the left, at the end of the hall, was the largest room. It had two windows, one that looked out to the view Euan had first seen, and the other into the woods themselves. It had its own bathroom, while the others would share the one at the other end or the one downstairs.

"I find it amusing they call this a lodge," Grace said.

Euan's first response was a quiet laugh. "Aye, but to them it would be."

"What do you think?"

"I think it would need a good deal of work to get up to the modern standards ye would expect," Euan admitted. Though he could live quite happily with it the way it was — this was a massive step up from their stone cottage — he knew Grace might struggle with it.

"It would, but nothing that couldn't be done. Would you be happy here? Is this what you'd want?"

Euan turned toward her and took her hands. "I know this place well. There used to be a lodge here, and I would come with Lochiel often when he would hunt. It was nae like this, but this is still home to me. What I will nae do is force ye into it if this is nae what will make ye happy, too."

"I think it's beautiful here. Quiet and peaceful, someplace to retreat and recover from our work without being surrounded by others. It's always the hardest part of a return, the way you feel out of place and out of time but are forced to pretend otherwise. We wouldn't have to do that here."

Euan reached up and stroked her hair. "Are ye sure about this?"

"Yes, but we should find out how much they're asking for it before we get too carried away."

"Aye, which would be the sensible thing to do," Euan said with a chuckle. "Let us go find out."

Euan took her hand and led her back downstairs to find Malcolm. "How much does Lochiel ask for this property?"

Malcolm looked at Euan and considered him for a moment. "If you were nae a Cameron this answer would be different, but as ye are, I can sell it to ye for £250,000. That includes the lodge and a fair amount of land around it."

Euan checked his reaction as he forced himself to remember that those numbers meant different things now. He looked to Grace, as it was her money being spent and not his own.

"I think that sounds more than fair. Would there be any Grade Listings that we'd need to be aware of if we make renovations?"

"No, I dinnae think so. Nae here, anyway. Ye won't be able to tear it down, but that's all."

"We'll need to meet with estate agents then?"

Malcolm chuckled. "No. It is Lochiel's estate, so ye will meet with me and a solicitor. How long do ye need to get money together for a down payment?"

"I can have the entire amount to you in a matter of hours. Just tell me where to have it wired."

Euan looked at Grace with the same surprise Malcolm did. "A young lady of means, it seems."

Grace smiled. "More like a young lady who has worked so hard and so much that she never had time to spend her money."

"I will ring the solicitor when we get back. How long are ye here for? It will take him a few days to draw up the paperwork and get here from Edinburgh."

"Another two weeks," Grace replied. "We have plenty of time."

Malcolm extended his hand to Grace, who took it and shook it. "Then allow me to be the first to welcome ye home to Achnacarry, ye long-lost Camerons.

CHAPTER 21

Euan was ecstatic as they rode back to their car with Malcolm. There were legal things to be worked out, of course, but he knew Grace would have all of those in hand. They were coming home. Aileen, too, was excited about returning to a place she knew so well, the danger gone, and no threat of her son being sent to war again. Somehow it seemed fitting that they'd be coming back here to live. The place where it had all begun would be the place it remained. That was, of course, if The Council would agree to assist them with the funds to bring the house up to standard in both modernity and the required Watcher security.

Grace spent the drive back asking practical questions, such as where the nearest grocery stores were, builders Malcolm may have worked with and could recommend, and anything else they'd soon need.

Once they got back to the cottage, Grace excused herself to go upstairs. She needed to reach out to The Council to ask for a meeting with them for the following day, and to do so she needed quiet and no distractions. When she came down again half an hour later, she gave Euan a small nod to let him know she'd gotten a response.

After supper, Euan stood up. "Mam, I am going to take Grace for a walk if ye dinnae mind."

Aileen raised an eyebrow but smiled and shook her head. "Begone with ye, lovebirds."

Euan chuckled and took Grace's hand once she stood. By the door, he picked up an electric lantern and a bag that he slung over his shoulder before they walked out. They walked in silence, headed for the bridge that would take them back to the other side of the woods, the same one they'd driven across with Malcolm earlier. Once across, they took a different path into the woods, not needing to worry about roads now. They crossed the clearing where his old home had been and continued to the edge of the trees and the loch. By going the way he normally would have come, he could make sure the spot he was searching for was exact.

"Wait here for me," he said before he disappeared back into the woods with the lantern, making quick work of the next part of his plan before re-emerging from the trees. "Grace."

Hearing him whisper her name from behind her, she turned around to find Euan there, dressed in his uniform, the clothing she'd been so used to seeing him in. She gasped as he made his way toward her and she didn't move. When he reached her, he slid a hand onto her waist and drew her against him.

"We have unfinished business here, ye and I." His voice was low, his lips close to hers. "There is no one to part us now."

"No, there's not," she whispered.

Euan drew her forward as he walked backwards, into the darkness of the woods and, once hidden in the darkness, he again pressed her back against a tree. "I still find ye captivating; still crave yer attention. I could never ignore ye and I dinnae intend to start."

His cheek was pressed against hers again but the tension she'd felt in his body the first time was gone, the war with himself over, and he was now free to do exactly as he pleased. Euan pulled back from her, turning his head to look at her in the moonlight filtering through the trees, before he pressed his lips to hers in the same sort of kiss he'd given her then, and felt her grip his shoulders before her hands found his hair once again. It aroused him just as much now as it had done then, though he felt a slight pang of fear as he once again placed that kiss on her neck, once again heard her enjoyment of it and felt her arch against him. Please God let her be here still! When he went to her lips again, she was there and met him in it, and Euan felt his heart relax. They hadn't taken her from him again.

He felt one of her legs slide up against his and he shuddered before he pulled it over his hip. There was nothing but need in this, and that was exactly how he wanted it. It was how it would've been then and how it should be now. He couldn't say if the intensity was due to the location and the desire to close this chapter or something else; but it didn't matter to him. In the end, he was left breathing raggedly against her neck as she held tight to him. When he regained his thoughts, he placed soft kisses against her collarbone.

"As much as I dinnae want to let ye go, I should change so we can go back."

"Not yet," Grace whispered. "Stay this way just a little while longer."

"Why?"

"Because for a moment I can pretend I talked you out of it and none of the rest of it ever happened."

Euan smiled and stroked her cheek. He could understand that desire, to take it all back if even for a few moments. "If ye wish. Shall I pretend for ye?"

"No, you don't need to act. We can just be here together and talk, and that will be good enough."

"I know just the place," he said, letting go of her. He grabbed the bag with his other clothes in it and the lantern, taking her hand to lead her out of the woods and back onto the road along the loch.

As they reached the rocks where they'd sat and talked the first time, Grace laughed. "How fitting."

"I thought so, aye," Euan said as he sat down on the same rock he'd occupied.

"Are you excited?" Grace asked as she joined him

"I cannae tell ye how much. Ye are right when ye say I need to be here. It may be different, but that is nae necessarily bad. I am my own man, no longer in service. I am free to do as I like and answer to no one. I will have a home grander than I could have ever imagined, and everyone will be safe. There are nae proper words for that feeling."

"I told you once, when we were right here, that you would have someone you loved and be happy, that I wanted that for you. You have it."

"Aye, ye did, but the difference is that I dinnae just have someone. I have ye. All the rest comes from that."

"If I'd only known then."

"We keep saying that, but somehow I think it had to be as it was. I think we knew deep down that there was something but could nae say what or make sense of it. Had we known, things would have been far different and perhaps I would nae be here now."

"Perhaps, but we'll never know."

"I am actually fine with that. Ye dinnae always need answers for everything, Grace. Sometimes it is best to just feel and accept that it does nae always go with reason, that whatever happened was what was meant to happen."

"We are taught the opposite now. There are answers for everything, and reason trumps emotion every time."

"What a shame that is. Such a thing takes so much of the magic out of the world, so much of the trust in yer intuition and in faith. I dinnae care what anyone says, there are always things for which there are no answers, and ye will nae find them no matter how hard ye search."

"Do you believe in magic?"

"Well, I am here in the future, and ye were back with me in the past."

"That is technology."

"Is it? Do ye really know it is, or is that what they tell ye?

Do ye think they know all the answers? Aye, they can do a great many incredible things, but ye said yerself that what happened with us was nae normal."

"The visions?"

"Aye. I asked if that happened to others, and Councilwoman Rochford looked at me as though I had lost my wits. They dinnae know everything." He took her hand and smiled. "Try nae to be so serious and let yerself believe in things ye cannae prove."

Grace chuckled. "I can try, but that's harder than it sounds. It's drummed into us from a young age that such things are foolish nonsense."

"The only people who say such are the ones who refuse to see what is around them and want to seem smarter than others."

Grace laughed now. "That might be true."

"It is true to me."

"Do you think I'm too serious?"

"Sometimes, but then I think ye have been taught ye must be. Ye believe that with such an important job there is no room for anything else, which is a lie if ever I heard one. There is a time for seriousness, and a time for nae."

"I suppose you'll be teaching me the difference?"

"Ach, no. Ye know the difference, I will just help ye to remember when ye are getting entirely too serious."

"And what about you?"

"Me?"

"You were always quite serious when I was here."

"When ye were here, I was working. Ye never saw me otherwise."

"Fair enough. I look forward to seeing it then."

"We can start now."

"What?"

Euan grinned and turned toward her, starting to sing a song that seemed innocent at first ... until it wasn't. Grace gasped before she started laughing, and by the time he'd finished, she was wiping tears away.

"That was horrible!"

"But ye are laughing, and I have plenty more where that came from."

"No, don't —"

Euan ignored her and started another, standing up and slinging the bag over his shoulder, then holding out his hand to her. Grace grinned and took it, standing up and taking the lantern in her free hand as they started the walk back. As they made their way, Euan sang filthy Scottish drinking songs, and they were laughing hysterically as they came through the door.

By the time they got upstairs and showered, Euan was exhausted and barely made it into bed. The pull of sleep felt so strong that as soon as he'd closed his eyes the blackness of sleep dragged him all the way down. Even so, there was a feeling of cool air on his face and the smell of wet earth. Confused, Euan opened his eyes and found himself where he didn't want to be: back at the battlefield. He didn't remember coming here but the ground beneath him felt solid and real. He felt real. Dreams never felt this way. There was always a detachment from the physical.

Euan heard a scream and turned his head toward it to see Grace, dressed in white once more, struggling with a man holding her and surrounded by many others. He scrambled up and began to hurry toward her, but the sight of who was holding her made his blood run cold and he slid to a stop.

"Duncan," he said in a choked whisper.

"Give him back to us! I dinnae know what ye did, but this is where he belongs! Bring him back!" he shouted into Grace's face.

"I can't! Duncan, please! I can't control that! Let me go!" Her voice was full of fear as she pleaded with him.

"Where is he, Grace!" Duncan growled at her as he gave her a hard shake.

"I don't know!"

"Ye lie now just like ye lied to him and to all of us then. But if he is nae here then neither can ye be."

"What?" Grace asked before Duncan turned her roughly around. What she saw made her gasp and struggle against him. "What are you doing? Stop!"

Euan followed her gaze and his heart dropped. The spectre, the one they'd seen before, was standing there and he reached out to Grace once more. No. No, no, no, no, no! He opened his mouth to shout, but fear choked him, and no sound left his lips.

Duncan shoved Grace forward with a violence that left her no chance to stop herself, sending her straight through it. Grace screamed in fear and pain, while Euan watched in horror as the white of the dress became red again, a wound opening on her chest before she dropped lifelessly to the ground. As she did, the spectre became solid while Grace suddenly appeared in spirit form. She was now dead and locked here instead of him.

"Thank ye kindly, lass," it said, smiling cruelly as it bowed to her. It was a smile the real Euan would never have given to Grace or to anyone else. It was borne of a malevolence the real man didn't possess.

"GRACE! NO!" Euan screamed, the sound finally erupting from him, and it drew everyone's attention to him.

Duncan smiled. "Speak of him and he comes, eh lads? I knew if we had her he would find her."

"Duncan, ye bastard! What have ye done?" Euan shouted in fury as he strode toward them, but he was seized by the other Cameron men and held fast.

"I am bringin' ye home where ye belong, Euan. That witch took ye from us!" Duncan replied as he pointed at Grace's now lifeless body.

"She saved my life, ye fool! She stopped me dying here! What have ye done!"

"She has traded places with ye, as ye can see, though this version of ye is nae the Euan we know, and we need to correct that. Bring him here, lads."

The men holding Euan dragged him forward even as he fought them. He had no idea what they meant to do, and he didn't want to find out, but no matter how hard he fought back it seemed to do no good. They pulled him face to face with the version of himself standing there: the Euan of the past, the one who kept dying, the one locked here still.

"It is time to put ye back together, Euan," Duncan said before he gestured to the other Euan.

"No! Duncan, stop! Dinnae do this!" Euan shouted as he resumed his fruitless struggle against the many hands that held him.

It smiled that same cruel smile before it pressed itself against him. There was pain, blinding, white-hot, and terrible, a feeling of drowning even as he screamed. There was a war between what he knew now and what he'd not known then and the knowledge gained was snuffed out like so many candles. All of it faded from him as he tried to cling to it in desperation. The last thing was his memory of her, of Grace, and he felt her ripped away from him before all knowledge of what had been there faded into blackness.

When he opened his eyes, he looked at Duncan and the other men laughed. There was only one Euan now. "There he is lads! Back where he belongs!"

Euan looked over at the ghost of Grace with an utter lack of recognition and cold indifference before his eyes landed on her body. "Who is this? What happened?"

"She put a spell on ye lad, but we were able to get ye back and turn the spell on her instead."

His indifference turned to contempt and anger. "Curse ye to hell, demon," he spat.

"Aye. Demon she was, but no longer. Come, Euan, we have a battle to fight in the morning. Let the English find their demon spy when the sun rises."

Euan turned to walk away with them, but somehow Grace managed to scream his name. "Euan, no! Please! You have to remember!"

He stopped and looked at her. "Dinnae speak to me. I will nae be tricked by ye again."

"Euan, I'm your wife! Please remember!"

"I have no wife, demon!"

The spirit buried her face in her hands and wept before he turned his back on her once more.

"Euan, please don't leave me here! You said you wouldn't leave! EUAN!"

The last was a scream of heartbreak and pain, something that made his world shift and sent him to his knees. His mouth opened, and he screamed before the ground opened beneath him and he fell. He landed hard, finding himself on a pile of bones clad in Cameron tartan. He scrambled backward in horror even as the light began to fade, the ground closing around him to forever trap him here.

"NO!" he screamed into the blackness.

Euan sat up in bed, screaming and drenched in sweat. He couldn't breathe and didn't know where he was. What bed was he in? What time? His body shook violently, and he felt someone touch his shoulder. "Dinnae touch me!" he screamed out.

Grace yanked her hand back, confused by his sudden screams and terror. "Euan! Wake up!"

When he heard his name called in that familiar voice, he whipped his head around to look at her. "Grace," he whispered. She was here, she was beside him, she was whole. Dear God, what had happened?

"Yes, it's me. Shhh, it's okay," she said as she reached out to touch him once more.

When he felt her hand on him, soft, warm, and solid, he broke down. Euan grabbed her and pulled her close, sobbing and still shaking. "Ye … they took ye … and …"

"Who?"

"Duncan and the others. They took ye back to Drumossie. They shoved ye through that spirit and it killed ye. Then, somehow, it forced me into itself and I became one with it. I forgot ye. I forgot all that had happened, and I had a battle to fight in the morning."

"No …"

"Ye begged me to remember ye, reminded me I had promised nae to leave ye and that ye were my wife. I told ye I had no wife. Ye screamed for me, and God help me, I turned my back on ye," Euan sobbed. "But something in it jarred me and I fell, the ground opened up and I fell into the grave I was meant for, on top of the bones of my brothers, and it started to close around me."

Euan's shaking intensified, and Grace held him tight. "It was just a nightmare. You're here now, we're fine."

"What is happening to us?"

"I don't know. Come with me tomorrow. I'm going to see The Council. Come with me."

Before Euan could answer, the door was thrown open and Aileen hurried in. "Are ye all right? What has happened?"

"A nightmare," Grace said, her voice calm and quiet so as not to agitate Euan further. "A very bad one, but just a nightmare."

"Ye poor lad. I have nae heard ye scream that way in a while," Aileen replied, her tone edged with a mother's concern.

"I will be all right, Mam. I just need a few moments to breathe." Aileen nodded and kissed his forehead before she left and shut the door behind her. Euan tried to even his breathing, but the shaking wouldn't stop.

"I would nae leave ye. I could nae …" he said.

"I know. My love, I know," she whispered to him. "You won't have to."

Euan looked at her in the darkness. It was the first time she'd ever called him that, a term of endearment of any sort, and the first time she'd used that word in relation to him. Love. Grace only said what she truly felt, and he knew she deliberately kept people at arm's length. Her life was too complicated to allow herself to love anyone. She might hurt them or, worse, they might hurt her. For someone who was always so out of her time, always in places where there was no one who cared for her and always faced rejection, such a blow would be great. For her to say that now was a testament to what he truly meant to her. He was the only one in all the world, in all of time, that she'd let into her heart. It wasn't a thing he'd ever take for granted.

"This will go away; I know it will. It will take time for both of us. It just happened."

Euan nodded to her, his arms still around her, needing her close to him. He needed to know she was real and not lying dead on the moor at Drumossie while her spirit was forever trapped there in his place.

"I don't think we're sleeping for a while. How about some tea? We can go sit outside."

"That sounds like a good idea," Euan agreed.

Grace slipped from bed, wrapping the arasaid around her because the night chill had settled into the cottage. "Come down when you're ready," she said before she left and went downstairs to put the kettle on.

Euan took a moment to try to regain control of himself, taking deep breaths and turning his focus to only that. After a few moments, the shaking eased enough that he felt he could reliably stand, and he got out of the bed. Walking into the washroom, he splashed cold water on his face before pulling the plaid from the chair where he'd tossed it when they'd come back.

When he got downstairs, Grace was pouring water into a pot and had pulled out sugar and cream. Sugar had been a thing he couldn't afford, but it came cheaply now, and he found he quite enjoyed a little in his tea. He stepped up behind her and nuzzled her cheek, kissing it before picking up the containers of cream and sugar, as well as the mugs she'd set out. Grace picked up the pot, and he followed her outside to where there was a small patio with a table and chairs.

The cool air on his skin made him shiver. Even in the summer the Highlands could be cold, particularly at night, and they were still in the early spring. It at least helped fully wake him and bring him back to the present. When they sat down,

Euan wrapped the plaid around his shoulders as Grace poured him a cup of tea. As he reached for it, she grabbed his hand and squeezed it before she lifted it and kissed his in the way he so often did hers. He smiled at her, it was such a small gesture on her part, but a sweet one that let him know he was never alone in any of this. Euan pulled her hand in his direction and placed a kiss on each knuckle of her hand before releasing it, which made her chuckle.

"Always have to one up me, don't you."

"When it comes to affection, aye," he replied. "But I thank ye for doing that."

"Everything will be okay," she said.

"I know it will. We can always say we have gotten through worse. Ye cannae get worse than death." Grace laughed, which got Euan to laugh too. "What a strange life we now lead, Watcher."

"That, I think, is the understatement of the century," Grace replied.

Euan was quiet for a long moment. "Ye were at Nairn." He didn't have to see Grace to know the look on her face. It was a piece of information he'd been holding onto for a while now.

"Yes," she replied, her voice barely audible over the lump in her throat. "How did you know?"

"While I was waiting for ye, I thought about it. That was why ye knew, was it nae? Why ye knew about the planned attack. Ye tried to warn me. Ye really did try to change the history."

"I did."

Euan looked over at Grace, her face pale, a sort of anguish written there he hadn't expected. "Is that why ye got upset that day? Why ye apologized to me but could nae tell me why?"

Grace closed her eyes in a failed effort to stop any tears. "Yes. I realized that I was the reason you were dead. They'd sent me to save a man I'd already condemned to death in another timeline."

"Grace, love, ye are nae the reason any of that happened. Ye did yer job. There is no guarantee I would have lived through any attack at Nairn had it happened. There is no guarantee that if we had been successful at Drumossie that we would have continued to be. It is none of it that easy. I read about what happened after the battle. I know that Lochiel tried to make another stand and failed. As an officer, I would nae have survived. I would have either died in battle or by execution. There was no quarter given for us."

"There is nothing easy in war."

"Aye, that is the truth of it."

"You were right."

"About?"

"I really am just a soldier in another kind of war."

Euan reached out and took her hand. "Ye are, but it is the most important war anyone could fight. As ye told me, think of all the lives ye save by doing as ye do. All the futures ye save, all the lives ye ensure are born and spend their lives nae aware of what war is because of what ye do. What *we* do."

"But what of those we could save?"

"Ye cannae save them because they are already dead. They were dead long before ye were born, their histories written just to be repeated. How many would ye kill in the future to save one life in the past? Ye feel guilt where ye dinnae need to."

"When did you become so wise?"

"When I realized there was more to everything than just my own existence." Euan lifted her hand and kissed it. "Let it go. Forgive yerself for it. I certainly dinnae hold any ill will toward ye for doing what ye had to when ye did nae know me."

"They knew I would go to you. They never should have sent me there. Councilwoman Rochford agreed and said they would consider it if it happened again."

"I think that is a wise change to make."

"I would do anything to save you. Anything."

"Ye did. I asked ye if ye would come to me if it meant yer death. I had no idea how true that would soon be. Ye said ye would and ye did. Ye tried to change the entire course of history to save my life. Thankfully for ye it did nae work."

"I couldn't understand it then. I couldn't understand why I felt that way."

"Neither of us could. All I knew was that I felt as though I had known ye always, even when I had nae. It was as though ye had come back to me somehow. Like ye lived in my soul. I still feel it."

Grace stood up and slid into his lap, resting her head against his shoulder as Euan wrapped his arms around her and his plaid around them both. "I hope I always stay there."

"There is no way ye would nae. Ye are part of me, just as I am part of ye. We are sewn together in so many ways there is no parting us now. I hope that when we leave this life one day, we can find each other again in another. Maybe we have. Maybe that is what this is now."

Grace smiled. "Maybe. Let's just say that's it."

Euan laughed and kissed the top of her head. "As ye wish it, so shall it be.

CHAPTER 22

When the knock came the next morning, Grace and Euan were ready. Caia bustled in and looked around with a smile. "This is very sweet," she said. "So, we are going to live in Scotland, are we? How exciting! I have always wanted to come here."

Grace laughed. "Maybe. We'll see what The Council says."

"They are waiting for you. I am taking you right to them." Caia held out her hands. "Have them back before you know it, Aileen!"

"Aye! See ye all soon. Give my regards to The Council."

Grace and Euan each took one of Caia's hands and then found themselves in Council chambers. A moment was given to let them adjust before they were spoken to.

"Good morning Euan and Grace," Councilwoman Rochford said. "How good it is to see you."

Grace smiled and bowed. "Good to see you too, Councilwoman. I won't even begin to act as though you don't know why I'm here."

Rochford smiled in return. "Very wise. Of course we know and of course we will assist you. We understand the desire for such a location and, as you know, we always think it is a good course of action."

"Thank ye," Euan said. "Thank ye for helping us. It feels right to me to be there."

"I am sure it does. Grace has worked extremely hard and it is our choice to reward her for it. She has not been profligate with the money she was given and seeks only our assistance in making the location as safe as it can be. We, naturally, have a vested interest in making sure it is so and remains so. The funds will be there for you when you need them."

"Thank you," Grace said.

"Councilwoman," Euan began. "I … something happened …"

Rochford raised an eyebrow.

"When we went to … the place … where it all happened, something strange occurred."

Grace frowned as Euan couldn't even say the name of the place now, and she could see that just thinking it made him feel panicked.

"What was that?"

Seeing Euan struggle, Grace intervened. "There was a sort of ghost there. It looked like Euan. We both saw it. I felt as though it was telling me I needed to help, and it held out a hand to me. Euan stopped me from touching it at the last moment."

"I cannae explain why, but I had this sense that if she did something terrible would happen to her," Euan said.

Rochford was silent for a moment, but her expression was worried. "It happens sometimes, and we do not know why. I can only assume that all the energy there feeds off itself. Then, the two of you walk into it with your own energy and memories, and things get confused. You suddenly see the other timelines and those appear as ghosts to you."

"Would something have happened if I had let her touch it?"

"Yes, and it is a good thing you stopped her."

Grace froze and Euan went pale. "What would have happened?" he asked.

"It is hard to say, but none of the outcomes would have been good. Best case she would have entered that timeline where we could get to her, but she would remember nothing of her previous interactions with you."

"That is the best case?!" Grace said.

"Worse is that the shock of the convergence would have

killed you. We cannot rescue you if you die in your own time. You know that. Worst case, it could have ripped you from time completely and it would be as though you never existed at all."

Euan squatted down, closing his eyes. "She would have been stuck there forever," he murmured.

"Possibly. Stuck there forever looking for you."

"She would nae have to. I would have followed her."

"Euan," Grace said, her tone shocked but gentle.

"No. I will nae stay without ye, Grace. If ye were to haunt that place, I would join ye in it. I swore to ye that I would nae leave ye and I meant it."

"You would not have a choice," Rochford said.

"What?" Grace asked as both she and Euan looked at her.

"When a Watcher and Companion are joined, a bond is formed between them. When one dies the other will follow not long afterward, anywhere from moments to hours. Had you died we would have lost Euan, too."

"Thank God for that," Euan whispered.

Rochford came around the table, looking at Euan in concern. "What has happened to you?"

Euan couldn't answer her, but Grace could. "He had a nightmare, a really horrible nightmare."

"What about?"

Grace looked at Euan. He'd only told her bits of it, and she wasn't sure if he had the strength to say it again, but he surprised her.

"I dreamt I was there again. That thing was there, my friends were there. They had Grace and wanted her to tell them where I was and what she had done with me, that she needed to give me back. She protested she did nae know and was told if I was nae there she could nae be either, then they shoved her through the spectre. It became solid as her old wounds opened, and she died only to become a spirit herself. They grabbed me and, somehow, I became one with the now solid being standing there. I forgot everything. Forgot

223

her. Turned my back on her and said I had no wife. Then the ground opened and sent me into the grave I was meant for. I landed on their bones and it closed around me."

Rochford frowned and then shook her head. "There is so much there. You saw what could have happened. You saw your own fears and your own guilt." She knelt next to Euan. "This will pass, I promise you. You were too close to it when you went there, and it had a profound effect."

"PTSD," Grace said, her heart sinking. Of course it was. He'd seen so much, done so much. She remembered then how he'd told her that night he'd sat with her in the dark outside of the cottage that he couldn't sleep. This had happened to him before.

"Precisely," Rochford said as Euan looked at Grace in confusion. "For both of you, most likely. But it will pass. You need to give it time, give yourselves time to recover. It is why we will not be calling on you for a while."

Grace sighed and closed her eyes. Both. Why hadn't she seen it? Perhaps she hadn't wanted to, but it explained what she'd felt at Culloden. "Is there anything we can do besides wait?"

"I think Euan would be well served by speaking with one of the Cognitive Specialists," Rochford replied. "There is much he needs to unpack, I think. His guilt for his survival for a start. Come, Euan, this will help." Rochford helped him to stand up and the doors opened, while Caia came in to escort him.

"Perhaps I shouldn't have agreed to take him there. Perhaps this is not the time to move ourselves there, so close to it," Grace said once he was gone.

"Grace, come walk with me. We should talk."

Grace looked at Rochford, curious. "All right."

Rochford turned and began to walk toward the back of the chamber as Grace followed her. Once they'd gotten through the doors, she found herself in a garden she hadn't known existed. It was green and lush, peaceful, a change from the pristine chambers within.

"We are assisting you because you are where you need to

be when you need to be there. If you were not, we would have denied your request."

"Things like this make it feel wrong."

"It is not, I promise. It is your own mind saying so, your own fear." Rochford stopped and turned to her. "You and Euan will die together, quite elderly and happy. You will simply go to sleep and not wake up. There is no painful or tragic parting in your future. Your granddaughter will follow you, as it always is in your line, for the Watchers tend to live long."

Grace looked at her in shock. "Are you allowed to do this?"

"I would not be doing so if that were not the case."

"Together," she whispered.

"Yes, as is the way with Watchers and Companions, like I mentioned a moment ago. We are not entirely sure why, but our best guess is that they are so linked by the experience that brings them together that the link is severed when one dies, and it takes them both. Remember, it was the same with your grandparents."

Grace realized she was right. Her grandfather had a stroke in his sleep they were told, and her grandmother had been holding his hand in the hospital when he'd died. She'd put her head down in what they'd all thought was grief, but they couldn't wake her again. Her body had failed later that day.

"We will always help you in whatever way we can. Your success is essential."

"Everyone's is," Grace said.

"No. Yours especially."

"What do you mean?"

Rochford sat down on a bench and Grace joined her. "You are the first and only Watcher to gain their Companion in the course of such a famous event. Most others are far more mundane. It is your line who always galvanizes the others. Your line who always leads. They are warriors, just as Euan is, and it is their bravery that makes them the premiere line. The best at what they do. One day, one of yours will even lead The Council itself."

Grace stared at her. "You …"

Rochford smiled. "Indeed. I cannot tell you what an honor it is to work with someone I always admired as a child. To know that everything I do now will lead to my own existence is strange, but this is a strange business."

Grace shook her head. "I can't."

"I know. It is a lot to take in and I do understand, but I want you to know you are making the right choice."

"You said 'our line.' The Evans line becomes important?" Grace asked as her thought process caught up with the conversation.

"No, it does not. The Evans line is dead."

"Wait, what? How? I'm right here!"

"Grace, the day you saved Euan's life and died in his place was the end of the Evans line and the start of a new one: the Cameron line."

"Does that happen with everyone?"

"No. You are a special case. I cannot tell you why, just know that you are. It is the Cameron line that sets the standard for all Watcher lines from almost the very moment of its creation. When you return you will no longer be the Evans Watcher. Watcher Cameron has taken her place."

Grace looked away from her, trying to process the information. A new line. A line started by her and Euan. The long line of Evans Watchers she'd come from would be no more and they'd become the Cameron Watchers instead. "Watcher Cameron," she said in a quiet voice. "How are you Councilwoman but also Watcher Cameron if I'm the first one and we're in the same Council? Were you an Evans Watcher and now you're not?"

"No, but that is a bit more complicated and something I cannot explain to you now. Not because I do not want to, but because I cannot."

"Okay, but if we're Watchers, how do you become head of The Council?"

"The members of The Council are Watchers first, just

as I was. When a member dies, their replacement is selected from the current group of Watchers. When the leader dies, the members vote for who among them will replace her. Then, another Watcher is selected to take the former member's place."

"There are still Watchers when you are old enough to become one?"

"Oh yes! And there are still Watchers even now. To them we are the past, and they guide us if we need correction. Of course, we do not put up any sort of a fight."

"How do you know that someone hasn't hijacked The Council and wants to destroy our work by coming back to the past and telling you the wrong thing?"

Rochford laughed. "An excellent question. A Watcher is always someone who has empathy, a desire to help others, a true desire to make the world the place it always should be. Someone with other intentions would quickly be found out."

"What's your name?"

"Alice."

"Nice to really meet you, Alice."

"At least out here we may be ourselves. I really am pleased I could tell you this. I always enjoyed hearing the stories about you. They were a bit legendary in our family."

Grace raised an eyebrow. "Really?"

"Oh yes. As I said, Euan is the start of much. We still live there, you know."

"At Achnacarry?"

"Yes. It is your request that the house always go to the next Watcher, and it does. I live there even now."

"You certainly don't sound like it."

"I did not grow up there, though I wish I had."

"Can I see it?"

"No," Alice said as an amused little smile played across her lips. "You know better than that. Even if I showed it to you, you would not know it now. It has been built onto and updat-

227

ed over the centuries so much that nearly none of what you will know exists. But I love it there."

Grace sat in silence for a long moment. "You won't tell me those stories even if I ask you, will you."

"No." Alice said, laughing. "All I can say is that the Cameron spirit is still alive and well, passed on through the generations. The next Watcher is born with it, without fail. You and Euan get up to some pretty grand adventures when you work together."

"This is really weird."

"I can imagine. But imagine what I felt! Directing my own ancestors into finding each other! If it failed, what would happen? When you two were in front of us to confirm your agreement, I cannot tell you how my heart was pounding."

"Luckily for you it went well." Grace knew that feeling all too well. It was the feeling she always had when her mission came to the critical point.

"Councilwoman Rochford, you are needed now," one of the other Councilwomen said, having come to fetch her.

"Duty calls," Alice said, winking before she stood up.

Grace laughed because that was Euan all over. He'd said and done the exact same thing in the library when they'd been summoned before The Council. It was good to see that part of him still existed. Cameron spirit, indeed.

"Stay away from Culloden and don't play with timeline ghosts, Grace," Alice called back over her shoulder with a grin as she disappeared back inside.

CHAPTER 23

Euan was exhausted when he returned to Grace and retreated to bed once they got back to the cottage, remaining there for the rest of the day and night. Aileen and Grace had gone for a walk with a very excited Caia before she went back, and when they'd returned, Grace had set to work on researching the logistics for the move.

The entire process would be complicated, and Grace realized it would be easier to buy what they needed here rather than ship it, especially since they'd be returning to the apartment each winter and would still need furniture there. The car presented a bigger problem, and that would need to be shipped here. They could always rent a car during the winter in California. Though, as it stood, they had two moves to contend with. The one at home to the larger apartment followed by the one here. But where would they stay while the improvements were made to the lodge? Here in a rented place, or back in California until it was finished? That would need to be discussed with Euan, though the more she thought about it the less she wanted to give up the beauty of a Scottish summer just to bake in California.

When Euan woke the following morning, and came downstairs, Grace was sitting at the table with a cup of tea, laptop open and studying something with an intent look on her face.

"Good morning," he said as he reached the kitchen.

"Good morning," she replied, looking over at him with a smile. "How are you feeling?"

"Much better, thank ye. I must have needed the rest."

"Aye, ye were exhausted, I could see it in yer face," Aileen said. "Would ye like some breakfast?"

"Aye, I would, thank ye. I am starving," he replied as he walked over to Grace, kissing her cheek as he sat down beside her. "What are ye looking at?"

"Logistics."

"I am good at those. I can help ye."

"Not that kind," she said with a chuckle. "This is about moving our lives from one continent to another."

"Oh, well, I cannae help there."

"No," Grace said. "I'm looking into hiring some moving companies to move us from one apartment to the other in California. I've already booked a shipping company to move my car here, and opened accounts in British banks for us to use. I'm going to leave our US accounts open with some money in them so that we can use them when we're there instead of the ones here."

"Ye have been busy!"

"You've been asleep for a long time."

"Aye, I have, I apologize."

"Not needed, love. You needed the rest." Leaning over, she kissed his cheek. "By the way? You are incredibly handsome this way. Fresh out of bed, hair down, mostly undressed," she whispered in his ear.

Euan grinned as she pulled back from him. "I will keep that in mind."

"Anyway, we have to decide where we want to stay once work on the lodge starts."

"Where would ye prefer?"

"Well, logically, it would make sense to be here in case the builders need to reach us. We'd be in the same time zone and area."

"It would leave us here for the best part of the year," he said. "Summers and autumns are beautiful here."

"I was thinking the same thing. Stay here for a beautiful, mild summer? Or go back to California and bake in 100 plus degree temperatures. It doesn't sound particularly appealing."

"Do ye think we could find another place for that long?"

"I've already spoken with the owners of the cottage. They have bookings for a few weeks after we leave, but they've agreed to let us come back and then stay on long term until the work is finished. It gives them a steady income booked solid and works for us. I told them I wanted to check with you first."

Euan nodded. "I am fine with all of it. We have things to handle back in California for those few weeks, so it should nae be a problem."

"I thought the same. I'll let them know."

"I know quite a few generals who would have committed murder to have someone this efficient managing the army," Euan said.

"Gives me something to do," Grace replied, laughing.

"Ye never can be still can ye?"

"Nope," she replied with an unapologetic grin. "I was thinking about speaking with Malcolm today and seeing if we might go down to Edinburgh to meet with the solicitor instead of waiting for him to come here."

"I think it would be great fun to see what has changed!" Aileen said.

"I agree. I could show ye about and tell ye what I remember."

"I'll send him a text message now," Grace said, picking up her phone.

Aileen brought a plate of eggs to the table for Euan, along with some toast and a cup of tea. "There ye are, love. I think I am going to go for a walk. It is a gorgeous morning and I would like to spend it out of doors."

"Have fun, Aileen!" Grace said.

"Aye be careful Mam," Euan called out as she shut the door.

"So, how did the visit go?"

"Well," Euan said before taking a sip of his tea. "It really helped me start to understand what I am feeling now. He would like me to keep coming, as he says it will take me some time."

"Will you?"

"Aye, I will. It is something I need to do. I will go again once the move is made."

"Good. I'm glad it helped," she said, reaching out to tuck some hair behind his ear. "I was worried about you."

"I know, but I will be fine, I promise ye. There has been a lot of change and no time to make sense of it all. He talked me through some things to help me manage it when I am overwhelmed and said it would lessen with time."

"It will. He's right."

"What about ye? The Councilwoman said ye were the same."

"Not nearly as bad, so I can wait a while. I did have an interesting conversation with her, however."

"Oh?"

"She said you and I are the start of a new line of Watchers, different from the others, and there are certain traits that the new Watcher in our line will always be born with. The Evans line is now extinct and has been replaced by the Cameron line. When we go back to work I'll be Watcher Cameron now, which will take some getting used to."

"I am nae sure if that is good or bad."

"Remains to be seen, I suppose."

Euan laughed. "What else?"

"She's a Cameron."

Euan stopped, the piece of toast halfway to his lips as he turned his head to look at her. "What?"

"She was a Watcher before she became head of The Council. She's one of our descendants."

Euan set his food down, trying to make sense of it. "That is ..."

"Strange, I know, but she told me about how strange it was for her to direct her own ancestors into finding each other, knowing each thing she did dictated her own existence. That must be strange, too."

"Aye, it would be."

"She did say that we're legendary in the family for the missions we work."

"Aye? What do we do?"

"She couldn't say."

Euan scoffed. "What is the fun in that?"

"I know! However, she did say she lives at the lodge now, and it was our request that the house go to the next Watcher in our line."

"I cannae tell ye how much that pleases me to hear. Our descendants are well in the future and still reside in the home ye and I are about to make together."

Grace smiled and stroked his arm. "She did say one other thing, and I think it will make you very happy to hear."

"Go on."

"She told me that you and I will live a long and happy life together, and when that life ends, we will go together, old in our bed. We will just go to sleep and not wake up."

"A long life. Something I was so sure I would never have. I will never need to suffer the pain of being without ye," he said.

"No, and neither will I. I hadn't made the connection with my grandparents and how they'd both died the same day, but it was their bond, the same bond we share now."

"Ye know, I was thinking about that after she mentioned it. Remember I told ye the other night that I felt as though ye lived in my soul?"

"Yes."

"It is more than just a bond, Grace. I really can feel ye within me. I know when ye are happy, when ye are sad or frightened, when ye need me. I feel those things and I can tell they are yers and nae mine. It is as though a piece of ye resides in me and connects us, and I swear to ye I felt it the first time I kissed ye. Suddenly I could feel ye in every bit of me, and it never went away."

233

Grace took a moment to think about whether she could feel the same, and to her surprise, she realized she could. "No, I can feel it too. How did I not notice that before?"

"Because it is as natural to ye as your own soul, as it is for me. We are part of each other in ways they dinnae know about, I am sure of it. It is why ye and I were so drawn to each other, why the things we felt for each other became so intense so quickly. There is more. We are more."

"You're right," Grace said, her voice soft. "I can feel that you're right. There's something more and we're the only ones who know."

"Aye, and no one else needs to either. This is about us alone, and it makes me wonder if this goes farther back somehow and that is why I felt as though I knew ye already."

"Maybe it does. I can't even begin to explain how comforting it is to me to be able to feel you there, like you're always with me even when you aren't."

"Aye, it is the same for me. Ye are right, however, it does make me profoundly happy to know ye and I will be happy together for so long. It is a balm to me, and a blessing."

Grace's phone pinged and she picked it up. "Looks like we go to Edinburgh tomorrow. Ready for this?"

"More than."

***

They set out for Edinburgh early the following morning, with Aileen and Euan starting to teach Grace Scots Gaelic as they drove. It was a drive full of laughter as she mispronounced things so that it meant something entirely different. Edinburgh had grown to a massive size since Euan and Aileen had seen it, full of people and buildings. The decision had been made to see the solicitor first and handle the business part of their trip before they gave themselves leave to have fun and explore the city itself. The documents had already been drawn up, it was just a matter of review and signing. As Grace pulled into the car park, Euan and Aileen were still looking out of the windows in awe, and it didn't change when they stepped out into the street.

"Heaven help us," Aileen whispered. "Would ye look at it now! So many people!"

"Aye," Euan said. "It was nae like this when I was here."

"At least we're in Old Town, so some of it will be the same," Grace offered.

Euan took her hand. "Aye. Let us get on with this business, and then I can show ye about."

They made their way to the solicitor's office, located in a grand looking building near Edinburgh Castle. They were ushered straight inside, where the solicitor awaited them, while Aileen remained in the waiting room. Standing up from behind the desk, he smiled in welcome.

"Good morning to ye, Mr. and Mrs. Cameron. A pleasure to meet ye finally."

"Good morning," Grace said, returning the smile and shaking the man's hand, with Euan doing the same afterward. "Thank you for agreeing to meet with us."

"I should be thanking ye for saving me a day of travel, though I will never complain about a visit with Malcolm. This shouldn't take long, the papers are already drawn up, they just need your signatures. I understand Malcolm gave ye the final amount for the wire, with duties and taxes?"

"He did," Grace replied. "I set it up yesterday morning first thing, so it should be waiting for you now."

"Excellent! Have a seat," he said as he returned to his chair. Sliding a packet of papers forward, he pulled out two pens. "These are the originals, and ye will get copies of all of it. I understand ye want the deed filed under a trust for privacy reasons?"

"Yes," Grace replied. "As I'm sure Malcolm told you, our employment with the British government requires it."

"It is the same thing done for celebrities, so it makes sense in your case. Let's get started, shall we?"

As Euan signed his name to documents that proclaimed him to be a joint owner of the property, he felt a surge of pride. He'd never in all his life thought he would own anything, and now he did. Land and the home on it. Land in Achnacarry. When they finished, the solicitor gave them a copy of the deed and sent the original with one of his assistants to be filed officially.

He picked up the phone on his desk and dialed a number quickly. "Hello, Malcolm! Aye, they're here. Everything is signed and sealed, the deed is on its way to be filed now and the money has been transferred," he said, pausing to listen to Malcolm. "Aye, I'll let them know. Thank ye, and please send Lochiel my regards would ye?"

The solicitor put the phone back down in the cradle and looked up at them with a smile. "Malcolm wanted me to let ye know he will be along with the keys tomorrow morning for ye. Congratulations, and welcome back to Scotland."

When they left, they made their way across and through Prince's Gardens to Edinburgh Castle. Paying to get inside of a place he'd once helped lay siege to amused Euan to no end, but it was fascinating to get a good look at what they'd been facing even if they *had* somehow gotten through. It was a true fortress, built to withstand attack, and it did so very well from a strategic high point. He enjoyed walking through the rooms and the great hall, captivated by the coats of arms in the stained-glass windows.

Afterwards, they proceeded down into Old Town, and into the Haymarket and Grassmarket, where Aileen and Grace took great delight in looking at the varying souvenir and trinket shops. Euan talked them through the bloodless capture of Edinburgh as they went, showing them the roads at the time and where things had stood then.

"These things are considered antiques?" Aileen mused as

they stepped into an antique shop. "I am older than they are," she whispered.

Grace laughed but quickly smothered it with her hand. "Well, to us they would be. Let's see if we can find anything here for the lodge."

"Would ye ladies excuse me a moment while ye look here?" Euan said. "I saw something in a window I wanted a closer look at if ye dinnae mind."

"No, go ahead, we can wait for you here," Grace said, smiling as he kissed her cheek and departed.

Euan held his mischievous smile until his back was turned, hurrying out to the shop he'd seen. When he returned, Grace was paying for some small trinkets she'd picked up for Caia and Vanessa. "Grace, Mam, come with me will ye?

"What is it?" Grace asked.

"I am told there is a rather grand church here and I would like to see it before we go to Holyrood."

Grace and Aileen left with him and Grace hailed a cab, as it was easier to just leave their own car parked where it was for the day. When they arrived at the church and walked inside, Aileen crossed herself and looked up in awe. The ceiling soared above them as light filtered in from windows along its bottom. The altar itself was ringed by stunning stained glass, and behind it was a beautifully decorated chancel wall. On the walls leading up to the sanctuary were carved pieces marking the stations of the cross.

"This is absolutely beautiful," Grace whispered.

"Aye, it is," Euan agreed. "It is exactly what I wished."

"Did you ever come here?"

"No. It was built long after I was gone."

"What a shame."

"Aye, but I am here now."

"Yes, you are," she said, smiling.

"I did nae come here just to see it, though I am glad I did."

"Oh?"

Euan smiled at her as he drew her closer to him. "Marry me," he whispered.

Grace let a soft laugh slip at his words. "I'm already married to you."

"No, nae really. We have a piece of paper saying we did something we never did, and it means naught to me because of it." Euan kissed her, church rules be damned, and then leaned in close to her ear. "Marry me truly; because ye want to, because ye love me as I love ye and want to spend yer life with me. I want to hear ye say the words, Grace. I want what we missed. Right here, right now, in my homeland. In the place where over 200 years ago a man ye never should have known let ye into his heart."

Grace closed her eyes, his words bringing her to tears, and simply nodded her head.

Euan reached up to smooth the tears from under her eyes and kissed her hand. "I do love ye, Grace. I know now that is what this is. I am sure of it. Nae infatuation, or fascination, or anything else. I love ye, and that is all there is to it. As I told ye yesterday, there is more between us, and we are coming back to each other instead of meeting for the first time. I have loved ye before and this is only a continuation of it. Ye dinnae need to say it, and I understand if ye dinnae, but I have to."

"I love you too," she whispered.

Euan looked at her in surprise. He hadn't expected her to say it. "Do ye?"

"Yes," she said with a nod. "I do. It's weird to admit, but I do. I think you're right about everything you said. There *was* something before."

Euan smiled at her. "Then that is all we need is it nae? It may nae be everyone's way, but it is ours."

A man in a cassock entered near the altar to set flowers out and caught sight of them standing there. "Ah, good morning to ye! Welcome to our church. Can I help ye with anything?"

"Aye, Father, ye can marry us," Euan said as Aileen's eyes widened.

"Have ye a license sorted, lad? We usually dinnae do it this way."

"We have already been married legally," Euan replied. "And in the church in California," Euan continued. It was a lie he hoped God would forgive him for, but it was the only way to get this man to perform the ceremony on the spur of the moment. "I want to marry this lass properly, in front of God in the land of my birth."

The priest smiled. "An unofficial renewal I can do. Come," he said, beckoning them forward. "Now, take each other's hands," he said when they reached him.

As the priest began to read the ceremony, Euan remained focused on Grace. There was no apprehension, no nervousness, no doubts. This felt right in every way, no matter how fast it may have seemed to come. There was no other possible explanation for what he felt deep inside when he was near her, when he'd met her. He was sure they'd already been tied together somehow, and when it felt as though she'd returned to him, it was because she had. Euan didn't know in what way that might be, but it wasn't something he felt a pressing need to delve into just now.

When the priest came to the part about rings, Grace looked panicked, but Euan pulled something from his vest pocket and slipped it onto her finger as he recited the vows as directed. A promise to love and honor her through everything. She looked up at him in surprise, but he smiled at her and pressed another into her hand – this one larger and very clearly made for a man. Grace slid the ring onto his finger and repeated the same words Euan had used, and he knew she meant them just as much as he did.

"May almighty God, with his Word of blessing, unite your hearts in the never-ending bond of pure love," the priest said as he closed the book. "Ye may kiss her if ye wish," he said.

Euan grinned and did so, but the gesture was rather chaste in front of a man of God, which amused Grace.

"Thank ye, Father. I feel it has been properly done now."

"God bless and keep ye both," he replied before he walked away.

"Ach, Euan, ye could have warned yer mam," Aileen said as she sniffled from nearby.

Euan laughed and hugged her. "Apologies, Mam, it was a bit spur of the moment."

"I am glad ye have done this."

"As am I."

"Where did you get these, Euan?" Grace asked as she looked down at the ring on her finger and studied the design, a delicate signet ring with the Cameron crest engraved into it.

"When we were on the street, I saw a set from another clan, so I went in to ask them if they had any others. They did."

"Is that where you disappeared to?"

"Aye."

"Sneaky."

Euan grinned. "Come, I want to finally see the inside of Holyrood."

"Finally?" Grace asked.

"Aye. As I told ye, my regiment took Edinburgh for the prince and, when we did, he stayed there. As an officer, I had the chance to sleep indoors, but I refused to do so if my men could nae have the same. Instead, I remained freezing my arse off in the park with them. I never got to see it before we left and I would quite like to see it with my *wife*," he said, adding extra emphasis on the word.

Another cab took them to Holyrood Park, and when they stepped out, Euan shook his head. "There was nae so much here then. We camped there," he said, pointing to a large green field stretching out behind the palace gardens. "Strange to see it so peaceful now, devoid of men and tents."

"I can picture it though," Grace said.

"I am sure ye have seen similar camps."

"I have."

"Come on," he said.

Once they'd paid and gone inside, they took their time walking through, examining all the objects. It was strange to Euan to see pieces of his past set out as artifacts to look at, but it was interesting to see what they'd found. Grace stopped in front of a case containing a court gown of his time, studying it.

"I could see ye in such," he said, his voice quiet as he stepped up beside her. "Ye would be beautiful in it. Sparkling in the light of the candles from the jewels on ye. No one here would have been able to resist ye. I can imagine ye floating through these rooms like a queen, without a care in all the world."

"Even queens have cares," she said, her eyes still on the dress. "I know, I've met a few."

"Aye, but in my mind ye dinnae. Ye have them eating out of yer hand, even the prince would yield to ye."

"If he yielded to me, I would be a Hanover."

"No, ye would be the superior being and he would see it. They all would."

"What would you have me do with such power?"

"I dinnae know. What do ye think ye would do?"

"Halt the rising. Send you all home and send the prince back to France with orders never to return."

"And leave the throne ye now have to the Hanovers?"

"I didn't say that," she said, the smallest mischievous smile creeping across her lips. "I would take over in his place, re-organize, resupply, and take this country back from England with a war we could win."

"I would like to see ye explain that one to The Council."

Grace laughed. "I know, but it is fun to think about isn't it?"

"Aye. I would follow ye, that is for certain."

"You never know, with our jobs you just might see me in this someday."

"Aye? Well, I will look forward to seeing ye in it before I take ye right back out of it," he said, giving her neck a teasing kiss.

"Stop it," she said, giving him a gentle nudge with her elbow. "Come on, let's see the rest."

The remaining two weeks went by in a flurry of activity. There were a few trips out, but much of it was spent just enjoying the peace of Achnacarry. Grace and Euan consulted with architects, builders, and designers to set the plans for the lodge with work to begin immediately. Grace paid handsomely to ensure that the work would be done before winter, and for this year, they'd be spending the entirety of the time in Scotland. This would allow them time to make the lodge truly a home with furniture and other things. The following winter they'd begin their lives of dividing time between two continents. While a security firm was enlisted to make sure they had the most up to date security systems at the lodge, Euan left that part to Grace. It was something she understood that he didn't, and the next round of security improvements would be made by Council experts.

The night before they were to return to California, Grace stood on the banks of the loch, watching the setting sun turning the water into a sheet of white.

"I've asked my mother to come visit once we're back," she said as he approached her.

"How did ye know it was me?"

"I know the sound of your footsteps by now."

"Cursed Watcher," he said, laughing as he wrapped his arms around her. "Ye are nervous about it."

"A little," Grace admitted. "Not because of you, but because of their reaction to all of it. Suddenly I'm married, they weren't there to see it, and I'm moving to Scotland for most of the year."

"It is, in the end, still far less change than ye have experienced. Ye said they know what ye are."

"My mother does. My stepfather doesn't. He wouldn't understand it."

"Stepfather, I had forgotten. What happened to yer real father?" He had a feeling, based on the disdain with which she'd said it, that there was far more to the story than she would tell just now.

"My father died when I was a baby."

"Oh, love …"

"I don't remember him, and she won't talk about him. She married this man when I was about five. I'd rather not talk about him."

"Is this why ye were so determined to have everything arranged before we left?"

"Partly. I wanted to set everything in motion so there was no way for them to stop me."

"Ye think they would have or even could have?"

"I don't know," Grace said, sighing. "I didn't want to leave anything to chance. I suppose that's my job talking."

"I think it is wise. Yer heart was telling ye something and ye listened to it. Ye always should."

"I wish we weren't leaving. I like it this way, just us."

Euan kissed the top of her head. "We can always return sooner than planned if ye find ye cannae bear it."

"I'll have to tough it out. There are things we need to see to there that can't be moved up, and the cottage is occupied."

He held her in silence for a long moment. "This will be yer home soon enough and ye will nae need to leave it if ye dinnae wish to."

"It already is."

Euan made a sound of contentment at her declaration. "Sometimes I wonder if ye were nae always meant for me but simply born in the wrong place."

"I think you could argue that might also go the other way."

"It could, that is true. Though, I suppose it does nae matter now. Whatever happened, I have found ye."

"Just like Cupid, you shot me," Grace said, deliberately making a terrible joke.

"I did nae do anything of the sort!" Euan protested. "It was Duncan who shot ye, nae me!"

Grace laughed. "I know. I just like to tease you about it."

"Careful, ye. I am nae sure ye want me to hand ye back any of that teasing," he replied. "Now, come away and stop putting off packing yer case. We have a plane to catch in the wee hours.

CHAPTER 24

It took a couple of days for all of them to get adjusted back to California time, and it resulted in naps and strange hours kept. There were meetings to sort out the logistics on this side, and they began to start packing things up for the shift to the new apartment, which would happen just before they left, as well as the few things they'd be shipping to Scotland. All the items remaining in California would stay in boxes until they returned the following winter.

Grace invited Vanessa to lunch, wanting to tell her first, and Euan decided to take Aileen out to a movie to leave the two friends time alone.

"Moving? To Scotland?" Vanessa asked as she sat across the table from Grace, her expression both shocked and sad.

"Yes. It's so beautiful there, Van! I want you to come and visit as soon as we're all settled in."

"I would love to, it's just ... well ... you won't be here. At all."

"I'm gone a lot anyway; it won't be that different. I'll be back in the winter."

"I suppose there's always video calls, right?"

"Of course!"

"What made you take such a drastic decision?"

"Euan needs to be there. It's home, where he can truly relax. We can spend a day outside and never see anyone else, and I really love that. We need that kind of peace when we aren't working, so it just made sense. I fell in love with it from almost the first moment. It's just … magical. You'll see for yourself when you visit."

"You aren't just doing this for him, right?"

"No, not at all. He wouldn't do it if I didn't want to."

"I'm just worried is all. He's taking you away from anyone you know."

"He isn't isolating me, Van. I know what you're getting at, and it isn't anything like that. He wants you to come visit, he wants us to keep in touch."

Vanessa nodded. "If you need help though …"

"I know, and I appreciate it. Please don't worry, I'm going to be fine."

"You're one of my closest friends, Gracie. It's my job to worry about you. Someone has to."

"I'm not that bad."

Vanessa raised an eyebrow.

"Okay, well, not all the time."

"Uh huh."

Grace rolled her eyes and then smiled. "Yeah, yeah, yeah."

***

The morning her parents were to arrive, Grace was a bundle of nerves, and Euan did his best to keep her calm. He was less worried about meeting them, which seemed strange to him, but she seemed to be concerned enough for them both. As soon as he met them, however, he understood why Grace felt the way she did.

The two people who came in weren't what he'd expected. Grace looked very much like her mother in some ways, and she radiated the same sense of kindness that infused her daughter. Grace's stepfather, on the other hand, was something entirely different. Euan had never met anyone who seemed so false before he even said a word, and it set him on edge.

"Gracie, good to see you," he said as he gave her the most meaningless embrace Euan had ever seen.

"Cac tairbh." *Bullshit.* Grace muttered under her breath after he released her, softly enough that only Euan could hear her.

Euan blinked and then laughed louder than he meant to. That his wife should choose to swear in Gaelic wasn't a surprise to him, but it was funny all the same. Those words had been, of course, among the first he'd taught her when Aileen wasn't around.

Grace shot him a sly smile and winked before she hugged her mother. This affection seemed entirely genuine, and Euan could tell that Grace loved her mother a great deal.

"Gracie, it is so good to see you," her mother said.

"You too, Mom. But here, I want to introduce you to someone. Mom, Richard — this is Euan." As her mother reached out to shake Euan's hand, Grace finished what she was going to say. "My husband."

Grace's mother froze in place and stared at Euan before she looked at Grace, her mouth open.

"You got married without your family there? That's pretty damned typical of you, Grace. Or, maybe this is a joke?" Richard said, his tone already confrontational.

Euan frowned. "It is nae a joke, I assure ye. Grace is my wife. It is good to finally meet ye. This is my mother, Aileen."

"Good day to ye both," Aileen said, her smile forced after having seen the same thing Euan had.

"Grace," her mother whispered, her hurt clear.

"Mom, I didn't exclude you deliberately. It all happened so fast. You know how work can be."

The woman's face changed as she caught the implications of what her daughter was saying. Euan could tell she was well aware that this was the way of things but had perhaps hoped it would be otherwise or that Grace would put it off to marry in front of family.

"Work."

"Yes. I met Euan at work."

Her eyes moved back to Euan, studying him in way that made him aware that there would be questions later. Euan offered her a smile and a slight bow of respect. "It truly is good to meet ye. Grace has spoken of ye fondly."

She seemed to compose herself and reached out her hand again to shake his. Euan took her hand and shook it gently. "I'm Anne. Has she?"

"Somehow I doubt that," Richard groused, and Grace rolled her eyes. "So, you were busy with whatever it is you do, you meet this guy, and you get married. But you don't even have the decency to tell us you were dating someone?"

"Richard, please," Grace's mother pleaded.

"No, Anne! I'm tired of this shit from her. We come here to see you, and you drop this bombshell? You can't even invite your own parents to your wedding? You don't introduce him to us first, so we can judge what kind of a guy he is and if he's even good for you? Not only that, he doesn't have the honor to even talk to us first?"

Euan's jaw tightened and Grace was quick to place a hand on his chest to stay him before Euan could make a move to defend the honor just called into question. "This is why I didn't! Why should I if this is how you were going to treat him? And, need I remind you; I am not your property. You don't get to judge anyone and decide whether they're good enough to marry me. That's my choice."

"I'm your father!"

"You are NOT," Grace shouted at him. "You like to play it for show when it suits you, but you have *never* been my father. To you, I was just someone in the way unless you could brag about me to make yourself look good."

"Grace!" Anne said, shocked.

"I'm done with this, Mom, and I'm not going to pretend anymore. I don't have time for it." Grace turned her attention back to Richard. "Euan has more honor than you'll ever possess. Apologize to him or get out of my house."

Anne looked at Richard, angry and clearly not interested in leaving because he couldn't be civil. Richard offered Euan his hand but, when Euan took it, Richard tried to squeeze it hard enough to hurt him. It was a game with which Euan was quite familiar, and he returned the move. Richard winced and pulled back; it had been a mistake to even try it against a man who had trained for battle with swords.

The power game was not missed by Grace, who shook her head. "Exactly. Get out of my house, Richard."

"Excuse me? You had better remember who you're talking to."

"I do. My *step*father," Grace said, emphasizing the first part of the word. "A man who didn't care about me and still doesn't. If I had invited anyone, it wouldn't have been you. I would've told her to come without you."

"She never would have come without me. I wouldn't have let her."

"So then why would I invite you?"

"Because, whether you want to admit it or not, I'm still your father. I married your mother."

"You are *not* my father," Grace said again. "Stop saying you are. You're just angry because you have no control over me, not that you ever did. I owe you nothing because you're nothing to me. You may be her husband, but you aren't my father."

Richard lashed out suddenly, hitting Grace hard enough to send her sprawling to the floor, and she cried out in pain.

"Richard! Stop! Don't do this!" Anne shouted at him, but he ignored her.

"Ungrateful little bitch! I raised you, not your sainted father. ME! I put up with your attitude while your grandmother puffed you up to make you think you were better than everyone. Guess what, Grace? You aren't! You're just a spoiled, selfish bitch who likes to break the hearts of the people who love her."

Unlike the last time he'd seen Grace hit, Euan knew she could feel the pain of this one. She tried to push herself up from the floor but failed, and there was no defiance in her eyes as she squeezed them shut to keep her world from spinning.

As Euan started to move toward Richard to make him pay for daring to strike Grace, Aileen immediately put herself in front of him, her hands on his chest.

"Euan, no," Aileen said, her voice taking on the firmness of a mother. "Dinnae do it, it will only make things worse. Ye cannae do that here. Remember that."

Euan checked himself and backed up, then knelt to check on Grace. When she moaned and remained down on the floor so she wasn't sick, he rose again and turned to face Richard.

"How dare ye lay a hand on her. What makes ye think ye have that right?" His voice was deadly calm, and Aileen remained between them. Euan knew she'd heard this tone of voice from him before and what that tone portended for the man in front of them if she didn't stay there.

Anne was in tears now, torn between her daughter and her husband, while Richard smirked at Euan. "And what are you going to do? I have every right. I'm still her father, whether she wants to believe it or not."

"That does nae give ye the right to strike her," Euan replied, his hands tightening into fists. "Ye have no right to disturb so much as a hair upon her."

"You're talking awfully tough for someone who couldn't be man enough to come to her parents, or at least demand she tell us before you married her."

Euan smiled, but it was dark and menacing. "If ye were truly a father to her ye would know ye could nae demand Grace do anything she did nae want to do. Ye are trying quite hard to goad a man into a fight when ye have no idea who I am or what my abilities may be. Ye will lose, I promise ye. Now, I suggest ye leave as ye were asked to do."

Richard stepped up closer to Euan, attempting to threaten him, and Euan moved Aileen behind him for safety. The two men were nearly the same height, but Euan still seemed to tower over him.

"I don't even believe you're actually married. I think she's just doing this to upset us and cause drama. She's good at that. She disappears and then contacts us later with some bullshit excuses. Now she disappears and turns back up with some Eurotrash and says she's married? How convenient."

"Oh, I assure ye, she is actually married. If she were nae, she would nae have this," Euan said as he grabbed Grace's EU passport from a nearby table and showed it to him. "Note that the name on it is Cameron."

"It could be faked. I still don't believe it."

"She wouldn't go that far, Richard!" Anne said.

"Wouldn't she? She just loves to upset us!"

"No! You love to upset *her*! You love to poke and prod until she fights back, and this is what you do! You blame it on her!"

"Now you stand up for her! You're on her side now?"

"No, it isn't li —"

"Shut your mouth! You're just as worthless and ungrateful as she is. Like mother, like daughter. Stupid and deceitful. The only difference is that the daughter is too stupid to be respectful and learn her place the way her mother has. Every time I hit her, she deserved it."

Rage flowed through every bit of Euan. She deserved it. Every time. This man had laid hands on Grace more than once, and he was proud of it. The punch Euan landed against Richard's jaw sent the man crumpling to the floor and Anne cried out. She made a move to go to him and Euan stopped her, blocking her path with an outstretched arm.

"Ye leave him there where he belongs, for he does nae deserve yer comfort. How could ye when ye just saw what he did? When he just told ye what he has always done? Ye deserve better than this."

Anne looked at Euan curiously but returned to sit down in the chair.

"Get out of our house, ye wretched piece of filth, before I have the authorities here."

Richard stumbled up. "I had better see you at home in an hour, Anne," he spat before he made his way out.

Euan turned and went to Grace to help her, grabbing a towel to wipe the blood from her nose and mouth. "Shhh now. I am here with ye. He will nae touch ye again."

He'd never imagined this, never imagined that she'd lived with this. No wonder she was distant from others and didn't want to talk about this man. Her actions that morning at the loch suddenly made so much more sense. The cold stare as yet another man used violence against her. The defiance of his expectation when she didn't cower in fear or from the pain she was unable to feel. The simmering rage that had made her dig her fingernails so deeply into her palms that they'd bled.

Anne stood up and returned with ice from the freezer to place against Grace's face. "Oh sweetheart, I'm so sorry," she said through her own tears. "I didn't think he would ever do this again and I —"

"He isn't allowed to come here anymore, and he isn't allowed at our new house," Grace said, cutting Anne's attempted excuses off before they began.

"What new house?"

"In Scotland. We have a home there where we will be spending most of the year," Euan replied.

"Grace! You can't go so far!"

"I can and I have. It's all done now. Deeds are signed, keys, builders, all of it. You can come and see me, but not with him. He's never allowed near me again, and if that means I can't see you because he won't let you go alone, then I guess that's the price we must pay. You know you deserve better. Leave him, Mom. Please. You'll miss so much if you don't. You don't have to put up with him anymore. You don't owe him anything!"

Anne sobbed at the threat of being cut out of her daughter's life more than she already had been. "I don't have anywhere else to go, Grace!"

"You can stay here," Grace said. "We won't be here, so you can stay here. I'll take care of you. You don't need him."

"You never talked like this before."

"I did, you just weren't ready to hear me! I promise you can stay here. Security will keep him out. Everything will be paid for, so you won't have to worry about that. You can get a job and learn who you are without him telling you what that is."

"You sound like your grandmother."

"I take that as a compliment."

Anne sighed. "All right, Grace. I'll think about it."

"Ye should think about it here," Euan said. "Dinnae go back to where he is tonight. It will nae be safe for ye."

"He's right, Mom."

"Who are you?" Anne asked.

"Euan Cameron. Yer daughter's husband."

"Yes, but who are you really? Where did you come from? *When* did you come from is probably a better question."

"I am of the Camerons of Achnacarry. I was an officer in Lochiel's Regiment before my lovely wife prevented my death on the battlefield."

"What battlefield?"

"Culloden," he replied, remembering to use the modern name for it.

"Jesus Christ!"

"I am nae Him, as far as I know, but I did come back from the dead, so I suppose it is a possibility," Euan quipped, which made Grace laugh and then wince, hissing with pain.

"Euan." Aileen said, her tone one of gentle chastisement for his mild blasphemy.

"Sorry, Mam."

"Let's just try to salvage this visit somehow," Anne said.

Euan helped Grace off the floor and braced her until the dizziness passed. "Are ye well," he whispered to her.

"Mostly."

"I am so sorry for this. I had no idea, and I never would have let him come here if ye would have told me."

"It doesn't matter now."

"Come with me, lass. Let me help ye get cleaned up," Aileen said, taking Grace's arm and walking her back toward the bedrooms.

"I am sorry I raised my voice to ye," Euan said, looking at Anne. "It was nae polite or respectful."

"No, you were right to do it. You were protecting her, and I understand that."

"I will nae apologize for what I did to him."

"You shouldn't."

"As I said, ye are welcome to remain here tonight where ye will be safe. I have a feeling he will take it out on ye if ye return. I have seen plenty of men just like him."

"Thank you, I will. I don't think Grace would allow otherwise."

"Probably nae. Would ye like a wee dram to settle the nerves? I know I need one."

"Actually, yes."

"I know just the bottle," he said as he offered a small smile before he went to the cabinet.

As the rest of the day wore on, Euan watched as Grace did the best she could, but by the early evening it hurt too much for her to speak and her skin was marred by an ever-darkening bruise. Euan helped her to bed, and Grace took something that would take the pain away but also make her sleep. He remained with her until she was sleeping, stroking her hair as he lay beside her.

He couldn't help but wonder how many times this had happened. How many times when she was a child and too small and weak to fight back? How often had she taken to her bed in pain and injury caused by someone who pretended to love her? Had it ever been worse than this? He wasn't sure he wanted to ask her. He wasn't sure he wanted to know.

Once he was sure she was asleep, Euan made his way back

out to the living room where he found Anne and Aileen on the couch, talking quietly. Aileen smiled at him as he joined them.

"Is she asleep, then?" Aileen asked.

"Aye, she is."

"I'm really sorry," Anne said. "It shouldn't have happened."

"No, it should nae have, but it did," Euan replied. "I am less bothered for my own sake, as I have met men far worse than he, but more for Grace."

Anne sighed. "Grace was always different. When I was pregnant with her, I hoped she was a boy, because I knew if I had a daughter she would be pulled into this strange life. Of course, when she knew about it, she wanted it more than anything."

"What was she like?" Euan asked, his tone becoming gentler.

"Focused. Beyond her years. She was an adult in a tiny body. She always had such a hard time relating to children her own age and preferred the company of adults. It drove Richard crazy."

"Why?"

"Because she was a child and wouldn't just accept what he said as law. She questioned it, and when she outmaneuvered him in an argument, he would hit her to end it."

Euan winced and looked down.

"The day he hit her and she didn't cry, but instead stood back up and stared him down ..." Anne began, but paused for a moment as her emotions rose at the memory. "He kept hitting her until she stopped getting up. I sent her to live with her grandparents then."

"How could ye watch him do that?" It broke Euan's heart to think of a tiny Grace being beaten to within an inch of her life because she refused to back down, the beginnings of the same strength he'd seen in her when he'd challenged her at the loch the first day they'd met. "How old was she?"

"He hit us both. He would say he was sorry for hitting her or me, and I hoped it would stop, but it never did. I got her out and she was safe. She was 10 when that happened."

"But she has never forgiven ye," Aileen said.

"No, I don't think so. It happens less now —"

"But it still happens," Euan finished, though he was bothered by the fact that Grace had lived with that abuse for years before she was pulled out of it.

"Yes, sometimes."

"Grace is right, ye deserve better. No woman deserves a man who harms her," Aileen said. "Ye should take her offer, lass. Get away from him and make a new start. Become yer own body again."

"What about Grace's real father?" Euan asked.

Anne looked up and, for a moment, the pain that registered there surprised him. "Nathan," she said, his name whispered in a strained voice. "He was a wonderful man in every way, and I loved him with everything I had."

"What happened to him?"

"Car accident. Someone was drunk and hit him on a canyon road. It was instant they said. Grace was too young to remember him. She was maybe 6 months old then. God, I wish she could have known him. Everything might be so different."

Aileen nodded in understanding. "Euan's father died when he was young, too. How did ye meet Richard?"

"At a friend's party. He was the friend of a friend of a friend, so no one there really knew anything about him. He was great at first and told me he loved children. It was all a lie. As soon as we got married, he was pushing me to send Grace to live with her grandparents so he could have me to himself and we could have our own child. It's funny that he accused you of having no honor for marrying Grace without us there, because he did the exact same thing. He pushed me to marry him, and I did. My parents weren't there because I knew what they would say."

"Did ye always know what yer mam was?" Euan queried, interested in how it had all come to this.

"Always, but always in chunks that were appropriate for me

at the time. She was the same with Grace when she started asking questions. My mother told her the truth, and that it would be Grace's turn to do the job when she died." Anne paused to wipe tears away. "I adored my parents, and I hate that Grace didn't get the same from me but got it from her grandparents instead. They're the ones who sent her to school at Oxford."

"What?" Euan's shock was clear. Grace had gone to Oxford? He knew of the place, of course he did, it was an elite institution of learning even in his time.

"She had to qualify, of course, but she did, and they sent her there. I think as much to get her away from Richard as anything else. He loved to brag about her, but he didn't actually care about her."

"What did yer mam say about the abuse of the both of ye?"

"Oh, they wanted to get me away from him, but I wouldn't go. My father wanted to kill him, but my mother stopped him. They were just happy when I gave Grace to them, so they knew she was safe. Eventually they stopped letting her come to us because, inevitably, he would hurt her again. Then I had to come to them by myself to see her."

"Christ," Euan murmured. "No wonder she did nae seem to care about leaving her family here."

"Why would she? You've seen it. I can't blame her," Anne said before she started crying. "I failed her in every way, and it amazes me she still wants anything to do with me."

"The part of her that is ye still exists in ye somewhere," Aileen said as she placed a hand on Anne's arm. "The fight, the confidence, the spirit. Find it again. Ye must."

"Do you love her? Really love her?" Anne asked Euan, moving the topic away from something so painful.

"With everything I am. Why do ye ask?"

"Because it isn't always that way. My father told me once that he hadn't been in love with my mother when The Council first joined them but had become so later. I never wanted that for Grace even though I knew that was how it worked."

"I have always loved her," Euan admitted. "I always will."

"How did she find you?"

Euan took a deep breath and released it. "They sent her to stop me from continuing with the rising against the Hanover king."

"You were a Jacobite."

"No. Nae exactly. My chief was, and so I did as he bid me. A king was the same no matter his name, as far as I was concerned."

"Did she manage to stop you?"

"No, she did nae."

"Then, how?"

"She took the musket fire meant for me, and the bayonet, too." To say it still hurt, still conjured the image of his dead wife on that table. Anne gasped and Euan nodded. "It was as terrible as ye are imagining."

"I don't think my mother went through that."

"What did she tell ye?" Euan asked, looking at Anne with a confused expression.

"That she was sent to keep my father from dying in a railroad accident. She managed to pull him out of the way in time."

"I hate to be the one to tell ye, but she would nae have simply pulled him away. She had to die. That he came with her means she did."

"What? No …"

"Aye. That is how it happens. They sacrifice themselves to save us. That is how the choice is made. Yer mam was struck by that train in his place."

"But that means —"

"It means Grace died too, aye. Nae instantly, as yer mam likely would have, but amidst the horror of war. She did that because of what she was starting to feel for me. I cannae say if yer mam was the same, but she must have felt something for him."

"Oh my God," Anne whispered, the horror she felt at the thought of her daughter dying, much less dying in such a way, quite clear.

"I will tell ye this: I will never hurt her. Ye have my word.

Perhaps the word of a man means naught to ye now, but it is all I can give. I will never ask her to be less than she is, and I will honor her every day because it is no less than she deserves. I am sorry ye were nae there to see her marry, and that it happened this way, but this is how it is done. We had a certificate saying we were married even when we had nae, but we are now. We went to a church in Edinburgh and did it properly. She married me because she wanted to, nae because she was forced."

"No, I know you mean it. I can see that very clearly. Believe me, I know what it looks like when someone says things they don't mean."

"I am sorry ye must."

"You're trained in battle then?"

"Aye," Euan said.

"Have you killed people?"

Euan raised an eyebrow at the very blunt question. "We were at war, so, aye."

"He definitely would have lost a fight with you, then. I kind of wish he would've tried."

Euan looked shocked for a moment, and then laughed. "Nae sure ye would have wanted to spend yer visit cleaning the blood from the floor. The only men who act as he does are the ones who are weak but want to seem strong by terrorizing those unable to fight back."

"You are just like Grace," she said.

"Why do ye say that?"

"Older than your years. Full of conviction, a drive for justice, and a desire to protect. I think you're everything she could've wanted, everything she did want but didn't know she did. She'd closed herself off to protect herself, and it would've taken someone special to get through that. Thankfully, The Council found him."

Euan smiled, but it was Aileen who spoke. "Aye, Euan has always been that way, but then he was asked to be a man at an age where he should have still been a boy."

"I still managed to get that in, too," Euan said.

"Aye, ye did, that is true. But I always felt ye were destined for greater things. It was in yer eyes. Ye were meant for a bigger life beyond the woods of Achnacarry, and ye have found it."

"I have nae always found it," he replied, thinking about all the times he'd died before now.

"No, nae always, but that has been fixed and ye are now where ye were meant to be."

"I will worry far less about her now, knowing she's with you," Anne said.

"Aye, I will be there to assist her in her work and keep her safe."

A knock at the door made the two women jump, and Euan rose from the couch as the door opened. When he saw Caia come in, he frowned, wondering whether he'd missed the call to action. "Caia? What are ye doing here? I thought we were nae being called for a time?"

"You are not, but I am here for Grace. Just a quick trip. She cannot go around with that bruise on her face, right? People would think you did it."

"That is a fair point I had nae thought of," Euan said.

"Hi Aileen," Caia said with a wave.

"Caia, love," Aileen said.

"Hi Grace's mom. I'm Caia, Grace's Guardian."

"Anne," she replied. "Nice to meet you, Caia."

"Right, so, I will just go back then?"

"Aye, ye know where to find her," Euan replied. "She took something to make herself sleep though."

"No problem. I can still handle it," Caia said as she walked back toward the bedroom.

"Would ye like a cup of tea, Anne?" Aileen asked.

"That actually sounds lovely, thank you."

Aileen stood and walked toward the kitchen, patting Euan on the back on her way past him. "I will put the kettle on. Naught better for getting to know each other than talk over a good cup of tea."

CHAPTER 25

ASHRIDGE HOUSE, ENGLAND
JANUARY 1554

"**G**ood, but ye need to turn yer hands this way," Euan said as he adjusted the young woman's hands on the hilt of the large sword she held. "Keep yer grip relaxed so ye can adjust it as needed. Now, try it again." Euan watched as she reset her feet and then brought the blade down and across. "Aye, very well done, Yer Highness."

"I think my sister would be most upset if she knew about these lessons," she said.

Euan shrugged. "Ye may one day be sovereign, and it would be wise for ye to learn to defend yerself instead of relying solely on others as she does."

"I will not be if she marries and has a child."

"Has she done either of those things as yet?"

"No."

"Then ye still have a chance," he said, winking.

"There is talk of her marrying the Spanish prince."

"Even if she does, I would nae fret."

"Why?"

"What do ye stand to lose if she does? Ye may nae be a queen, but ye would still be a princess and live well the rest of yer days without the pressure of running a country. I am nae sure that sounds entirely bad."

"No, I suppose not."

"Your Highness!" The voice of an older woman rang out across the hall, and the younger woman turned to look. "It is time for you to prepare for your lessons. I am sure Cameron has other work he should be about."

"Coming, Blanche," she replied, before she turned to look at Euan and smiled, handing back the sword. "Thank you, Cameron. I really do enjoy our lessons."

Euan bowed to her. "The pleasure is mine, Princess Elizabeth."

He watched her hurry off to join Blanche Parry, the woman who had been with her nearly every moment of her 21 years, and he smiled. He'd heard of Elizabeth, but the stories he'd heard were nothing like what she was here. Perhaps time changed her, but for now he found her to be pleasant and exceedingly intelligent.

He'd worked a good many missions with Grace now, becoming more comfortable with each one. They worked well together, complementing each other, and it made them more effective. It had surprised him at first to see how different she was when she was working compared to the way she'd been with him. Alice had been right: Grace had been seriously thrown off when she'd met Euan. The Grace he worked with was calculating, focused, and able to adapt to any situation or change without hesitation. He saw now what Alice had meant about Grace's ability to fit the pieces together and make it all work; Grace was brilliant. Turning, he scooped up the blades and left the hall.

***

Elizabeth walked into her chambers to find Grace tidying up. "Oh! Good morning, Grace."

"Your Highness," Grace replied with a curtsy before resuming her work.

"Your Highness, a letter has come for you," a young girl said as she brought it in.

Elizabeth took it and opened it, frowning as she read. "Leave me," she called out. As everyone turned to obey the order, Elizabeth amended it. "Except for Grace."

"Your Highness," Blanche began to protest, but Elizabeth silenced her with dismissive hand movement. Blanche's lips pursed, but she obeyed.

Once everyone had gone, Grace spoke. "How may I help you, princess?"

Elizabeth moved to sit in a chair and studied Grace. "Cameron is handsome, do you not think?"

"I would be telling a lie if I said I did not."

"Are you having a tryst with him?"

The question caught Grace off guard, and she didn't immediately answer.

"I thought so," Elizabeth said, smiling.

"Your Highness, I —"

"I will not tell anyone, if that is what you fear. In fact, I rather envy you."

"How did you know?"

"I saw him kiss you once when you thought no one could see. I hope someone kisses me that way."

Grace smiled and shook her head. "So do I."

"What is he like?"

"Like?"

"You know …"

"Oh. Well, he … he has not made me regret a thing, let us just say that."

Elizabeth giggled a bit. "Are you in love with him?"

"Maybe," Grace said, her smile becoming teasing.

"Do you think he loves you?"

"I cannot speak for him, but I would wager he does."

"Oh, you lucky thing!"

"Perhaps someday you will find that for yourself."

"Perhaps," Elizabeth said, her voice and countenance dejected. "But I have no intention of marrying anyway, so it does not matter. Come and read this letter I just received. I need your advice and that is why I kept you behind," she said, holding out the letter to Grace.

It was the moment Grace and Euan had been working and waiting for. Grace took it and read it over before looking up and feigning surprise. "A rebellion?"

"Yes. It seems Sir Thomas Wyatt and the others are not happy about my sister's forthcoming marriage and want to be rid of her."

"That is treason."

"Only if they fail."

"Even if they succeed."

Elizabeth leaned her head back against the chair. "So, you think I should not give my consent?"

"I most certainly think you should not. Even if you do not give it and they succeed, they will put you on the throne. If you give it and they fail, it is proof you knew of it. That proof would be —"

"Treason," Elizabeth finished.

"Yes. You would end up in the Tower with Lady Jane."

"Like my mother."

Grace was silent for a moment before nodding. "And sharing her fate. She would not have wanted that for you."

"What should I do?"

"Let me take this. I will destroy it and then, if the worst happens, there is no proof you ever received it."

"Except that it was delivered here."

"Letters go astray all the time. Oh no, this one accidentally fell into the fire before you read it or even saw it. How terrible," Grace said in a flat voice before a dark smile appeared on her face.

Elizabeth returned the same smile. "Take it. Get rid of it."

"As you wish, Your Highness. There is something I must tell you."

"Oh?"

"Do not fall for these promises. Say nothing. Commit to nothing. To do so will save your life. Do not rush to sit upon the throne of England, for you will find your way there eventually if you are patient. You need only outlast your sister."

"If she marries and has a child, I will not sit there at all."

"There is always a chance. Heirs die. Sovereigns die."

"You sound as though you know what is to come."

"Maybe I do." Grace was quite aware of Elizabeth's interest in the occult and wouldn't hesitate to make use of it.

Elizabeth sat up in a quick movement. "Do you? How do you know?"

"I cannot tell you how. Trust me when I tell you that you will outlast your sister, you will take the throne for yourself, and you will do it without a rebellion. You have no need of them. Until then, consider any responses you make to any questions carefully, for all can be used against you. No matter how bleak things may seem, just know it will all come out right."

"What else do you know?"

"Just that you will be a beloved queen. More than that I cannot tell you. I need to go and rid you of this letter. The longer it remains here the more likely it is that you got it and read it."

"Yes, of course. Thank you, Grace."

Grace started to walk toward the door and stopped. "One last thing. In these uncertain times, when treachery is used to eliminate those in the way, it may serve you well to draw lines at the end of any correspondence you send if there is space left upon the parchment."

Elizabeth looked at her curiously. "Why?"

"It makes it impossible for anyone to add anything to your letter after the fact." Elizabeth gasped and Grace smiled before she hurried out of the room.

265

Later that night, Grace walked down a darkened corridor on her way to seek out Euan. She needed to give him leave to move to the next part of the mission. Out of the darkness, someone grabbed her and placed a hand over her mouth, pulling her backward into the blackness of an unlit corner. Before she could scream, she felt a familiar kiss on her neck and closed her eyes, relaxing back into Euan.

"Hello love," he whispered to her in Scots Gaelic as he removed his hand from her mouth. "I have missed ye."

"And I you," she responded in the same language, knowing that now their conversation must be entirely in Gaelic.

"Did ye get it?"

"Yes, and it has been disposed of. Evidence of her being privy to it no longer exists."

"Well done, lass. I suppose that means it is my turn?"

"It does. You have been meeting with those you need to?"

"Aye. Everything is ready."

"Be careful."

"It is nae as though they can kill me," Euan said, amused.

"I am not sure how that works with hanging, drawing, and quartering, but let us not find out."

"I have no intention of doing so, believe me."

"I will miss you."

"And I ye, every moment, as usual. Now, kiss me goodbye Watcher, and let me do my job. I have a rebellion to implode."

Grace smiled and gave him a long kiss, trying to drink in the feel of him as he pulled her against him. She wasn't sure when she'd see him again, but she would be here until he returned. They didn't leave a mission separately.

"I love ye, always remember that."

"I love you too," she whispered before he walked away from her, disappearing into the darkness like a phantom and taking her heart with him.

When the news of the rebellion broke days later, along with the news of the chaos within its ranks, Grace knew Euan had been successful. When Mary's men came for Elizabeth, Grace reiterated her message about choosing her words carefully and having faith even when it seemed bleak. The departure of Elizabeth and her household to London left Ashridge nearly empty, with nothing but wind and snow to replace the multitude of voices now silenced.

With no one left to serve, Grace made her way out onto the wall to look out across the grounds. She wondered where Euan might be, what he was doing, if he was safe. She placed her hands on the stone, impervious to the ice and snow, and closed her eyes. She could feel his hands on hers, feel his body behind her, and it wasn't until he spoke that she realized it was real.

"I am nae sure, but it feels a bit like victory out here."

Grace smiled and opened her eyes, looking down at his hands covering hers. "Does it? It feels a bit like winter to me."

Euan wrapped his arms around her, laughing. "Aye, it is that too. It is good to have ye in my arms again."

"It is good to be there again. Congratulations on the successful destruction of a rebellion."

"A bit strange to be on the other side of that but thank ye. It was nae that difficult, really. Nobles are far easier to play against each other than they ought to be."

"Sometimes very true," Grace said as she turned around to face him.

"Do ye wish to know how I did it?"

"Do I ever?"

Euan grinned. "No, ye dinnae, and this would be no exception. I thought I would ask anyway, just in case ye did."

"You just want to brag."

"Perhaps a little, aye."

It was Grace's turn to laugh now. "You can brag about it in debrief. Let us go home."

"I thought ye would never say so."

Grace shook her head in amusement and then closed her eyes to contact The Council.

"Watcher and Companion Cameron reporting mission completion."

"Copy, Watcher Cameron. Are you requesting immediate extraction?"

"Absolutely."

"Extraction process beginning. Congratulations on a job well done and welcome home, Camerons."

EXCERPT FROM THE NEXT BOOK IN THE SERIES, "ENEMIES OF THE MIND!"

"Euan?" she called out as she picked up the candle and tried to look around. The flame seemed to make no difference, the darkness remaining just as heavy.

"Grace," he said as he suddenly stepped out of the blackness and in front of the candle.

Grace screamed in shock and almost dropped it, then took a deep breath. "Do not scare me like that! What is going on? Did we lose power?"

Euan didn't answer, looking at her in silence. It was only then that she noticed his face was dirty, there was blood on it. From behind him, more men suddenly stepped into the meager light, all of them with the same faraway look. Grace gasped and took a step back, but they followed her forward. In the flickering light, the ones she could see all had pure black eyes, no white to be seen.

"Euan, what is wrong with you?" she asked, her voice small and quavering with fear.

"They cannae help ye. No one can. They cannae stop us now. Welcome back, lass."

The voice, so familiar but so cold, only added to her terror before a hand shot forward and covered her mouth. She screamed against it but there was no sound, the blackness consuming it even as it consumed the light. The candle dropped to the floor and went out as she fought to pull forward and away. There was nothing but their laughter as a multitude of hands dragged her down into the dark.

Acknowledgments

To my wonderful husband, Myles – There aren't enough thank yous in the world. Without your support, encouragement, and understanding this never would have happened. Thank you for everything you've done, I love you.

To Anaïs – Thanks for understanding seeing mommy at the computer so much, and thanks for the hug breaks you so often forced me to take even when I didn't want to. Tha gaol agam ort.

To my "core readers" – You guys are the best. Thank you for your feedback.

To Julie Miller, Barry Drake, Mary Johns, and Lana Yakimchuk – The four of you have been with me since day one. You have had my back, encouraged me, let me bounce ideas off of you, and I couldn't have done this without you. You love these characters and this world as much as I do, and it shows. You are invaluable to me, and I adore you all. Thank you.

To Rebekah Kujawsky – Bekkers, thank you for being there and being my friend.

To my parents, Lisa and Duane – Thank you for your encouragement on this project and for the freedom as a child to let my mind go where it would. It laid the foundation for this and is the best gift you could have given. I love you both.

To Tara Lyn Joseph – Thank you for your photo editing

skills! You are an absolute angel.

To Rebecca Roberts – My red pen lady! Thank you so much for your expertise!

To Bekki Cox-Marsiglia – Thank you for listening, for reading the same book 20 times to catch the things my eyes could no longer see, and all the pep talks. I promise I'll go outside!

To Hilary Parsons – My surrogate grandmother. You were so excited when I told you about this and were one of my biggest cheerleaders. I'm broken-hearted that you didn't live to see the finished copy, but I know you're cheering me on from the other side.

To Árstíðir – Thank you for the beautiful music on your album "Nivalis," which featured in such heavy rotation on my writing playlist for this book. You gave Grace and Euan their theme song with "In the Wake of You."

To Devin Townsend – Thank you for the ass-kicking music which informed many of Euan's early scenes, the Battle of Culloden scene, and others. There's a reason he becomes a massive fan of yours in Book 2.

To Donald Cameron of Lochiel, XXVII Chief of Clan Cameron – Thank you for meeting with me and giving me the benefit of your vast historical knowledge. You helped the fictional members of Clan Cameron come to life.

Last but not least – To Euan Cameron – The smoothest muse a woman could ask for.

ABOUT THE AUTHOR

A California native, Eilidh Miller, FSAScot, has a BA in English and studied history as an undeclared minor to better inform her literature studies. A Fellow with the Society of Antiquaries of Scotland, Eilidh is very active within Southern California's Scottish community, spending a great deal of time volunteering with the charitable organization St. Andrew's Society of Los Angeles.

A long-time historical reenactor, Eilidh loves research and educating the general public about historical events, as well as entertaining them with tidbits no one would believe if they weren't documented. She extends this same energy to her work, extensively researching the historical periods she includes in her writing to ensure that the information she presents is correct, even going so far as to travel internationally to access archives and scout locations.

She resides in Southern California with her husband, daughter, and her feisty Shiba Inu sidekick.

You can keep up with Eilidh on Twitter, Instagram, TikTok, or her website www.eilidhmiller.com. You can also join her reader group on Facebook, Eilidh Miller's Reading Lodge, to keep up to date on the next release, get exclusive content, teasers, and enter contests!

Made in the USA
Las Vegas, NV
24 July 2022

52115797R00163